1

This work is dedicated to my Aunt Laura Edith Henson. No one living remembers her, I have never heard anything regarding Laura except that my father had a sister who died as a baby. Her grave lies between my Grandfather and Grandmother's on a hillside overlooking Chesapeake, Ohio

Brave Daughter Table of Contents

Chapter One

The little Missouri clapboard church house was crowded. The evidence of that could be seen by the numerous wagons and horses tied to the several hitching rails. A spring thunderstorm was rumbling across the countryside, with an occasional bolt of lightning and accompanying thunder. Each step Laurie Burdock's horse took placed a brief imprint of its hoof on the ground, which quickly filled back in with muddy water.

Mr. Jasper Burdock's funeral had brought out all of the family friends and neighbors, although it wasn't entirely clear which was which. He and his family had lived among them for the better (or worse) part of seventeen years, after he arrived with his wife and a small baby. Mr. Burdock had been a "sharecropper" (meaning that he farmed someone else's land for a portion, or share, of the crop).

The Burdocks had attended this same church for most of the years they had lived there.

The late arrival, wearing an oil cloth rain slicker, dismounted, tied up her horse, and tried to stomp off the mud from her boots as she climbed the steps of the church. Under the roof's overhang, the young woman pulled off her boots; moving into the vestibule, she shed her rain slicker and hung it on an unused peg provided for that purpose; inside, through the half-open door, she heard the Preacher waxing eloquently about the late Mr. Burdock. She shook her head, freeing a cascade of lovely long dark hair, and her dark eyes flashed as she listened to the Preacher's words.

The Preacher took a deep breath and began reciting the number of years and different offices of the Body of Christ that Mr. Burdock had served. He stopped mid-sentence as a lovely young woman trudged resolutely up the aisle.   As she neared the altar in front of the casket, she knelt in prayer. The Preacher was surprised to see this daughter of the deceased kneeling in prayer, but continued along the same theme of extravagantly eulogizing Mr. Burdock. The funeral service continued, even including numerous testimonies by church members about the good works of Mr. Burdock.

It soon became obvious to the Preacher, and to at least the parishioners seated in the first few rows of seats, that Laura Edith Burdock was quietly weeping at the altar. The Preacher, Reverend Silas Jones, walked around the open coffin and stepped down from the pulpit. He then moved slowly to the side of the beautiful young woman, and offered his hand to help her to arise from the floor. Wishing to alleviate what he understood to be her deep sorrow for her deceased father, Reverend Jones said, "Laurie, your tears of sorrow will be dried by our dear Savior as he wraps His loving arms around you to provide comfort in this time of loss."

Still sniffling, Laurie took his hand and stood up. Turning to face the Preacher, she said, in a strong firm voice, "Pastor, those weren't tears of sorrow, at least not in the way you're thinking them to be. I have been beseeching my Lord and Savior to forgive me of my sin, of my sin of hatred for this monster. This is the only person I have ever hated in my life, and I haven't ever been able to forgive him. I think now that he is dead, I can finally forgive his sins against me."

At that moment, there was a flash of lightning nearby with a loud clap of thunder, almost as if Heaven had supplied the exclamation point.

The congregation was stunned at Laurie's words, and nearly everyone in attendance sat in silence, most with their mouths open.

The Preacher himself was greatly shocked, and was speechless for several moments; he then asked, "Laurie, this is very surprising. What is the nature of Brother Burdock's offense against you? Surely, it must have been a misunderstanding?"

Laurie's dark eyes clouded, and she replied, " I didn't misunderstand! My father would come in late, after everyone else had gone to bed. He was almost always drunk. He would come to my bed and try to… to…. I can't bear to describe what he would do -- or try to do. I finally started staying in the barn 'til after he'd come home and gone to bed; I'd sneak back in to my bed only when I thought it was safe. That wasn't all I hated him for. He'd also beat my mother; you should have seen the black eyes and bruises on my mother. Those of you who did see them failed to do anything to help her. Some of you drank with this monster, laughed with him, and ignored the brutality he poured out upon my dear mother. You need to get on your knees and beg for forgiveness from the God of Creation just the same as I did for my sin."

Now there was silence in the house of the Lord, until a man several rows back stood up and spoke. "Laurie, Mrs. Burdock – Evelyne -- I'm guilty of that. I knew, or thought I knew, but never said anything because I figured it was none of my business. Please forgive me; I should have at least spoken to Jasper. The Apostle Paul told me what to do. He said if you know what is right and don't do it, then that is sin. I know it is too little and too late, but I am so sorry and so ashamed."

Others began to murmur amongst themselves, and heads dropped, with all the eyes looking at the floor, and not a few had begun to shed tears -- of sorrow, of regret, of contrition.

Even the Preacher was silent as Laurie turned around and faced the congregation and spoke again, "May the Holy Spirit convict you,

you know who you are, of not speaking out for my mother; but you didn't know about me. The last couple of years when Dad came home drunk, I had to fight off his advances and leave the house until he sobered up. I've been so unhappy in this place, I know I can't find peace here, so I'm leaving. I'm going west with the Porter family. They lost their farm recently, and with all those children they need help cooking, cleaning, and caring for the babies. In exchange they'll feed me and provide me with a seat in their wagon to go in search of a new life. Good-bye to you all, and be kinder to one another."

It was silent in the House of God, and then behind her, the Preacher said, "Laurie, you're right; many of us knew, or certainly should have known."

Raising his arms as if to Heaven in supplication, Reverend Jones began to pray: "Heavenly Father, have mercy on me, a sinner. I have failed in my job to be the shepherd of your flock. I ask for your forgiveness and your mercy. I ask for the ability to continue on in this ministry. I will call for a vote of the Deacons to ask for their permission to remain and will serve in any capacity or office of the Body of Christ which the Board of Deacons decides. In the name of our Lord and Savior, Jesus Christ, I pray. Amen.

"We have a Hope for eternal life, now we have a hope that Brother Burdock somehow received forgiveness for his sins during the short time he laid on the ground with a broken neck until he departed this life. It is appointed once for man to die, and then the judgment. We pray for Mercy on him at the Judgment seat of God. In Jesus's precious name, Amen."

Some men in the congregation made their way to the coffin, closed the lid, and carried it to the waiting wagon. The congregation quietly broke up, some speaking to others in hushed tones, and then they either went home or went to the cemetery to bury Jasper Burdock.

Evelyne Burdock went to her daughter and silently put her arms around her. Evelyne's other children stood close to their mother, some of them watching Laurie and others watching their mother.

Evelyne finally spoke, "Laurie, is there any way I can convince you to stay here with me and your brothers and sisters?"

"Mother, I can't stay here. All through school, the other children used to call me an Indian squaw and worse, because of my dark hair and eyes. Now, after today, everyone will look down on me even worse. Mother, before I go, I must know. I don't look like my brothers and sisters. Are you and Jasper Burdock really my parents?"

"Oh, Laurie, I am so sorry I failed you as a Mother!"

"No, Mother. You loved me and taught me right from wrong. Your only failing was not leaving Father."

"Laurie, I am your mother, but Jasper was NOT your father."

Laurie's siblings in unison turned their heads to look at their mother. Several of them had unfavorable thoughts about their own father.

"I always wondered about that since I have a darker skin, almost black hair, and dark eyes, while my brothers and sisters have brown or blond hair and blue eyes, like you do, Mother."

"I never told anyone any of this, but my parents went west in search of a better life. We stopped for a few days at an Army fort in Colorado. Unfortunately, there was a fever epidemic. Both Mom and Dad died of the fever. There was an Indian Scout there named Sam. He and his wife had a young son, about a year old. They had taken us in, and Sam's wife died of the fever too. He and I cared for my parents and his wife until they died, one at a time, and then we buried them.

"I wrote a letter to my oldest brother, Bob, when Dad died. Bob couldn't leave the farm until he got the crop in, so his family would have food to eat, then he set out for Colorado.

"After Sam and I had cared for the people we loved and had lovingly buried all three of them, we were tired and emotionally drained. As I cared for his son, Sam and I fell in love -- or thought we did. Looking back on it now, I see that it was really just a way to gain companionship, and comfort to soothe the loss. But, we thought we were in love.

"Sam went back to his tribe -- I think they are Utes – and brought one of his sisters, a girl of about twelve, back to stay with us. About two days after his sister arrived, Sam had to lead a mapping patrol, which was to be gone about three months. I didn't know I was pregnant then. Within a week, my brother Bob arrived from Missouri to get me and Mom, but Mom had already died. Bob took me back to his home and I met Jasper Burdock there. When I married Jasper Burdock I was eight months pregnant, and you were born that Spring. We moved here when you were very young.

"Jasper wasn't a bad man except when he was drinking. I always wondered if he felt second best by marrying a pregnant girl. But I did my best to be a good wife, even when he beat me up."

Laurie almost started crying again at hearing her mother's story. "I have to go now; the Porter family is over there and ready to leave for the wagon train. Thanks for telling me. I love you, Mother!"

Laurie's fourteen year old sister, Mildred spoke, "Oh, Laurie, I will miss you so! Please write and come back if you can!" Then she whispered to Laurie, "Father tried to do something to me once, too! I got real scared, but I ran under the clothes line and Father was taller than me and drunk, so he never saw it and ran right at it. I thought it had killed him when he hit the ground. He left me alone then. You remember when he had the raw welt on his neck about six months ago?"

"Laurie, we all love you so much. Please write if you can. Be very careful! There are lots of dangers in the world," advised Evelyne Burdock.

The grieving mother kissed and hugged her daughter in the empty church house, and Laurie rushed to the vestibule, put on her boots, grabbed her rain slicker, wiped tears from her eyes, and ran down the steps to her waiting horse. She climbed on, turned the horse away, and never looked back.

Chapter Two

Tommy Thompson came back to the house in Denver at supper time, as James Watson was washing his hands before sitting down to eat.

"Hey, Dad, don't let my stomach make me forget that I want to talk to you at supper; it's about horses."

James chuckled, and said, "Tommy, you are way too young to start getting forgetful!"

"Oh, I just have a bunch of things on my mind that I've got to do after supper. I have three customers to deal with this evening."

Just then, Abigail Watson rang the supper bell for the residents of the boarding house and the rush began to feed upwards of twenty-five people (if they all showed up for supper). The Watson, the Temple, and the Elder families usually ate at the long table nearest the kitchen, because it was large enough for all of them, and, later, the employees who were serving food could sit there, too.

Jim and Pete Elder had things to discuss over supper, too, so the menfolk settled at the far end of the long table. Jim's cousin, Phillip Temple, wasn't at the supper table, as he was delivering some farm equipment which had been sold by the family General Store; but he knew he'd have cold left-overs to eat later that night.

"What's on your mind, Tommy?" asked Jim during a lull in his conversation with Pete.

"We need to get some more horses. I could sell two or three horses a week, and probably rent another one or two, if I had them."

Jim thought for just a bit, and said, "Well, we could go on another buying trip back toward Kansas, and check all the farms along the way, like we did last time."

Tommy smiled and said, "Actually, I thought about that, but maybe there's a better way. I heard there are a whole lot of wild horses up in the mountains between Wyoming and Montana. We could get a group together to go capture a bunch of these horses, and make a bundle of money, 'cause we wouldn't have to pay anything for them, and we could sell extra ones we don't want to feed cheap."

Jim laid down his fork and replied, "Tommy, that's Indian country, and the Indian wars are still a problem. The U.S. Army can't go along to protect you. Plus, those horses are wild animals. It would take a lot of work to break them to ride. I know that you're young, and you'd like to add some adventure to your life, but I think there is too much to lose and too little to gain."

"Fair enough, Dad; that's all true. But, then, what about buying horses from the Indians?"

"That's a better approach, but what happens when you meet a war party? We don't have Johnny [Little Bear] to intercede for you. And Indian ponies, the ones they'd want to sell, anyway, are probably not much better than wild horses, I fear."

Pete Elder joined in: "Better to buy horses from people of your own background. You've each got the same words to describe good points and weaknesses of horses, and they won't object to letting you examine them the way we do. We barter differently than Indians do, too, I 'spect."

"I think the best plan would be to take two wagons, and buy hay and horses. That trip will be exciting enough; you don't need to go looking for trouble," advised Jim.

"You make a good argument, Dad; you, too, Mr. Elder. I guess I was looking for adventure, but not trouble, for sure. How soon should I start and how many horses should I buy?" asked Tommy.

Jim thought a minute and replied, "It's Spring, so you might find a good deal on some last year's hay, but I don't think you'll find enough horses, cheap enough, to make you happy. If you managed to buy a hundred horses, or even fifty, you'd have to herd them; that's too many to lead, and it'd take too much rope. Also, to herd that many horses that don't know each other would be really hard. You'd probably need to rent a corral, and, as you buy them, put them in the corral, and feed them there for several weeks. Such an operation could take all summer. That's a lot of beans and bacon."

Tommy took a chance. "Sounds like a good plan. How about I leave in a few days, and take the two men we hired last summer?"

Jim grinned and said, "On your own, without even your Uncle Pete?"

Tommy grinned back and nodded.

"Okay, there always has to be a first time," sighed Jim, feeling the weight of fatherhood on his shoulders.

Three days later, Tommy, Davie Barton, and Timmy Elliott departed Denver, driving two wagons, with two saddle horses tethered behind, and with lots of supplies, headed East toward, eastern Colorado and western Kansas.

Relying on advice from farmers, the town of Norton, Kansas, was selected as the center of their purchasing operation. Spring flowers and blossoms on apple and cherry trees made the trip a pleasure, as it had been a long, cold, drab Winter in Denver. A corral was rented, and slowly the small herd of horses began to grow. However, hay was scarce; it would be another month before any of the grasses were high enough to cut, dry, and collect for hay.

But luck was on their side; an old farmer, who they met by chance on the road, told Tommy about a big farm about fifty miles over in Nebraska, where the owner had died and the family wanted to go back East. The family had sold most of their livestock, but still had a barn full of hay.

As quickly as they could, the three young men took their two wagons and one of the saddle horses on the trip to Nebraska. When they arrived, they discovered the owner had been sick for some time before he died, and no effort had been made to run his operation other than to feed the horses which hadn't been sold yet. His barn was full of nice alfalfa hay, and there were ten horses for sale at a very reasonable price. They needed just one day to load two wagons of hay and tie ropes to the ten horses in order to lead them back to Norton.

Since Norton was named for a Union soldier killed in the late Sectional War, the young men never mentioned that they were all originally from the South, and only Davie really sounded southern; but they never saw any overt discrimination.

Toward the end of June, the boys had purchased forty horses, and they decided they had found all the horses for sale in that area. Since they had all the hay the wagons could carry, and hadn't spent nearly as much money as they had budgeted, they decided it was time to head back to Denver. A little rest for them, and some time for the horses to get to know each other, seemed to be in order.

Tommy led the way into a family-owned restaurant. The building had been freshly painted a crisp white, and the shutters a nice contrasting pine green. The three young men sat down to enjoy a home-cooked meal at a table with what appeared to be a new red and white checkered tablecloth.

Before they could even order the food, a local man burst into the restaurant carrying a newspaper and blathering like he had lost his mind. All that anyone could understand was the word "Indians," but that got everyone's attention. When he had been calmed down enough, he read the newspaper loudly enough for everyone in the room to hear; the message was bone-chilling. Indians at a place called the Little Big Horn had won a battle with Colonel Custer and the 7th U.S. Cavalry. There were no survivors among the soldiers. This had happened on June 25th, 1876, only about two weeks beforehand.

Everyone was terrified that the Indians were headed their way. Tommy looked at Davie and Timmy and said, "I don't think I told you, but that area was my first choice to try to round up some wild horses, but my Dad talked me out of it."

Ignoring the subject, Timmy asked, "Tommy, you always call Jim your Dad, but your name is Thompson and his is Watson. How is that?"

Tommy started laughing and replied, "My real Dad had a Livery Stable in a little gold rush town in Montana. He slipped and fell from the hay loft while throwing down hay for the animals. Since my Mom had died long before that, I had no family, so Jim and Ms. Abigail took me in, helped me to run my business and, when the gold mine ran out of gold, we all went to Denver together and went into business there. Jim has been a great substitute Dad; in ways he feels more like my Dad than my actual father."

Davie spoke up, "I sure am glad you didn't drag us up North and get us kilt!"

"We may not be out of the woods yet," added Tommy.

At that moment, a Deputy Sheriff came into the restaurant and announced, "No one knows where this huge band of Indians is headed. They have in the past attacked stagecoach stations almost this far East.

Of course, there are a lot of different directions they could go. The Sheriff has deputized a bunch of town folk; then he sent deputies to the nearby towns and three to different locations North of town to watch for Indians. If we should suffer an Indian attack, everyone should seek shelter in Stewart Adams' heavy barn. We are moving guns, ammunition, water, and some food supplies into the barn. We also have moved the hand pumper inside if we need to fight fires. Again, this is only IF we are attacked, but we don't expect to be attacked."

Tommy was already thinking; he told the other two young men, "If we get word that the Indians are on the way, then we must deny them our horses. One of us should go to the corral, throw open the gate, and fire his revolver into the air; that'll drive the horses out. The horses will either return to their original homes or just scatter. If the Indians want our horses, they'll have to work for 'em!"

They finally got their food and it was as great-tasting as they imagined, but it took a long time. All three young men wrote a letter to a loved one, just in case, and Tommy collected them from both Davie and Timmy and, along with his own letter, plus the remainder of their money, they dug a hole inside the corral and buried everything. The last thing they each did was to put a note in each boot saying to search the corral.

Then, they waited. The days passed agonizingly slowly. Finally, two weeks later, news was received that the Indians must have gone to Canada, because the US Army couldn't find them. Tommy decided it was time to return to Denver.

They dug up their money and letters, packed their belongings, boarded their hay-laden wagons, and started for Denver, with Timmy herding the horses. It went surprisingly well. The horses had ample time to become a herd, and a large stallion had become the leader, so he was fitted with a halter and was led by the second wagon. Timmy rode along and kept the group together, and it wasn't hard. The next day, Davie took his place, and on the third day out, Tommy had the job.

The trip back to Denver was slow, and all three young men were on edge until they saw the outline of the city set against the Rocky Mountains. At the boardinghouse, general store, and livery stable, everyone was very happy and relieved to have them all back home, safe and sound.

Chapter Three

The Porter family's wagon was slow and cumbersome. The heavily loaded old Conestoga wagon creaked and rattled whenever its wheels ran over a rock or encountered any unevenness on the trail, which was almost constantly. Laurie walked alongside it with Jeffrey Porter, age ten.

They weren't part of a wagon train, but were just following the trail west toward Denver. Mrs. Porter wasn't well, although no one seemed to know what the cause of her ill health was. Mr. Porter was a big man; he didn't appear to be very smart, but he seemed nice enough, except for the way he looked at Laurie from time to time. Laurie liked the children, especially Jeffrey. He always wanted to be different, and walking alongside the wagon seemed to stir his sense of adventure. Laurie didn't like all the jolting and vibrating in the wagon, but Mr. Porter was the main reason she walked.

The Porters' plan was for Mr. Porter to find work once they got to Denver; then they would decide about going further once they saw the city.

From time to time, another wagon or a wagon train would pass them by, as the Porters traveled very slowly to make it easier on Mrs. Porter. Sometimes they would have time for socializing, and occasionally were invited to join another passing family for supper. Most of the time, it was just dusty and monotonous on the trail. Laurie spent a good deal of her time thinking about how she might find her real father, Sam, the Ute Indian. She spent a lot of time thinking about what he might be like, as well as what her half-brother might be like.

About half-way across the state of Kansas, the rickety old wagon broke a wheel. Fortunately, it happened within view of a small farming community. The family camped by the wagon, while Mr. Porter rode one of the horses into town to ask for help. Mr. Porter was able to secure a job at a local farm, where he earned enough money to pay for the wheel repair, although it took him a month to do so; but at least the family could get food at the farm through some of the older children working at what they could while Laurie tendered their mother and the smaller children.

They were still in Kansas when they learned of the Battle of the Little Big Horn. It was difficult being out there on the plains all day, anxious to get on with their journey, trying to occupy themselves as best they were able and waiting on a replacement wheel. When it was finally put on, it wasn't a new wheel, but their old wheel with some new parts.

Still, there was no Indian attack, and eventually, the wheels on the wagon began turning again -- slowly, but turning – heading West.

By the time they reached the Colorado line, Mrs. Porter was doing very poorly indeed, so poorly that the next day she breathed her last and quietly died. Laurie helped Mr. Porter bury her, and thereafter took over the job of taking complete care of the children, which meant she had to start riding in the wagon. This made the travel more uncomfortable, and emotionally draining trying to keep the four children consoled and busy. It was crowded in the wagon, with the entire group in it, even Jeffery, but it seemed to Laurie that Mr. Porter touched her a lot more than seemed just accidental, and certainly more than was at all necessary.

One night, after they put the children to bed, Mr. Porter suggested that it would be a good idea for he and Laurie to get married. Laurie explained that she didn't love him, she wasn't interested in getting married right then, and she didn't want to take on a life as a mother of four children. She didn't say that she thought he was creepy.

Mr. Porter said nothing more for several days, but he seemed to be watching her constantly and bumping against her even more. Then, one night after putting the children to bed, he crudely suggested they could live together as man and wife and didn't need to get married. When Laurie flatly refused, Mr. Porter began to try to convince her that she would like it. Laurie was totally blunt and unequivocal in letting him know that such a situation was against the clear teaching of the Bible, and that she would never, ever, agree to it.

Later that night, when the children were all asleep, Mr. Porter approached Laurie and said, "Laurie, I need a wife and you need a husband. You also wanted to go to Denver. But if you won't marry me, then just get your bag and go! You can't stay with me!" (Of course, he knew full well there was no place to go out in the middle of the Colorado plains with no horse, no water, and no food.)

Laurie got up from in front of the campfire and silently walked to the wagon. She didn't have much, so it was easy to put it into the old sack which she had brought with her from Maysville. Mr. Porter's smirk began to fade as she packed all of her possessions in the world and started walking up the trail in the direction of Denver. Mr. Porter called to her as she was starting to fade in the night away from the light of the campfire, "Now, you come back here. You know you can't make it on your own out there."

Laurie silently kept going, telling herself that she would rather starve than to go back to being the captive of a crude, coarse man who was trying to take advantage of her situation. The awful memories of Jasper Burdock came rushing back into her mind, and she knew she couldn't stand to even look at Mr. Porter any more.

Laurie walked steadily, and a bit faster than the old wagon could go, hoping to put as much distance between Mr. Porter and herself as possible.

Laurie walked all night and, at morning, as the dawn's light brought a dim glow to the plains, she saw two trees off in the distance. Laurie was too tired to keep up the pace she'd been walking, and definitely didn't wish to take the chance that Mr. Porter might find her, so she walked the short distance to the trees and found a place where she could rest in the tall grass and be out of sight.

After taking care of children and cooking all day, she had been tired. Then after walking all night, too, she was exhausted. However, the walking had at least kept her warm enough to ignore the cold night and the wind of early April on the plains. Laurie had no difficulty in falling right to sleep.

She awoke in the early afternoon when she heard the rattling and clanking of a wagon. The tall grass had kept most of the wind off of her, and the sunshine had warmed her in her curled-up position. Laurie cautiously raised herself up on one elbow and peeked through the cover of the tall grass. There came the Porter wagon, with Jeffrey holding the reins. No doubt Mr. Porter was back in the wagon, maybe tending to one of the smaller children. About that time, Mr. Porter emerged from the covered portion of the wagon and sent Jeffrey back inside.

Laurie was somewhat relieved that they were managing without her; after all, she felt a real sense of responsibility toward the little children. Now that the Porter wagon had passed, Laurie knew that she could return to the trail and (hopefully) find a ride so she could earn her own way West.

After the Porter wagon had gone out of sight, Laurie took her bag of possessions and walked back to the lonely trail. After thinking a bit about her vulnerable situation, and the real possibility that she might die as a result of her decision to leave the Porter wagon, Laurie marched off resolutely toward the West.

Laurie walked briskly along, facing a lowering sun and no possibility of shelter. It suddenly dawned on her that if she continued into the night, she might meet up again with the Porter wagon. So, she continued to walk, but also to look carefully at the sparse vegetation off on either side of the wide wheel-rutted track through the plains. Just before twilight, Laurie noticed a small stream, just a trickle really, beside the trail, going alongside the trail for a short distance before veering off again. She reasoned that water would provide her with a path to follow back to the trail, and the water would be larger further along and accompanied by more substantial grasses and maybe even trees.

Fortunately, it was a cloudless night and, though the moon was in the first quarter phase, the Milky Way provided ample light for following the stream. After about twenty minutes, Laurie came upon a small grove of trees around a pool of water. At the furthest tree from the water, Laurie found a bunch of thick soft grass. Again, she made herself a small bed, hidden from the view of anyone who might happen along. It was a bit more difficult going to sleep this time due to that wind. Tired, but not as exhausted now, thoughts of snakes, pumas, and unfriendly Indians surfaced in her mind. Finally, after a long time, Laurie drifted off to sleep.

The next morning, the sunshine woke her up from a very restful sleep. As she lay there, Laurie began to think about other shelter issues. She had been very lucky. The weather had been warm and there had been no rain (though she did still have her oil cloth rain coat which she had been sleeping under). But sooner or later, that could change.

Then, she heard it -- small noises, getting closer, like someone walking up on her, but trying to be quiet. Laurie's first emotion was pure fear. But then she reasoned that no one could know she was there; maybe it was someone else seeking shelter, or even a rescuer. Laurie rose up on her elbow, but couldn't see above the tall grass, and it was too thick to peek through. Slowly, carefully, quietly, she began to get up on her knees.

There, right in front of her, looking directly at her, stood two female deer. Once the deer saw Laurie, they snorted and bolted off into the grassland. Laurie had been as shocked as the two deer had been. After her heart began to beat at a more normal rate, Laurie began laughing.

Then she stood completely up and began to investigate the pool of water. She saw no snakes, just a few frogs. There were a few deer tracks around the edge, but nothing larger than the holes made by small sharp hooves. Laurie knelt and using the palm of her hand as a cup, she thirstily drank as much water as she could. That relieved her thirst, but did nothing for her hunger.

Laurie took out her spare clothing and a small piece of lye soap and did her laundry. That didn't take long since she had few pieces of clothing beyond that on her back. Next, Laurie twisted the clothing to remove as much water as she could and spread the clothing on a few bushes and tall grass nearby. The clear cloudless day was making short work of her wet clothing.

Finally, Laurie decided it was safe to take a bath and wash the clothing she was wearing. After getting undressed and bathing in the cold pool of water, Laurie washed the rest of her meager wardrobe. As her clothing dried, she covered herself with her old rain coat. By about Noon, Laurie was clean, wearing clean, but slightly damp clothing, and had the rest clean and packed into the flour sack she was using as a bag.

Laurie was now confident there was no possibility of encountering Mr. Porter again, so she followed the stream back to the trail and turned Westward, once again striding briskly on her journey.

Laurie noted small wildflowers alongside the rutted trail, and even observed some more deer off in the distance as they raised their heads and looked curiously at her. She worked hard at trying to ignore her deepening hunger. She thought about the times when she had helped her mother gather dandelion greens and turnip greens to cook for supper, so it was a little surprising when she spied a small patch of turnips alongside the trail as she was looking for wildflowers to get her mind off of her hunger. Laurie stopped short when she saw those distinctive turnip leaves; turnips don't grow wild. Surely some traveler must have spilled some seed out of their wagon.

Looking around the trail, she found a sharp rock, picked it up, and began to dig around one of the larger turnips. Soon, Laurie had a large turnip in her hand. It still had considerable dirt attached, so she carefully wiped it time and again. After a while, the turnip looked pretty darn clean, so she began gnawing on it. Laurie had never cared much for turnips, but this one tasted mighty good. After about an hour, Laurie wasn't nearly as hungry as she had been. Now, she was mostly thirsty. Laurie dug up all the turnips she could find, which was only six. She decided to wait until she found water before trying to clean them, so once again off down the trail Laurie went.

As Laurie walked along considering her situation, she decided that the turnips were like Manna from Heaven with which God fed the children of Israel. Now, if she just had the staff of Moses, she could smite a rock and have water. Thinking about these things made her laugh and then pray for deliverance. Laurie had been in the grasslands for not yet forty hours but she still felt it was the right choice. It was her refusal to accept a life like the one being thrust upon her which had gotten her into this predicament.

Chapter Four

As Laurie walked briskly down the trail thinking about how she might overcome these circumstances, almost day-dreaming, she could have sworn that she heard singing. The singing got louder, and she could almost understand the words; they sounded vaguely familiar. Then Laurie detected the weak sound of a distant wagon, and the singing again, louder this time. Yes, she knew that tune....

"Mine eyes have seen the glory of the coming of the Lord;

He is trampling out the vineyards where the grapes of wrath are stored;

He hath loosed the fateful lightning of His terrible swift sword:

His truth is marching on.

Glory, Glory, Hallelujah!

Glory, Glory, Hallelujah!

Glory, Glory, Hallelujah!

His truth is marching on.

I have seen Him in the watch-fires of a hundred circling camps,

They have builded Him an altar in the evening dews and damps;

I can read His righteous sentence in the dim and flaring lamps:

His day is marching on.

Glory, Glory, Hallelujah!

Glory, Glory, Hallelujah!

Glory, Glory, Hallelujah!

His day is marching on.

I have read a fiery Gospel writ in burnished rows of steel:

As ye deal with My contemnors, so with you My grace shall deal;

Let the Hero, born of woman; crush the serpent with His heel,

Since God is marching on.

Glory, Glory, Hallelujah!

Glory, Glory, Hallelujah!

Glory, Glory, Hallelujah!

Since God is marching on.

He has sounded forth the Trumpet that shall never call retreat;

He is sifting out the hearts of men before His judgment-seat;

Oh, be swift, my soul, to answer Him! Be jubilant, my feet!

Our God is marching on.

Glory, Glory, Hallelujah!

Glory, Glory, Hallelujah!

Glory, Glory, Hallelujah!

Our God is marching on.

In the beauty of the lilies Christ was born across the sea,

With a glory in His bosom that transfigures you and me.

As He died to make men holy, let us die to make men free,

While God is marching on.

Glory, Glory, Hallelujah!

Glory, Glory, Hallelujah!

Glory, Glory, Hallelujah!"

Laurie had turned around and was watching as three wagons got closer and closer. From the time Laurie had first identified the song, she had begun to sing along.

By the time the singers had finished the song, all of them had spotted Laurie standing at the edge of the trail, watching them approach, and they could tell she was singing, too.

Laurie stood still until the first wagon pulled up in front of her and stopped. The whole family had come out from under the cover and were looking at the peculiar sight -- a beautiful young woman, holding a flour sack, with no evidence of how she had gotten to this isolated spot in the middle of the remote grasslands of Colorado.

The family was black. When the first wagon stopped, the other two did likewise; a representative from both wagons got down and started coming forward; they were black people also. No one had uttered a single word since the conclusion of "The Battle Hymn of the Republic."

Finally, the big black man driving the first wagon, spoke up, "Missy, you be a fer piece from civilization."

Laurie smiled and replied, "I noticed that. I was earning my way to Denver by taking care of some children. Their mother died, and we buried her a good long piece back. Their father seemed to think that he and I should be husband and wife to raise his children. I had different ideas. He gave me two choices, and I took the one what got me where you see me."

The man laughed loudly, and then he said, "Good fer you! I figger you must be doggone stubborn enough, you woulda made it even if'n we'uns hadn't come along. How long you been standing here?"

Laurie was more than a little annoyed at the implication that she had been standing there waiting to be rescued, and replied, "I've been walking the better part of two days so far, and I've spent the last two nights on the Prairie. I found a pool of water, where I had a drink and washed my clothes. I also found a small turnip patch a ways back, and I've eaten one turnip, plus I have five more in my bag."

The man's countenance turned sober and he said, "Missy, I do believe you could've walked out to some town. I'm sorry that I thought you had been standing there waiting for a ride."

Laurie quietly replied, "I would truly like to get a ride. I'd be happy to work for my keep. And my name is Laurie Burdock,"

One of the two other men who had been listening spoke up, saying, "Now, Joe, we agree we wuzn't havin' no white folk with us, since that other wagon train wouldn't take no black folks."

Joe quickly replied, "Now, Isaiah, this here is different. This ain't business, its lovin' our neighbors like the good Samaritan did."

Laurie quickly injected, "Hey, if it helps, I'm half Indian!"

Everyone in earshot looked at Laurie and considered her words, as if it might make a difference. The other driver, who hadn't yet spoken, said, "Well, that should make everyone happy. My wife's grandfather was Thomas Jefferson! So, she's part white, too. If'n we don't take this lady with us, and then I guess my wife has to leave, too. I ain't leavin' my wife out here in the wilderness."

Joe was starting to get flabbergasted with these men. "Now, we ain't a-leavin' nobody in the wilderness, even if they was all the way white. Jesus told us to love our neighbor, and them other wagon train people have the problem, NOT us'n."

Laurie asked, "Excuse me, but I don't have any way to carry any water with me; so may I please have something to drink while you talk?"

30

Joe's wife jumped down off the wagon, got a dipper, and drew water from a barrel lashed onto the side of their wagon. Laurie quickly walked to her while she was drawing the water, thanked her, and gulped down the water, and thanked her again. Joe's wife drew another dipper full, and the scene was repeated.

Laurie said, "Oh, that was delicious water. That pond water was warm and funny tasting."

Joe's wife said her name was Daisy, and she took Laurie around and introduced her to the other families. Afterwards, Laurie asked Daisy, "What can I do to earn my way around here?"

Daisy put her arm around Laurie and said, "Sugar, there's plenty to do, especially when we start getting ready to stop for the night. If you see someone with their hands full, just volunteer to help and, if someone needs any help, they'll ask for it."

That evening, Laurie was able to help with some of the smaller children while their mothers made sure the older ones bathed and washed their clothing. It was noted by the little group that they were getting low on lye soap. Laurie had never made lye soap before, and she found it interesting that the little wagon train carried its own ashes.

They had a small old barrel full of hardwood ashes collected from fires where there was ample hardwood for the campfire. A portion of the ashes was put into a pot; water was added, and the pot was placed over a fire until the water boiled for a few minutes. Next, beef fat was placed into the pot; the mixture was stirred until the fat had turned into soap. Then it was ladled into some small rectangular boxes to cool and thus became bars of soap. Boiling the water and ashes caused the lye to separate from the ashes, and that then turned the beef fat into soap.

After supper, and before bedtime, the men started singing again:

"Go down, Moses,

Way down in Egypt land

Tell ole Pharaoh

To let my people go.

"When Israel was in Egypt land --

Let my people go --

Oppressed so hard they could not stand --

Let my people go.

'Thus spoke the Lord', bold Moses said;

If not, I'll smite your first born dead!

Let my people go."

Laurie was very impressed; the men had started the singing, then the wives joined in. They made a beautifully harmonious choir. Laurie applauded, and cried, "More! More!"

Joe, Daisy, Isaiah, Hope, Samuel, and Flossie (the granddaughter of Thomas Jefferson) were all excellent singers and, like most performers, they loved an appreciative audience. The children all went to sleep listening to beautiful spiritual songs sung with heartfelt emotion and great harmony. Finally, Joe announced, "This has been enjoyable, but let us continue on the road to Canaan's Happy Land tomorrow?"

Everyone thought Joe was right, and they all liked his metaphor. Soon, everyone was sleeping peacefully, except Laurie. Thoughts about these strangers she was traveling with, her future, where she was going, and how she might find her father when she had such a small amount of information to go on.

Chapter Five

Missouri had been a slave state, and well invested in both the so-called Civil War (that wasn't what most of Missouri called it!) and a guerrilla war with abolitionists from Kansas. While the Civil War had concluded while Laurie was just a baby, the guerrilla war continued for several more years. The towns and countrysides in Missouri contained many people with a deep hatred for Yankees and, by association, black people. Laurie had grown up in a white community, and had been exposed to mean and unflattering stories about both Yankees and Negroes (as black people were called in those times among "polite society"), but not frequently.

These three families forming the wagon train seemed to be the opposite of the picture drawn by most of the adults who Laurie knew. This caused a conflict in her mind about who to trust and who not to trust. Just before she fell asleep, Laurie decided that she was seeing more Christian fellowship in these three families than several white people she knew or had known.

The next morning, Laurie awoke early and was surprised to see Isaiah up and working on building a cook fire. "Good morning, Isaiah! Need some help?"

A surprised Isaiah looked up and replied, "Not much wood for a fire out here on the prairie. You might could walk over to that small group of trees and see if'n you can find some wood there. I ain't found much."

"Sure," replied Laurie and started for the half-dozen trees about 200 yards away. At the same time, Isaiah had found some remains of an old wagon a few yards up the trail and was trying to pry some boards from it to help cook breakfast.

Laurie did find a few dead limbs, but only one arm load. She returned to the campsite and deposited the branches next to where Isaiah had been piling some small amount of burnable refuse which he had found. Laurie walked over to where Isaiah was trying to break up the old pieces of a wagon and suggested, "Why don't we just drag the whole thing over to our camp and burn it there?"

Isaiah looked up and said, "Sounds like a good idea. If you'll grab that corner right there, I'll pull from here, and I think we can move it easy enough. There ain't much left of it no way."

Soon, Isaiah had a small fire started, and he told Laurie, "Go wake the rest of the folks up, especially the women, and when they get ready, I'll feed the wagon to the fire."

Laurie went to each wagon and woke everyone as gently as she could; telling all the wives that Isaiah had the cook fire started. Soon everyone was stirring, getting dressed and washing their faces and hands. Daisy quickly began to heat a big iron skillet, and put a piece of pork fatback in the skillet which sizzled and popped a bit. That increased as the skillet got hotter. Daisy turned to Laurie and said, "I think we ought to fry up some turnips, what you think?"

Laurie grinned and replied, "I never cared much for turnips until I got real hungry so let's eat'em while we're not so hungry and save tastier things for when we really are starvin'!"

Daisy laughed and handed Laurie a knife and a turnip, "Peel half of the turnips and slice them as thin as you can get them without cutting your hand."

While Laurie was peeling and slicing the turnips, Daisy got out a large pot of cooked beans and put some in another skillet, along with another small piece of fatback. All this time, Isaiah was tending the fire by shoving some more wagon remains into it slowly to keep it going, but not so the fire would get out of hand.

34

Daisy put a coffee pot onto a bed of coals at the edge of the fire. Soon, the first skillet was sizzling and popping with the fatback-flavored sliced turnips.

In no time at all, everyone was eating fried turnips and thick hot beans, and the adults were sipping coffee. Several of the travelers commented that the turnips added quite a good change to the beans they had been eating for over a week.

That day as the wagons rolled along, they sang:

"Swing low, sweet chariot,

Coming for to carry me home;

Swing low, sweet chariot,

Coming for to carry me home.

I looked over Jordan, and what did I see?

Coming for to carry me home;

A band of angels coming after me,

Coming for to carry me home.

Swing low, sweet chariot,

Coming for to carry me home;

Swing low, sweet chariot,

Coming for to carry me home.

If you get there before I do,

Coming for to carry me home,

Tell all my friends I'm coming, too.

Coming for to carry me home.

Swing low, sweet chariot,

Coming for to carry me home;

Swing low, sweet chariot,

Coming for to carry me home.

I'm sometimes up and sometimes down,

Coming for to carry me home,

But still my soul feels heavenly bound,

Coming for to carry me home.

Swing low, sweet chariot,

Coming for to carry me home;

Swing low, sweet chariot,

Coming for to carry me home.

The brightest day that I can say,

Coming for to carry me home,

When Jesus washed my sins away,

Coming for to carry me home.

Swing low, sweet chariot,

Coming for to carry me home;

Swing low, sweet chariot,

Coming for to carry me home."

Joe had a deep rich baritone voice and he must have known the
words to all the Gospel songs which had ever been written. When the

road was particularly rough, and the wagons made a lot of noise, Joe would drop back to the middle so he could lead the singing, and that way everyone would be no more than one wagon away. It was a wonderful way to cross the plains, and made the time go very quickly.

One day, Laurie spotted a large patch of dandelions. She, Hope, and Flossie picked dandelion greens until they had enough for everyone for two days. The cooked dandelion greens were a little bitter, but they went very well with the normal staple of beans, and kept the limited menu from being quite so boring and monotonous.

After about a week and a half with the Smiths, Joneses, and Washingtons, the little wagon train came to the small town which grew up around Fort Morgan (and which had remained even after the Army had closed the fort). And, of course, they called the town Fort Morgan.

Seeing a small wagon train of black people wasn't so much a surprise, but seeing a beautiful light-skinned woman traveling alone with such a wagon train got a lot of people's attention.

When asked about how far away Denver was, they were told that it was just a few days by wagon. Laurie got everyone's attention at supper that night and announced, "I've been thinking about it. Y'all aren't planning to stop in Denver, and, while I was planning to go to Denver, my mother told me that she met my father at a fort in Colorado and I think it was close to Denver. So, I think that, since I am already here, where there was an Army fort, maybe I should try to make sure that no one here remembers my father. Then maybe I can catch another ride on to Denver if I learn nothing in this place. I've really enjoyed your hospitality, your companionship, and your singing. I'll hate to leave, but finding my father is why I came to Colorado."

Daisy got up and walked over to Laurie and hugged her. Then she said, "You're a really sweet girl, and we've enjoyed traveling with you. We understand you're trying to find your father; we just wish there was more we could do. You be careful around these town people. They'll be suspicious of you coming into town with a Negro wagon train."

The next morning, Laurie walked the short distance into town, and started looking for work. Meanwhile, the three wagons started down the trail which led past Denver and across a Pass through the Rocky Mountains.

Chapter Six

Laurie felt as alone as when she was out on the prairie before meeting that Gospel music singing group of former slaves. They had truly been friendly and pleasant to travel with. Obviously, there were some very troubling attitudes about black people. While it was true that Laurie didn't have many years of experience dealing with different types of people, other than her own family, fellow church-goers, and a few nearby neighbors, she was puzzled about how some people could decide to write off an entire race of people when the only ones she knew personally were so nice and clearly practicing Christians.

A few people in Fort Morgan were out and about this Spring day, but no one seemed to pay much attention to her. That is, they all seemed busy with something. Laurie decided to inquire about possible work at the only restaurant in town, the Prairie Kitchen, but, when she entered, the place was empty. Laurie walked to a doorway which had no closeable door and peeked into the kitchen. A woman sat there peeling potatoes; when she saw Laurie, she stopped and asked, "Would you like to order something to eat?"

The question reminded Laurie that she had no money, so she replied, "Actually, I don't have any money, so I was looking for work."

The lady hesitated a few seconds, and then said, "If you wanted to earn your dinner, I can work that out with you. If you need a full time job, I can't help you."

Laurie quickly replied, "I am looking for full time work, but I need to eat until I find a job … or a couple of small jobs. I'm here alone; some nice people gave me a ride in their wagon, but they've gone on West. I came this far because I'm trying to find my father."

The restaurant lady returned to peeling potatoes, and then said, "I wish you a lot of luck with that! You'll surely need it! It's a big country."

Laurie grinned and, nodding her head, said, "I know you're right. But, I really needed to leave Missouri anyway. At least this search'll give me something to occupy my spare time!"

The lady laughed and said, "My name is Teresa Jacobs. If you'll take over peeling the potatoes, I've other work I need to do for supper."

(Teresa Jacobs was fast approaching middle age. She had been an attractive woman and still was – except for some well-earned wrinkles and a small amount of thickening around her waist and hips. Teresa had a quick smile and a positive attitude about everything. She was several inches shorter than Laurie, but there was a twinkle in her eye. She had a somewhat ruddy complexion, and her mousy brown hair was streaked with gray.)

"I'm pleased to meet you, Mrs. Jacobs. My name is Laurie Burdock. I'll just put my bag over here in the corner, out of the way."

"I'm likewise pleased to meet you, Laurie. I do still call myself Mrs. Jacobs, though Mr. Jacobs has been dead several years. But please call me Teresa."

"I'm so sorry, Teresa," said Laurie as she picked up the paring knife and began peeling the potatoes.

Mrs. Jacobs pulled out a wooden bin from a shelf, picked up a tin cup, and, obviously poised to dip something from the bin, she stopped mid-motion and said, "Laurie, it suddenly dawned on me. You probably have no place to stay yet."

Laurie looked up and replied, "I actually hadn't thought about that yet, but you're right, this is the first place I stopped in after leaving the wagon that brought me here. Do you have any suggestions?"

"Well, child, if I'm going to put you to work, you'll have to start early some days, so you'd need to be close by. I live in a few rooms on the back of the restaurant, and there's a storeroom back there which is mostly empty. There's a bathtub in the next room over, with a small sink and pump. You can stay in the storeroom and bathe in that other room. If you're industrious, you can heat some water while we're cooking, or after the cooking if the fire is still going. Otherwise, I guess you can take cold baths."

"That's so generous of you, Mrs. ... Teresa! I'm used to cold baths back in Missouri. We didn't have much of a source for firewood."

Teresa Jacobs picked up a pot and dumped a couple of cups full of dried beans into the pot, then held the pot under the small water pump at her sink and pumped the pot full of fresh water. Then she opened a wooden box and reached her slender hand into it and came back out with a small amount of salt which she tossed into the pot of water. Next, Mrs. Jacobs sat the pot on a wood stove and added some wood to the fire, which had died down to some red coals. Satisfied that the beans could be neglected for some time, she moved on to a smoke closet where she retrieved a ham. Teresa put it into another pot, added some water, then placed the lid on the pot before putting the ham on the stove beside the beans.

Laurie watched the operation while busily peeling potatoes and remarked, "I'm a bit surprised that you are putting dried beans on to cook at the same time as the ham."

Mrs. Jacobs looked up and replied, "Well, the beans are for tomorrow, and I want some of that ham in them; but most of the ham

41

will be served with tonight's supper. When you finish peeling the potatoes, quarter them and put them into that pot." She pointed to another pot and lid sitting on a shelf.

Laurie nodded and tried to work even faster.

Soon, Teresa had moved on to canned corn, and Laurie was washing and slicing green tomatoes for frying. She also washed and sliced onions, and then turnip greens. Teresa had her preparations down to a science. In less than three hours, the restaurant was ready to serve a full menu: Smoked Ham, Fried Chicken, creamed corn, turnip greens, sliced onions, fried green tomatoes, and stewed potatoes, plus biscuits and cornbread.

As customers began coming in for the evening meal, Teresa Jacobs went to a lot of trouble introducing Laurie and explaining to people that she was looking for full time work or, failing that, maybe a couple of small part time jobs.

Laurie was kept busy bringing fresh bread to the tables, along with serving a variety of coffee, water, buttermilk, and sweet milk (sweet milk being the euphemism for fresh cow's milk which hadn't been churned to separate the butter from the liquid).

Colonel and Mrs. Davenport were among those who ate their supper at the Fort Morgan's only family restaurant that evening, and Mrs. Davenport told Laurie that she would like to hire Laurie two or three times a week as a part-time housekeeper, if she didn't find a full time job. Mrs. Davenport explained that, due to their advancing years, both she and her husband were unable to keep the house as tidy as they preferred. Two other elderly ladies eagerly made the same offer, and Laurie agreed to help each of them as often as she was able. The three part-time housekeeping jobs would pay enough for Laurie to survive on, but not enough to have much of a savings.

Teresa told Laurie that, for working two hours on weekdays and four hours on Sunday, Laurie could help herself to leftovers after supper. So, for six days a week, Laurie would clean houses between 8 am and noon, then go to the restaurant at 3 pm and work until 5pm. In fact, it worked out that she worked there about three hours a day so as to be on hand to take her own meals as well. Most days, there was some of everything left over. As the days passed, Teresa Jacobs learned to appreciate and to like Laurie more and more, and they spent a great deal of time together.

As time went on, Laurie began to clean Mrs. Jacobs' rooms some, too, plus she worked even longer hours at the restaurant.

Teresa began to notice that she had several new customers, all men. They seemed to be paying a lot of attention to Miss Laurie. That night, after clean-up, Teresa said to Laurie, "I need to speak to you about something which really isn't any of my business."

Laurie looked at her rather oddly and replied, "I can't imagine what you are talking about, Teresa!"

"Laurie, you are a very attractive young lady. I can't help but notice that your complexion is a bit darker than most. If I had to guess, I would say that you have some Indian blood in your background. Please don't take offense; you have a very lovely skin."

Laurie grinned and replied, "Thank you, Teresa! My classmates back in Missouri used to call me an Indian squaw. My mother fell in love with a Ute Indian after both of her parents and his wife all died of fever about eighteen years ago, but they got separated. I'm hoping to find this man, since the man I had known as my father was very disappointing."

Mrs. Jacobs studied on what Laurie had said for a minute, and went on, "Many white people look down on the children of mixed race unions, even more so when those parents weren't married.

"If you enjoy working here with me, I wonder if you would object if I took advantage of your beauty."

Laurie got a puzzled look on her face and said, "How would you do that?"

Teresa showed a little mischievous grin and replied, "I want you to change clothes."

"But I do! I only have three dresses, and I wear a different one of them every day, to keep what I'm wearing clean."

"I guessed that your wardrobe is limited, and I know you're always clean and neat in your appearance. But what I want is for you to have new dresses." As Laurie opened her mouth to object, Teresa went on, "I'll pay for Mrs. Arthur to make you two nice dresses, which you'll wear alternately on Sundays – and at no cost to you for them."

"Teresa, how is my wearing them on Sundays going to help you enough to pay for two dresses?" asked Laurie.

"Haven't you noticed the Marshall and his Deputy have started coming to Sunday dinner? Several other men who haven't eaten here more than two or three times in the past year are coming regularly now, and they're all paying a lot of attention to you."

Laurie slightly bristled, and burst out, "I don't want to do anything to encourage any man to try pushing himself off on me! I've experienced that and I don't like it!"

"Laurie, I would never encourage anything like that, but a lot of men, especially those out here in the West, are single or, in the case of older men, widowers. In my restaurant, I really don't think you'd be offended by them, but you might find several suitors that you liked. If you simply treat them with gentle respect, I think most of them would do likewise. If you're willing to try this, Mrs. Arthur is a very good seamstress, and she told me that she would make you two nice dresses

44

for just a small amount of money and a couple of Sunday dinners. I insisted that there be no other dresses in town of the same pattern."

Laurie was still a bit unsure, but so far everything Teresa had done for her had been really nice, and she really did like Teresa.

Mrs. Arthur turned out to be very nice as well as very talented. In addition to making the dresses, she suggested a new way for Laurie to wear her hair that looked very attractive. Laurie's own attention to her looks had always been limited to being clean and neat. As a result, her hair -- which was almost straight, but had some body to it -- had always just been tied back out of her eyes.

Mrs. Arthur showed her how to put it up in a coiled bun, and how she might curl it with a curling iron. "You simply put the curling iron on a hot stove for a few minutes, and then curl your hair around it for about five minutes, repeat with a different section of hair" she said, demonstrating it on her own hair. Laurie wasn't much interested in the curling iron, but she really like the coiled bun, especially leaving a few strands looser so as to keep the look from appearing too hard.

Laurie decided to wait to debut the new hair style until the look would include a new dress.

It was soon thereafter that Mrs. Arthur delivered the first new dress, and it was lovely! The fabric was a special one she had gotten quite a long time ago, on a visit to Denver, but never found the right use for -- a mix of purple lilac flower sprays and pretty green ferns, on a deep green background. It was a pattern unlike any other fabric in town (as Teresa had asked her to ensure), and, fortunately, it was just enough for the one dress; that is, it was enough for a slim figure such as Laurie's.

The fitted waist wasn't tight, but showed just how small Laurie's waist was, especially with its purple grosgrain ribbon belt. The upper part of the dress was just billowy enough to be conservative and decent, and just snug enough to make it clear that its wearer was a female, while the softly pleated skirt provided small folds of material to give Laurie flexibility for moving around and working. It made a very attractive package.

The next Sunday, after breakfast, Laurie changed into her new dress and rolled her long black hair into a neat bun.

Nearly every customer who came in after church for Sunday dinner complimented Laurie on how attractive she looked. Teresa did all of the kitchen work, leaving Laurie to circulate among the customers and do all of the dining room work. Quite a few heads were turned, and men who had never said more than asking for some drink or condiment began trying to engage Laurie in conversation. As suggested by Teresa, Laurie smiled politely at everyone, thanked people for each compliment she received, and refused to engage in any conversation other than menu-based. It hardly seemed like work; it was fun!

Chapter Seven

The battle of the Little Big Horn, and Crazy Horse, was a hot topic around Denver for a long time. Tommy became known as the young man who barely avoided being scalped by Indians. He tried to counter the stories with the truth, but it was impossible. Everyone wanted to have known someone who should have been at the scene of the battle, but avoided it simply by Divine Intervention. But, on the positive side, it was good for business. People referred customers to him because of this notoriety, even as illogical as it was.

Summer was slipping away, and, though Tommy had enough horses and wagons, he did need more hay for them. So, once again, Tommy, along with Timmy Elliott and Davie Barton, set out to buy as much hay as they could cram onto two wagons. If they found any horses for sale, well, that would simply be a bonus, but wasn't their primary objective.

The trio headed east toward Kansas along the main trail. About four days after starting out, Tommy and company passed through a small but bustling community (which eventually became the civilian town of Fort Morgan). The young men stopped there, in order to have a break and to enjoy sleeping on clean sheets and eating food other than bacon and beans.

During their brief stop, Tommy observed a lovely dark-haired young woman walking down the street. As he watched her smooth almost athletic form glide over the wooden sidewalks and around people busy talking or loading supplies into their wagons, he was enchanted.

Not wanting to be caught staring at her, he idly turned his attention to look further down the sidewalk and saw a curly-haired toddler who was gazing about in wonder. Then, as Tommy watched him, the child, who had escaped his mother's attention for a moment, noticed a dog on the other side of the street and ventured out into the street to go to the dog.

Suddenly, Tommy noticed that a wagon was coming down the street, being driven much too fast for the area it was in; it was being pulled by a very spirited team, which its driver was showing off for the local crowd. Tommy started to race to the toddler to pull him to safety, but realized he was too far away to reach him in time. He looked on in horror, feeling hopeless.

But then, almost out of nowhere it seemed, that lithe athletic form he had been admiring darted out into the street, effortlessly swept the child up in her arms, jumped back up on the sidewalk, and deposited him back safely behind his mother (who had no idea what had just transpired, but who would hear about it later from others who had witnessed the miraculous rescue).

The lovely young woman continued on her way as if she had done nothing out of the ordinary and saved children's lives at the risk of her own every day or so. Tommy had been enchanted before; now he was truly smitten.

After the three young men had secured their teams and wagons, and had a bath and changed into clean clothes at the local hotel, they went to the lobby and inquired about the best place to eat in town. The clerk recommended two places: the local saloon, and a restaurant called the Prairie Kitchen. Since none of the young men drank or smoked, they eliminated the saloon and decided the Prairie Kitchen would likely be their best choice. The clerk pointed in the direction of the restaurant, and the three started walking down the street.

By the time they walked into the restaurant it was getting towards the end of the supper hour. They went to a round table, set off a bit by itself, so that they could talk without bothering anyone else. Tommy was talking to Davie when he suddenly felt a presence at his side. When he looked up, his mouth fell open involuntarily, but he quickly closed it, and said, "Good evening."

Laurie looked down at the cowboy-looking young man and thought to herself, this was the most handsome man she had ever met; she smiled and asked, "What will you gentlemen like for dinner? We have Fried Chicken and Pot Roast tonight."

Davie was quick to make his decision and order the fried chicken, and Timmy took only slightly longer to order the same; both of them also asked for potatoes and cooked greens, too (no beans tonight for them!), and biscuits. It was clear that these two men were ready to eat.

Laurie turned her attention to Tommy and said, "And, Sir, what will you be having tonight?"

Tommy stuttered a bit, and had to ask, embarrassed, what the choices were again, as his brain felt as if it had completely shut down. Laurie dutifully repeated them without any hint of irritation. Her matter-of-fact response was enough to give Tommy a little of his confidence back.

Tommy recovered enough to ask, "Miss, may I ask your name?"

Laurie smiled and replied, "Certainly, my name is Laurie Burdock."

Tommy was trying desperately to think of something to say or ask, so she wouldn't go away, which he knew she would if he just gave her his order; finally he blurted out, "I saw you save that child this afternoon."

Laurie begun to be embarrassed and replied, "Oh, that was nothing. I didn't really save anyone, maybe I kept the mother from being frightened, but really it was nothing."

Tommy was shaking his head. "No, it wasn't nothing, you really saved that child's life. I could see it all very well. There was a real good possibility that little boy would've been run over by that wagon. I deal with horses a lot, and I can tell you, seeing that child out there in the street in front of those horses really scared me."

Laurie flashed her politest "customer smile" and said, "Well, in any case, what would you care to eat this evening?"

Tommy saw that she was finished with idle conversation and was all business now, so he decided on Pot Roast, with potatoes and cooked greens, and corn bread. Laurie took the order to the kitchen, and Davie smirked and said, "I think we'll come back this way on the return trip!"

Tommy, for the very first time, had a new thought pass through his mind, different than any he'd ever had regarding any other young lady -- "Oh, my, I hope she isn't married." Tommy was a much sought-after young bachelor in Denver. He had an excellent reputation, both as a business man and as a clean-cut Christian. Lots of Denver mothers tried to play matchmaker to become Tommy's mother-in-law; but it was no use. Tommy seemed to take a different girl to church each Sunday, and, while he enjoyed attending church socials, clearly he had found no special spark with any girl to retain his interest for long.

Tommy knew he didn't have much time to devote to following up with his interest in Laurie while he was in town, but he managed to ask one person he met about her. The fellow he asked was a young man only slightly older than Tommy.

After the standard introductions, Tommy made his usual inquiry about horses or hay for sale; but the man knew of none in the area.

Then, as he was about to go on his way, Tommy added, as if it were merely an after-thought, "Mr. Dawson, I just happened to remember... I met a young woman working in the Prairie Kitchen, and wondered who I could get to give me a formal introduction to her? She has a real nice bit of color to her skin, like she spends a good deal of time outdoors."

Mr. Dawson looked intently at Tommy. "I guess you're talking about Laurie Burdock?"

Tommy was encouraged. "Why, yes, that's her."

Mr. Dawson made a slight frown and said, "I don't reckon you know that that girl is an Injun? Some folks consider her to be attractive, but, personally, I prefer white women."

Tommy was taken aback. "I guess she might have some Indian blood in her, I don't know, but I'm sure she is no Indian. Besides, what difference does that make?"

Mr. Dawson shrugged his shoulders and went further. "She may be a very pretty woman. But they say that when she came to town, she was with a Negro wagon train. And everyone knows how those people are; you know what I mean. No tellin' what the sleepin' arrangements were."

Tommy was running out of both time and patience with the guy, but didn't want to get into an argument, so he just mildly asked one final question, "Does she go to church?"

Mr. Dawson said, "No; that is, at least I never heard of her goin' to church. She works as a domestic, doin' housecleanin' for folks, I've heard tell, when she ain't at the Prairie Kitchen."

"Thank you, Mr. Dawson. I need to be on the trail. Please keep a watch for horses and hay for sale, and let me know when I come back this way if you learn of any."

51

Mr. Dawson smiled and nodded as Tommy turned away and headed toward the wagons. Tommy made a mental note to inquire about this Laurie Burdock from someone else the next time he came near to Fort Morgan. He didn't need to hear any more opinions involving stereotypes about whole groups of people, whether based on race or religion or whatever.

Tommy's two helpers already had the wagons all hitched up and their belongings all loaded, too (not that there was very much in the way of baggage), as well as provisions of food and water (for men and for horses).

Tommy climbed aboard one of the wagons, released the brake, slapped the reins on the horses' backs, and yelled, "Giddup!" And, so, they were off, to Nebraska and maybe to Kansas.

Chapter Eight

Besides working at the Prairie Kitchen, Laurie cleaned house several days a week for the retired US Army Colonel Davenport and his wife, and cleaned two other houses one day (or sometimes two days) a week for two elderly ladies, one a spinster and the other a widow. She also did an occasional washing of laundry for each of the three customers, to earn a little more. She scrupulously saved as much of her money as she could, so that she could continue to search for her father.

One day, during her "cleaning" day at the almost spotless home of Colonel and Mrs. Davenport, after Laurie had completed dusting everything in the house and moping the floors, she went into the living room where the Colonel was at his desk, looking over some old papers and smoking his pipe. Laurie didn't particularly care for the smell of any tobacco, but she readily admitted the pipe smoke was much milder than the cigars which some men smoked.

"Colonel, I've completed dusting and moping the entire house -- not that it needed it. Mrs. Davenport keeps it awfully clean herself. I was wondering if you need anything further before I leave?" asked the young lady.

Colonel Davenport looked up from his papers and asked, "Laurie, do you have a few minutes to visit with an old man?"

Laurie smiled and replied, "Colonel Davenport, I always have time to talk to you! Besides, I have at least an hour before I need to be at the Prairie Kitchen."

The Colonel was pleased, and it showed, "Thank you, Laurie. It is always nice to speak to a young person, especially one as attractive as yourself. It allows me to think about myself when I was much closer to your age.

"Dear, I have heard gossip that you are part Indian, and that your goal in being here is to look for your father. I wonder if your father might be an Indian? Please stop me if I exceed the boundaries of friendly inquiry."

Laurie gave a matter-a-fact reply: "The man who I had always known as my father was a drunkard. After his death, my mother told me that she was nearly ready to give birth to me when they married. She seemed to think that somehow this influenced him in a negative way, causing him to drink. Whether it did or it didn't, I don't know, but I do know that he was a really mean drunk.

"My grandparents, that is, my Mom's mother and father, had decided to leave Missouri and go West when Mom was young, to make a better life for themselves and escape the poverty back home. My mother told me they reached Colorado, where they stopped at a Fort. While they were there, her father had come down with a fever. There was fever all over this Fort, and Mom and her mother needed help in caring for my grandfather. A young Indian couple was the only assistance available, and soon, Mom's mother and the Indian woman caught the fever as well. Not long after that, my grandfather died, then the Indian woman died, and finally my grandmother died as well.

"My mother had written a letter to her older brother, my Uncle Bob, asking for help. But Uncle Bob had to harvest his crops first, so that his family would have food for the coming Winter, so it took him a while before he could leave Missouri.

"The Indian couple had a young son, less than a year old, so after his mother's death, Mom took care of him. That gave the Indian man a chance to go back to his tribe and bring back his younger sister to care for the child, as a more permanent solution.

"Mom said that, thrown together so closely, after both suffering such great losses, and neither having family around for help or comfort, the two of them fell in love, or thought they were in love.

"After a short time back from his tribe, the Indian man, who was a Scout for the Army, had to lead a mapping patrol, which was estimated to be gone for three months. In the meantime, Uncle Bob showed up at the Fort and took my mother back to Missouri. After she returned, she discovered she was with child -- me."

Colonel Davenport had been listening carefully to every word. Then he said, "I was here at Fort Morgan about twenty years ago, when it was still a Fort. I had just been promoted to Colonel, and I was sent here as my last assignment in the Army. I retired here after thirty years of service. I remember one scout who spoke English better than the others. I don't recall his name, but as I remember, he was a Ute Indian. That was a tribe which was generally peaceful."

Laurie excitedly interrupted, saying, "My mother said she thought Sam was a Ute!"

The white-haired old Colonel's face lit up with a smile, "Sam, that's it! Sam Running Bear!"

"Praise the Lord! This can't be merely luck; in His wonderful love for us, He has directed my footsteps here to you!" exclaimed Laurie.

"Young lady, while that does seem like more than a mere coincidence, I fear that I have to tell you that I haven't seen Sam Running Bear in almost twenty years. And, of course, as the Post Commander, I didn't keep track of the lives of the Indian Scouts, nor even where they were, if they weren't needed for some reason. You see, there would always be a few Scouts living at the post, and so there was always at least one available for each mission. But I do recall San

Running Bear as being an exceptionally fine Scout, which is why I remembered his name, if that's any comfort to you."

The practicality of the information, and the fact that is was from a long time before, didn't dampen Laurie's spirits much. She was very excited to have confirmed her mother's memory of her real father. Laurie replied to the white-haired elderly man, "At least I have found the Fort, and confirmed my mother's memory, and now I actually have a name and a starting place.

"Oh, my, I just realized as well – that also means that my grandparents are buried here somewhere. Would you have any idea where that would be?"

It was a question which Colonel Davenport hadn't even considered, so he turned his thoughts to that issue now. He sat deep in thought, occasionally taking a puff on his pipe. After several minutes, he said:

"They'd almost have to have been buried in the old Fort cemetery. The cemetery was actually located outside of the Fort itself, and placed on a hill, because the South Platte River gets out of its banks sometimes. When Fort Morgan was decommissioned, much of its land became part of the town, and the Fort cemetery became the town cemetery.

"That cemetery is on a small hill, on the North side of town, near the trail where you came in from the East. I think most people call it Boot Hill now; I don't know that it ever had any other name. It's just the other side of the road from the river."

Laurie looked at him hopefully and asked, "Do you know if there are any records of who is buried where, or if there are any grave markers?"

Colonel Davenport carefully and politely replied, "Honey, I doubt if any record exists about your grandparents. The Fort is a long time closed, so, if there had been any records, they would probably be in Washington D.C. with the Department of War. But, frankly, civilian people who died while passing through the area rarely got more than an unmarked grave. I'd be greatly surprised if any record exists, even in Washington.

"You understand, the West is littered with unmarked graves, but it doesn't mean the people buried in them were unloved, or that they didn't get a nice funeral service; that's just the way it is. Grave markers cost a lot of money, and then there's the time it takes to get them brought in on wagons, and folks usually had neither the money nor the time to spare.

"But, that doesn't stop you from visiting their graves, even if you aren't sure exactly which ones they're in -- you'll still know that you're close to their final resting places, and that might give you some comfort. Just go up there, and have a look around. It's not far."

"Thank you, Colonel. And I do understand. I helped bury a woman out on the plains, and we had no way to permanently mark her grave. We only stuck a large stick in the ground, but that may even be gone by now."

Colonel Davenport nodded his head and, added, "Out here in the frontier, death can often come more unexpectedly, and sometimes violently, without the person having any allies to help prevent it. Both medical men and lawmen are spread mighty thin across this land, and many people coming here – or through here – have no family or friends with them. And many of the niceties of civilization are absent as well. People in tough situations must get tough, and, many times, must choke down their emotions in order to make rational decisions."

"I don't doubt, Colonel, that you're correct. You've had a lot of experience making a lot of tough choices, I'm sure. However, I've chosen to follow this mission to its conclusion – or mine. I crave a father's love, and I want to give a daughter and sister's love. Who knows? It might do some tiny bit of good for both Indians and white people by forcing them to face members of their own families who belong to the other race."

"That's quite laudable," replied the old Colonel, "but it's a lot more than race separating us. I believe it's our cultures and our different ways of life that divide us the most. Indians exploit the naturally-occurring animal life and vegetation, while white people exploit the land itself. This sets up a direct conflict and, due to our sheer numbers, the Indians must change and give up their way of life. It's very sad, in a way, even though I do believe that the Indians can benefit a lot from the knowledge that we bring."

Laurie grinned and said, "I've greatly enjoyed our talk, which I found very helpful, but now I need to hurry back to the Prairie Kitchen and start helping prepare for supper, or I'll be late!"

"It was nice chatting with you, dear. Hurry on, and don't work too hard. Mrs. Davenport and I won't be over again until after church on Sunday."

The next day, when Laurie had completed her cleaning chores at the widow's home, she walked the two or three miles to the little hilltop cemetery. There were less than half a dozen actual grave markers, with crudely carved names and dates, none of which were more than fifteen years old.

There was also evidence of other grave sites, some sunken where the absence of care allowed the earth to settle below ground level when nature had reduced the wooden coffin and the remains to the dust from which they came. Other grave sites indicated having benefited from care provided by someone, as they were the opposite, being small hills where soil had been heaped on the grave as the earth settled,. Surely, Laurie thought, her grandparents would rest in one of the sunken grave sites. There were about dozen of these in evidence. The neglected grave sites made Laurie feel sad and lonely, and she drew no comfort there, so she didn't linger long.

Chapter Nine

Davie had watched Tommy and his reaction to the tall, dark-haired Laurie back in Fort Morgan, and asked, "Tommy, I guess we're coming back this way when we return to Denver?"

"Well, maybe, if it's convenient, and it don't take us too long to find all we come for," replied Tommy rather unconvincingly. Davie had noticed that Tommy had kept looking on both sides of the street as they went out of town, trying to gain one more glimpse of the mysterious young woman, he was sure. Davie wasn't easily misled, and he felt confident they would be stopping in Fort Morgan before reaching the outskirts of Denver.

As luck would have it, within only two weeks, they had both wagons piled high with hay, and had even bought two yearling horses. Best of all, as far as Tommy was concerned, Fort Morgan was indeed right on their path back to Denver.

Tommy had been driving the lead wagon, with Davie driving the other, and Timmy riding with Davie. Their saddle horse and the yearling horses were trailing along behind attached by a rope halters. The night before they would be arriving back at Fort Morgan, after they stopped to camp and eaten their beans and bacon, Tommy announced, "I think you two can handle the wagons just fine. I think I'll take the horse and ride on ahead into Fort Morgan. If you two don't show up tomorrow night, then I'll ride back and look for you. But, I'm sure, nothing is going to happen to you along this trail."

Davie looked over at Timmy, winked, and said, "I think the Boss is in love!"

Timmy, taking the cue, added, "Ooh, darlin', won't you come to Denver with me? Did I mention that I like Indians?"

60

Tommy began to turn red, and said, "You two just do your jobs, and don't worry about me. I can take care of myself."

His comments were met with snickering, but they said no more, and Tommy went to his selected sleeping place under the wagon.

The next morning, after breakfast, they broke camp and started on their way toward Fort Morgan. Tommy took off at a gallop, and soon distanced himself from the wagons. In a short time, Davie and Timmy were unable to even see his dust.

Tommy decided the General Store would be a good place to learn something about Laurie, so he easily found it in the small town. Tommy tied his horse to the hitching rail, dusted the trail dust off of his clothing with his hat, and climbed the steps to the board walk. He entered the store and looked around. A small bell attached to the door had announced his arrival.

Tommy saw a man behind the counter, and went over to him, saying, "Good morning, Sir! Beautiful day today, isn't it?"

The storekeeper raised his eyebrows and replied, with only a hint of sarcasm, "I reckon it's a nice enough day, though it is already afternoon." At overhearing that, a woman who was cleaning up around the store gave a quickly muted tiny giggle.

Tommy's face added a tiny bit of color as he realized his greeting had fallen flat. "I guess it is, at that. I've just ridden in, so I wasn't paying no heed to the time of day it had got to be. What I was looking for, sir, was a bit of information."

"Hmm, I woulda sworn that you were trying to sell me something."

Tommy's color got a little bit deeper red, and he stumbled over his words just a bit. "I was trying to start a conversation, so I could ease into my question, but, since I reckon that didn't work, I'll just blurt it out. I'm interested in one of your customers, and I figure that a man who runs the General Store knows just about everything about the folks in town that there is to know. She's a tall black-haired young woman, and her name is Laurie. I wonder if you could tell me anything about her?"

The storekeeper replied, "I can't tell you nothin' about her."

The woman stopped cleaning, and said, "I can tell you about her. Her name is Laurie Burdock and she works at the Prairie Kitchen, and for old Colonel Davenport and his wife, and she cleans house for someone else, too, I think. She's half Injun. She arrived here some time back on a wagon full of Neee-gros." (She kind of sneered the word, drawing it out as she said it.)

Immediately, Tommy discounted anything further she might say about Laurie's character, but he still had more to ask. Then he said, "I was wondering how I might go about meeting her, proper-like. Does she have any family in town who could introduce me to her?"

The woman sniffed, "Huh, ain't you afraid of being scalped or stabbed to death?"

"Well, not really. I'm not married, and I find her attractive and hard-working. I thought I might be able to meet her at church or something."

"You're a brave fella. No, she's got no family here. There ain't no other Injuns in this town. I don't know which tribe she belongs to, either; she might be the daughter of Crazy Horse, for all I know."

"Well, maybe you could tell me where to find this Colonel Davenport's house?" Tommy asked.

"The Colonel and his Missus live up the street near the church. Their house is the big, pretty white house with the green shutters, up that-a-way." (The woman gave a hand gesture, in the general direction of the church and the house.)

Relieved that the conversation was finally ending, Tommy said, politely, "Thank you, Ma'am, for all your information." Then he turned to the man behind the counter, whom he assumed to be her husband (since he had deferred to her and hadn't uttered a word since she began talking), and said, "Thank you, too, Sir, and good day to you both."

As Tommy exited the store, he overheard the man say, "Strange young fellar, ain't he, Sarah?" Tommy didn't linger to hear Sarah's response.

Tommy traveled on up the street toward the church, and easily found the white house with green shutters.

He went up to the front door and knocked. An older white haired man opened the door, and asked, "Good afternoon, young fella. Is there something I can do for you?"

Tommy sensed he was in the company of a distinguished gentleman, and made an extra effort to be polite and respectful. "Good afternoon, sir; would you be Colonel Davenport?"

"I am, and who do I have the pleasure of addressing?" replied the Colonel.

"My name is Thomas Thompson, but everyone back home in Denver calls me Tommy. I'm pleased to make your acquaintance."

"And how may I be of service to you, Mr. Thompson?"

"Actually, I came to inquire about an employee of yours, a Miss Laurie Burdock."

Colonel Davenport wasn't at all surprised to see a nice young man inquiring about Laurie, but he was slightly reserved in his answer,

63

since he didn't know the young man. "Well, young fella, Miss Laurie works up there at the Prairie Kitchen nearly every day of the week, and only works here a couple days a week. Why don't you just go up there and talk to them?"

Tommy, who had respectfully removed his hat, answered, "I've been up there, sir. That's where I met Laurie, when I had dinner there, but she was working and there wasn't any real introduction, so I started out looking for some relative who could give me a formal introduction, but I was told she has no family in town. No one seems to know if she attends a church here or not, but I gather that she doesn't, so meeting her at church and getting the preacher to introduce us doesn't seem to be the answer either. So I'm trying to find a way to get introduced to her, properly."

Colonel Davenport weighed what Tommy had said, gave it some thought, and finally said, "Mr. Thompson, please come inside."

The Colonel showed Tommy to a chair in his sitting room, and they both sat down. The Colonel picked up his old pipe (which had gone out, since he had drifted off to sleep until Tommy had knocked on the door), searched around and found a match, and struggled with it a short while before relighting his pipe. He puffed on it several times, and, when it was clearly lit, he put it down and addressed Tommy.

"Young man, you seem like an honest and decent fellow. But you must understand that I'm not going to reveal any information that has been given to me in confidence.

"Laurie is a recent citizen of Fort Morgan. She apparently had some difficulty with a family she was traveling West with, and disembarked in the middle of the plains. Fortunately for Laurie, three Negro families came along with three wagons and gave her a ride. Laurie has come West looking for her father, and the first clue she was given was that he'd been at a fort in Colorado.

64

"Well, this is a town which grew up around Fort Morgan, so it kept the name when the fort was decommissioned by the US Army. Laurie left the wagons of the kind folks who had rescued her and she stayed here, so she could check out the Fort Morgan area to see if her father had any connection with it.

"Laurie found work at the Prairie Kitchen, and also works for, I think, three families, including my wife and myself, in need of housekeeping assistance. Laurie is a bit quiet, and, I think, sad, but she works hard and well. I think she is saving to extend her search for her father.

"I don't think your plan for an introduction is going to work, or, even if you could get someone to introduce you, I don't think it would do you a lick of good. I think Laurie is a good Christian girl, but I don't think she has time to go to church, since, as far as I know, she works every Sunday. And, besides that, she doesn't appear at all interested in meeting young men. She's got too much on her mind in finding her father to think about much of anything else, if you see where I'm going."

Tommy gave that some thought, and replied, "I suppose I just need to make a pest of myself, and see where that gets me."

Colonel Davenport leaned forward and said, "Young man, if you'd accept a piece of advice from an old man, it seems to me that maybe, if you could offer her some assistance in her search for her father, that might do you more good than anything else you could undertake."

Tommy looked down at the floor for a few moments, considered what the Colonel had said, and replied, "Well, Sir, it's like this. I have a business in Denver. I travel out this way from time to time to purchase hay, feed, and horses for my livery stable. I'd truly like to help Laurie with her search for her father, but, frankly, I don't have the know-how to search for anyone, nor do I have the time."

"My, my, you seem mighty young to be a real businessman!"

"Well, Sir, you see, it was like this -- my father had the business, and then, when I was only a young boy, he died in an accident. A friend of my father took me in, raised me as if I were his own son, and helped me run the livery stable until I was old enough to do it by myself. He's always given me good advice over the years, and has been as good a father as a man could want!"

Colonel Davenport picked up his pipe, puffed on it a few times, and resurrected a tiny coal in its tobacco which blossomed into gray-white smoke. He took the pipe from his lips, and said, "I guess that is all I know to tell you, Mr. Thompson. I wish you all the luck in the world. I think someday Laurie will make some lucky man a mighty fine wife."

Tommy rose to leave, and thanked the old Colonel for all of his information and encouragement. Then he tipped his hat and closed the Davenports' door behind him.

Tommy mounted his horse and rode slowly over to the feed store to talk to the proprietor. Mr. Fred Dawson was waiting on a customer, so Tommy wandered around inside the store looking at various things like chicken feed, oats, and vegetable seeds. When Mr. Dawson finished with the customer, Tommy asked him if he had heard of any horses for sale, and explained that they had a full load of hay and would be starting to Denver soon.

Mr. Dawson hadn't heard of anything which interested Tommy, so he purchased some oats for the two teams, the yearlings, and the saddle horse. After he had paid for the oats and put the bag across the saddle, he wished Mr. Dawson a "Good Day" and reminded him that they would return in several months looking for the same kind of information.

Tommy led his horse, rather than rode, and walked the few blocks to the Prairie Kitchen, where he tied the horse to the hitching rail.

Tommy went into the restaurant, but he was too early for supper. No one was in the dining room, so he stuck his head into the kitchen doorway. Two women were busy working on getting ready for the evening meal, and neither one had noticed him. Tommy spoke up and asked, "Am I too early for coffee?"

Both women jumped a little at the surprise sound of a man's voice, and Mrs. Jacobs answered, "If you'll give us a few minutes, I'll put on a pot. Just have a seat at one of the tables in the dining room, and one of us'll bring it to you. Would you like a piece of cake to go with it, or anything else?"

Tommy raised his eyebrows and asked, "What kind of cake?"

Teresa Jacobs replied, "I have some yellow cake with lemon frosting. It's left over from lunch, so it's still fresh. I do have a slice or two of chocolate cake, with chocolate icing, but that cake is probably pretty dry, since I made it three days ago. I've kept it in the pie safe, with a small saucer of water sitting in there, trying to keep everything moist, but, as I said, it's been there a while."

Tommy quickly replied, "I'm not too keen on lemon, but I'm right partial to chocolate. Even stale chocolate is better than lemon, to me. My adopted mother runs a boarding house in Denver, and I often eat the leftover cake. I actually prefer my desserts a little chewy, and not quite so fluffy and light."

Teresa grinned at his enthusiasm for stale cake, and asked, "Do you want the cake now, or later, with your coffee?"

Tommy again quickly replied, "It doesn't really matter; now is fine. I'll go on out to the dining room where I can watch for my two friends, who should be coming into town soon."

Tommy chose a window table where he could watch the trail from the East, and sat down in one of the chairs with arms.

In a very short time, Laurie came out of the kitchen with a big slice of cake on a plate, a napkin, and a fork. She carefully sat the cake plate down in front of Tommy, placed the napkin to the right of his plate, and placed the fork on the napkin.

Tommy looked up at her and asked, "Are you sure that I'm not left-handed?"

Laurie didn't miss a beat, but replied, with a small smile, "If you were left-handed, you wouldn't have sat on the right side of the man you were with the last time I served you." Then she turned and walked back into the kitchen.

Tommy sat quietly eating small bites of the cake, trying to make it last a long time. He was only about one-third of the way through it when Laurie returned with a large cup of coffee. She sat it down on Tommy's left, and asked, "How is the cake?"

Tommy was looking at her when she asked and, before he answered, he looked back down at the cake, almost as if he were surprised it was still there,. "The cake is very good," Tommy replied, "I was trying to make it last so I might have more opportunities to talk to you before I have to leave."

Laurie smiled and said, "I'm flattered. What did you want to talk to me about?"

Tommy had been about to take a drink of coffee, but he immediately set it down. "My name is Tommy; that is, Thomas Thompson, but Tommy for short. I've been going around town trying to find out how I could get someone to introduce us, to make it formal. But, unfortunately for that plan, I've learned that you have no family in town and you apparently don't attend church here. I even spoke to Colonel Davenport, thinking maybe he could introduce us, but he told me that I was probably wasting my time since you were on a mission to find your father."

Laurie paused a bit before replying, as she ordinarily didn't engage in any personal conversations with customers. However, somehow she felt comfortable with this young man. "The old gentleman is correct; I'm committed to finding my father, or at least looking a lot harder than I have been able to so far. I'm trying to earn enough money for at least the next step of my search. While I'm here, I have a job, food to eat, and a place to stay; but once I leave here, I'll have to pay my way to the next location my search takes me.

"And I normally do attend church, that is, I used to, but I'm just so busy working now that I usually don't have the time, or, when I do have some spare time, I always seem too tired to go."

Tommy finally was able to take a drink of the coffee; it was hot and strong – he liked that.

"Well," he replied, "how much longer will your search involve staying in Fort Morgan?"

Laurie answered, "I'm not sure. I went to the local cemetery recently, and that was not productive. I didn't think it would be, but I needed to mark it off the list. My father was associated with the US Army here while it was still an active Fort, and Colonel Davenport was the Fort Commander back then.

"I believe he may have more information than he's given me so far, but I just have to give him time to remember it. He vaguely remembers my father, and, every once in a while, he remembers some little additional bit of helpful information, but it was a long time ago, and the Colonel has a lot of memories about many forts and many people and they can all get mixed up."

Tommy interjected, "I told the Colonel that I would just make a pest of myself while I'm here, and see if that does me any good in impressing you. The main problem is a shortage of time for me to do that. I've got to leave in a couple days to go back home to Denver, but I'll be returning here the next time I need more hay and grain for the horses."

Laurie looked a bit confused at that, and asked, "Isn't it a long way to come to buy food for your horses? I thought Denver was over a hundred miles away?"

Chapter Ten

Tommy started laughing and said, "I understand it might sound crazy. But, you see, I have a livery stable back in Denver, and I have about fifty horses -- unless the men working for me have sold some of them while I've been gone. Feeding those horses takes a lot of hay and grain, more than I can get locally, for the prices I want to pay, anyway."

Since Laurie seemed interested, he went on: "At the livery stable, I also rent horses, wagons, buggies, and tack -- you know, saddles, bridles, reins, that sort of thing. I also sell all of those things, and we board horses for visitors as well."

Laurie exclaimed, "Why, goodness, you can't be more than a year or two older than I am. How'd you manage to build a business like that?"

Tommy smiled ruefully, not wanting to lose any sliver of admiration from Laurie and admit he hadn't personally built it up from scratch, but he had always been an honest person: "I did it the easy way; I inherited it from my father. He died in an accident, and I was adopted by Jim and Abby Watson. Jim helped me and advised me. Jim never charged me anything for helping me, and never took even any small piece of anything which was mine. He's a great friend and father to me.

"The Watsons and me were in Montana then, and, when we moved to Denver, Jim wouldn't charge me anything for the costs he experienced in the move. We did use my horses and wagons to move as much furniture and folks as possible; there were seven or eight of us -- I'd have to stop and count noses to be sure – who made the move."

Laurie had been listening intently, and tried to imagine going such a long way with so many children. "That's a might big family to move any distance at all."

Tommy thought about it, and said, slowly, "Yes, I guess there must've been eight of us. But it wasn't all just one family. I guess I made it sound that way, but there was more than one family in our group. There was Pete and his wife Sarah, and their three little girls; Jim, Abby, me, and my brother; and Billy – no, that makes ten, not eight. Depending upon how you count, that could be four families, if you counted me separately. I counted Billy as a separate family, too. He was an interesting character. Billy moved to California a couple years ago."

Laurie was still a bit puzzled and asked, "Why did everyone have to leave at the same time?"

Tommy responded, "Well, it was a gold rush town, and the gold vein played out. The rest of the town left immediately, but Winter was almost there, and we had lots of property we need to move, so we waited for Spring. All of the people who left early had left large piles of fire wood behind, so it was easy to stay warm. They also left behind a lot of food stuff, because their wagons were full of furniture and other heavy belongings, and they only needed enough food to get them to Virginia City."

Teresa stuck her head out of the kitchen and called, "Laurie, can you come back here? We need to finish getting supper on." Liking the looks of the young man, and wanting to give them a chance to get acquainted, she had been giving Laurie and Tommy plenty of extra time to talk, but now she was at the point where she really needed Laurie's help.

"Oh, I'm so sorry, Teresa! I'm coming right now! This cowboy was wowing me with his stories!" She then winked at Tommy, and headed for the kitchen. That wink put Tommy on Cloud Nine. He just sat there, feeling an all-over glow, until he suddenly realized his coffee was getting cold. So he resumed eating his cake, faster now.

About the time Tommy finished his cake and coffee; he looked out of the window and watched two heavily laden wagons come creeping into town. It was time to go help the men.

Chapter Eleven

Tommy paid for his cake and coffee, then told Mrs. Jacobs that he and his friends would be back for supper once they took care of the horses. Teresa went back into the kitchen and commented, in an off-handed manner, "It's all right, Laurie, the good-looking cowboy is coming back for supper." But then she spoiled her studied nonchalance by giggling.

Laurie blushed, but stated firmly, "He IS nice looking, but I have my own plans, and they don't include any man at this time. Maybe you should wait on them when they come back."

When Tommy, Davie, and Timmy came in to eat, Mrs. Jacobs took their order and brought their food. It confused Tommy, since he had definitely gotten the impression that Laurie had been interested. Maybe the older woman was trying to keep Laurie working, or maybe Laurie just grew tired of the conversation? In any case, it had the opposite effect on Tommy than she intended, namely, he became more determined, not less.

The next morning, the trio hitched the horses up to the heavily-loaded wagons, and crept out of town, headed for Denver.

A few days after Tommy and his workers had left Fort Morgan; Laurie was again working at the Davenport home.

When she had finished sweeping, dusting, and mopping the house, she washed clothes and hung them on the clothesline out back. Laurie then went into the sitting room, and asked the Colonel if he could spare some time to talk to her

Colonel Davenport looked up as she entered the room, and he said, "Hello, my dear, you hard-working young lady. I'm delighted to see you, and of course I have time to talk to you. In fact, I'm always very pleased that you've come to visit with me for a while."

Laurie smiled and replied, "Colonel, you are just about the sweetest, kindest man I have ever met! You always bring a ray of sunshine to my day when you talk to me."

The white-haired old man grinned and said, "It pleases me to learn that I bring pleasure to you. Do you have something in particular that you want to talk about today, Laurie?"

"With all your wisdom, Colonel, I am looking for some advice. I wonder if you might have any suggestions on how I might proceed with the search for my father and half-brother."

"Laurie, my dear, it so happens that I've been giving that some thought recently, thinking about the half-brother you mentioned.

"You know, it seems to me that I did hear it said once that Sam had a son. As far as I can recall, though, I never saw him myself; the situation, as I heard it, was that Sam's son was being raised by his tribe. Not sure how I even heard about the son, or who it was that talked about him, since I'm fairly sure I wasn't a party to that discussion, but it was just something I overheard. That must have been, oh, at least eighteen or twenty years ago, which would fit the time period you described. Can't be absolutely positive, though; the years all sort of run together these days," said Colonel Davenport with a hint of sadness in his smile.

Laurie had been sitting in front of the Colonel when he first began to speak. However, as he started talking about her half-brother, she leaned forward and sat on the edge of the chair, listening intently to every word.

Colonel Davenport took some time to load his pipe, pack it down, and start the tobacco smoldering, before he began speaking again, this time with more certainty in his voice.

"You may have noticed a wagon in front of our house recently, if you passed by here on those days while you weren't helping us. We had visitors, a man and his wife, for about three days. The husband is an old friend of mine; well, a long-time friend, anyway, 'cause he's not as old as I am. He left the Army only about five years ago, so he's more up-to-date on current Army events than I am.

"Among other information we talked about, Jeb told me that a Colonel Edwards is in charge of watching over the Utes these days. The reservation he supervises is up in Utah, he said; there is an Army Camp very near that reservation.

"There is another reservation of Utes in southern Colorado, or maybe New Mexico, but when I brought up Sam Running Bear's name, Jeb said he believes Sam was serving in the more Northern area. The biggest obstacle is that the Indian Wars are up that way also, and it's possible there may be some Utes involved. Several tribes had banned together under Crazy Horse and defeated the Seventh Cavalry at the Battle of the Little Big Horn. You wouldn't want to go up that way with less than a large Cavalry escort, and, right now, that would be impossible to arrange."

"I hope my brother and father are safe and not involved in these wars," worried Laurie.

"I do have a suggestion for you, though. Since you can't go looking for them up there right now, I'd recommend that you write a letter to Colonel Edwards, and address it to the Department of the Army, along with a note that this Colonel's last known post was in Utah with the Ute Indians. In your letter to Colonel Edwards, just ask if he has any knowledge of an Army Scout named Sam Running Bear," suggested Colonel Davenport.

Laurie fairly jumped with excitement. "Oh, I saw the wagon, and I noticed two strangers, a man and his wife, eating at the restaurant a couple of days ago, but I didn't know they were your guests."

That very night, Laurie wrote the letter to Colonel Edwards, asking if he (or anyone at the War Department) had knowledge of a Ute Indian Scout named Sam Running Bear, or his son, whose name was unknown to her; she addressed the letter to the War Department, with the accompanying note about the last known assignment of Colonel Edwards, as recommended by Colonel Davenport.

Laurie also wrote a letter to her younger sister, and described the town where she was living. (Laurie did leave out all of the details about how she got there!) Laurie's last line in the letter said that her next letter would be to her mother.

As Laurie waited for a return letter or two (either from the War Department or Colonel Edwards, or from her sister, or from both), she asked everyone she could find who had been living in Fort Morgan any considerable amount of time, if they had ever seen or heard anything about any Indian Scouts who had been there at the fort.

Universally, however, no one had lived in the town before the US Army Fort closed except for four people: the Davenports, the widow lady, and the spinster. None of the women had ever had any contact with an Indian at all, leaving the Colonel the singular source of information. It appeared the Colonel had exhausted his memories of the times. (After all, eighteen years was a mighty long time in the Western frontier for civilian families to have been there.)

Laurie realized that she would have to do a lot more searching, which would involve going somewhere different, in order to continue her search for her family. So, in the meantime, all she could see to do was to continue saving what little money she could, in hopes of moving to Denver.

In the meantime, Mrs. Jacobs' idea of the new dresses was paying dividends. Business had increased at the Prairie Kitchen, especially at Sunday dinner. So many church members were coming that it caused many of their friends to follow. Teresa Jacobs had to hire another worker, and she started paying Laurie a small wage as well as give her room and board.

The second dress Teresa had ordered for Laurie had been delivered by Mrs. Arthur weeks before, and it was as lovely and as flattering as the first. This dress had a pale blue background, and was covered in darker Blue Bonnet flowers; it was a perfect complement to Laurie's dark hair and eyes, and "sun-kissed" complexion. Again, there was no other pattern that was even similar to its floral one, anywhere in town. The cut of this dress matched the first one's cut, also emphasizing Laurie's narrow waist with a grosgrain ribbon (this one a deep blue).

Stage coach drivers got wind of the "nice place to eat" in Fort Morgan, and a few even began changing their route so they and their passengers could eat at the Prairie Kitchen. Other businesses began trying to capitalize on the increased traffic, and a second, nicer saloon (with food also offered) was built just down the street from the Prairie Kitchen. The new saloon cut into Mrs. Jacobs' business a little bit, but she wasn't too worried, as she was having difficulty keeping sufficient groceries on hand even with the slight decrease.

Laurie was the center of attention on Sunday afternoons, with several men customers trying to flirt with her and gain her attention. But they were all wasting their time. When Laurie daydreamed -- which wasn't often -- the only man she ever thought about was the tall, handsome young man from Denver. (And she usually mentally scolded herself for thinking about him so often!)

About two months after mailing her letter to Missouri, she received a letter from her sister, Mildred, along with one from her mother as well.

Laurie had mentioned Tommy in her letter to Mildred, in what she imagined was an off-hand, casual manner. But that didn't fool Mildred; she was excited for her sister, and entreated Laurie to try to find her "another tall handsome fellar as well." Mildred was bluntly explicit in her letter: "The pickin's in rural Missouri are poor!"

Evelyne Burdock's letter contained mostly news about the family and neighbors, along with fervent assurances to Laurie that her mother still loved her and missed her. The news she wrote was, first of all, news of the children (their growing like weeds, their good health, their schooling, etc.), then news about neighbors, next was church, and, finally, local general news. Included in her mother's letter were updates about who had died, who got married, who had a baby, and that type of news. It was almost as if Evelyn Burdock poured everything she could think of into her letter.

It was comforting to read those letters and it made Laurie just a little homesick, but for her family rather than for Missouri. But, then, she missed Tommy, too.

She knew, however, that she wasn't ready to go back to Missouri, even to visit, for a good while to come, if ever.

She knew that she had to go on with her search, or she would forever wonder about her father and her half-brother, and worry about whether they were all right, or if she had missed her opportunity to be part of their lives and to have had an additional loving family in her life. She had come this far; she MUST go on!

Chapter Twelve

Tommy and his helpers arrived back in Denver a little over a week after they left Fort Morgan. It took them much longer to make the return trip because of their heavily loaded wagons.

Everyone was happy to see the young men back home safely, and that they had been successful with their buying trip. Jim and his cousin Phillip were especially happy to see that there was more than enough hay for Tommy's needs, meaning they would have plenty to sell at the General Store.

Pete Elder always worried about the young men when they went off without an older man along, someone who could add an extra degree of experience and sound reasoning to moderate the adventuresome spirit of the boys. Pete well remembered some of the errors of his youth, and the close calls he'd had because of them; he sincerely believed his escapes were nothing short of a miracle from God -- or at least a Guardian Angel.

Pete always believed that when Sarah agreed to marry him, it saved his life. Now, they had three little girls and a baby boy. (Actually, his oldest daughter could hardly be referred to as a "little" girl, but she would always be his little girl to him, no matter how old she was chronologically.)

The loose-knit (unrelated by blood, but very closely bonded) "family" members were an unlikely combination. Phillip Smith had been sent to prison for killing a man in Georgia. Jim Watson had been a Confederate soldier from Georgia during the recent War. Pete Elder had been a buffalo hunter, a cowboy, and even ridden shotgun on various stagecoach operations and gold mining endeavors. Everyone knew that, if you needed a tough job done, Pete was as good as they came.

One time, a few years previously, Jim and Pete were hauling a wagon load of gold from the small mine in Bannock, Montana, to Virginia City, Montana, when they were attacked by highwaymen. Jim had been injured, and only one horse of the wagon's team had survived. Jim tried to get Pete to take the horse and go for help (thinking that at least Pete would be safe). But Pete refused to leave Jim alone, since the highwaymen were still close by (or the two men thought they were, anyway). Jim and Pete formed a bond for life from that incident.

Jim's wife, Abigail, had been a widow before she met Jim, but she and her husband had been childless. Susan's husband was killed in a hostile Indian attack on a wagon train, the same wagon train in which Jim was moving his cousin Phillip (who was newly released from prison) to Colorado, and that's how Philip first met her. Pete's wife, Sarah, was the daughter of a Philadelphia banker, who most definitely didn't want her to marry such an unstable, reckless drifter as Pete.

Now, Abby Watson ran a boarding house in Denver with the help of Sarah and Susan, while Jim and Phillip ran a General Store. Pete, who could do anything, filled in wherever and whenever he was needed. They were, in daily practice (if not in the actual fact of blood kinship), one big happy family.

The children sometimes almost didn't seem to differentiate which of the adults were their parents. They may have actually thought the other children they were growing up with were their siblings! Each of the adult women treated all of the children as if they all belonged to her, and freely dispensed love and help to every one of them equally. (The men, too, didn't show any obvious favoritism.)

Phillip and Susan had three children: the two boys from Susan's first marriage, and the little baby girl born of their union. Tommy had been adopted by Jim and Abby when his father died; Jim and Abby hadn't been married long at that time, but now they had a little girl and a baby boy.

All of the local girls and young women seemed to have a crush on Tommy. He was ruggedly handsome, kind, a practicing Christian, and he owned a moderately successful business. Perhaps it was merely the prospective mothers-in-law who were wishing their daughter would snatch up Tommy, rather than the young women themselves, pushing for marriage, but it did create a sometimes slightly uncomfortable atmosphere for him, since he wasn't interested in being paired off.

After the work at the livery stable was all caught up following their return, Davie made a special effort to tease Tommy about his Indian girlfriend out at Fort Morgan. Much of his teasing was done in public areas, too.

Thus, soon, nearly the whole town was aware that Tommy had another reason for taking rest stops in Fort Morgan, although it was undeniable that it wasn't only a convenient place to stop, being about half-way home, it was also directly on the main trail from Denver to locations where farmers would be selling grain and hay.

On one particularly stressful day, Tommy was having a number of problems arise, with wagon wheels suddenly breaking, and horses that appearing to have developed various problems overnight, he wasn't at all happy to have Davie ask, in a jovial manner, when they were going back to Fort Morgan.

Tommy curtly bit out, "If you have nothing better to do around here, maybe you should look for another job. I'm getting awfully tired of your idea of fun."

Davie was taken aback, since Tommy was usually so mild and easy-going. He hadn't meant to be annoying, but he realized now that he had gone too far. He immediately replied, "Oh, Boss, I'm real sorry;

82

I guess I have been a burr under your saddle. I'll drop it; I swear, I didn't mean nothin' by it. I don't want you firing me; I like working here, and I'll work harder, really I will!"

Tommy realized how short he had been with Davie, and ruefully said, "Ah, Davie, I don't want to lose you. You're a good worker, and you know as much about the equipment and animals around here as I do. It's just that today nothing seems to be going right, and, in all honesty, I'm starting to get bothered by you constantly ribbing me."

Davie added, chastened, "I've always been one to pick on people, too much I guess, since sometimes I got into fights over it. Now, I ain't never objected to a good fight, but I don't want to ever fight you, and I like it here, a lot."

Tommy looked up from the wheel he was trying to fix and said, "Christians are supposed to show the Love of Christ, and aren't supposed to get into fights if they can help it. But, I will tell you, if I'd been Timmy last summer, I think I would have punched you for the way you kept picking on him."

Davie got a little sheepish, and replied, "He did. But I figured I had it coming, so I apologized and forgot all about it 'til you said something."

They both enjoyed a good laugh at that, and the atmosphere lightened between them. Davie grabbed hold of the wheel Tommy was struggling with, and together they were able to get the steel rim, which secured the spokes and wheel hub, in place.

Jim Watson loved to read. Mostly because of that, his general store regularly bought a large (for that time) amount of books. He would read them, and then put them out for sale to customers, or put them in a small library Abigail's Boarding House kept for its boarders. Many of the boarders really enjoyed reading from the broad selection of books they kept on hand, and Abigail would also sell books to the boarders, or trade for books the boarders had brought with them.

Jim even subscribed to two newspapers from back East: the Boston Journal, and the New York Herald. Frequently, the newspapers would be a month late arriving, and some never made it at all. Some of his employees enjoyed reading them, too, and then they'd be "recycled" over to the Boarding House library. (There wasn't much else to do with your spare time but read, back in the 1870s, especially if you didn't go to any saloon.)

Right before supper one evening, Jim was sitting in his office at the Boarding House, reading a newspaper story about a French policeman.

The article told about the Frenchman's experimenting with ferrotype (a tintype of photograph, which was much less expensive than the daguerreotype), in order to possibly create a cheap way to catalog photographs of suspects; his goal was to solve the problem of police officers having to remember what the suspect looked like. His name was Alphonse Bertillon.

The newspaper article also mentioned that this same police officer had discovered, in 1870, that everyone's fingerprints were different, and the article said he already had a workable plan for identifying criminals by their fingerprints.

Jim found the subject fascinating, and was devouring the article with great interest, when Abby came into the room. Abby had overheard Davie's good natured ribbing and questioning Tommy about a woman he had met. Abby, as his mother, wanted to know more about it, but she didn't think she was the appropriate person to ask Tommy about it, so she suggested Jim should ask at supper that night, since it would just be the three of them.

Jim, in front of Abby, brought the subject up with Tommy at supper one night, by first telling a little white lie, saying, "I couldn't help but overhear Davie teasing you about an Indian woman you met at Fort Morgan. Is that something you want to talk about, son?"

Tommy shrugged his shoulders and replied, "Sure, I don't mind. It doesn't look like anything'll ever come of it. Laurie Burdock is her name, and she's not an Indian. I don't know the whole story, but her mother isn't Indian and her father was, although I guess they never got married. So Laurie is only half-Indian. She's got dark hair and eyes, and a slightly darker complexion than us, like she'd been out in the sun a lot, and she's real pretty.

"Laurie came to Fort Morgan from Missouri after her stepfather died. Her mother told her then that he hadn't been her real father, that her real father was an Indian. All Laurie said about her stepfather was that Mr. Burdock had been a real disappointment, but I'm not sure what that means; maybe he beat her? Or beat her mother? Anyway, she came West looking for her real father.

"Laurie told me flat-out that she isn't interested in getting courted by anyone until she has found her father -- or given up her search, which don't seem likely to happen any time soon. I reckon she never had any fatherly love from this Burdock fella, ever."

"That is really truly sad," Abby said. "Fathers are supposed to love their children, and it seems to me that girls need that love to be shown them more than boys."

Jim spoke up next, saying, "I know you're a long way from thinking about getting marrying, Tommy, but you do realized the extra problems you'll face if you marry Laurie, whether she's full blooded Indian or a half-breed? There'll always be some jerk ready to say nasty thinks about Indians, whether out of ignorance or if for no other reason than to make you mad."

85

"Oh, yes, I know. I met a couple of those folks in Fort Morgan. I didn't have any trouble ignoring their comments. I can see, though, that if I had to put up with a lot of that kind of talk, it might get a whole lot harder to ignore, particularly about someone I loved.

"This woman is good, kind, hard-working, and smart. I saw her rescue a little boy who had walked out in front in front of a team of horses that was almost totally out of control. She just ran out into the street and picked the little boy up and brought him back and set him down by his mother and calmly went on her way. She moves very gracefully. Very handsome … no, she is a beautiful woman. She is pleasant and friendly to everyone.

"She works in a restaurant called The Prairie Kitchen. Laurie also does some housekeeping and clothes-washing for folks. She is saving as much money as she can so that she might travel to learn more about wherever it is that her father lives now. She doesn't seem to think about how difficult it would probably be for her, as a half-breed, to be welcomed in an Indian tribe."

Jim replied, "I doubt there's much danger of that. I expect she'll never find her Indian father; they don't exactly leave a trail for white men to track them down. And, besides, with the Indian wars still going on, there is a good chance he'll have been killed."

Just then, one of the General Store employees came into the room and stood quietly waiting to speak to Jim Watson. When Jim noticed her, he asked, "Did you want to speak to me, Elizabeth?"

"Yes, Mr. Watson, I do," the nervous young lady replied. "I come to tell you that my fellar has asked me to marry him."

Jim smiled and said, "I'm very happy for you, Elizabeth. Does that mean you want to take some time off for the wedding, and a honeymoon?"

86

Elizabeth took a deep breath and let the words out in a rush, "Oh, no, sir, Mr. Watson. It's just that my Henry wants to go back to Indiana and work for his older brother. His brother has been having some sickness, and needs help bad. We plan to marry soon, and, quick as we get our wagon and team paid for, we're goin' back to Indiana. So I guess what I'm trying to say is that I'll be quittin' and leavin' Denver."

"Oh, my!" exclaimed Jim, "You've been a great help in the store, and I'll hate to lose you. I'll never be able to find anyone who knows the stock and the system and prices as well you do. Do you have any idea how much longer you can stay working at the store before you have to leave?"

Elizabeth thought for a few moments and replied, "I don't see any way that we could leave in less than a month, and probably more like six weeks. I just wanted to make sure I let you know right away, so you could make plans; y'all have been so kind to me. And, if you need to replace me before we're ready to leave, well, I'll understand."

"Elizabeth, you needn't worry at all about losing your job. While I'm certainly going to start right away trying to find someone to replace you, I'd really like to have you at the store, too, if possible, to train them before you leave."

"Oh, Mr. Watson, thank you, thank you! I was so afraid you might want to fire me right away, and then we'd have to stay here even longer."

"Elizabeth, if, for any reason, I find that I need to replace you before it's time for you to leave for Indiana, I promise you I'll pay you two weeks' severance pay for your hard work and loyalty!"

Elizabeth was so overwhelmed with gratitude she started crying, choking out heartfelt thanks to Jim. She then hurried out to tell Henry the good news, and to remind him that she had been right about Mr. Watson. (Henry had been unsure about telling him so soon that she would be quitting her job, but that had been based on his own experiences with other bosses. Henry was much relieved to learn just how wrong he had been to caution her not to tell Jim.)

The next day, Jim was explaining to Phillip about the general store's need to find a replacement for Elizabeth, as Abby sat nearby.

Abby sat quiet listening to the men, thinking deeply. After they had finished their discussion of the subject, Abby suggested, "Jim, what do you think about offering the position to this Laurie Burdock that Tommy knows?"

Jim was visibly shocked; when he had recovered, he asked, "Abby, are you trying to play matchmaker?"

Abby smiled enigmatically, and replied, "There are a lot of lovely young women in this part of Denver. We know plenty of unmarried pretty girls whose fathers have money, and plenty of mommas who would love to see their daughters married to Tommy. But – have you ever heard Tommy talk about any of them like he does about this Laurie?"

Jim looked at her a moment, frowned, and said, "Tommy did say she was smart. If she were here, and if she finally gave up trying to find her father, then maybe she would find Tommy. Is that what you're thinking?"

Abby cautioned, "Well, she might not even want to leave Fort Morgan right now. So maybe we should talk to her about coming here to work at the store, without mentioning it to Tommy? So as to not get his hopes up if nothing comes of it."

Jim snorted, and replied, "I think meddling is a mistake, but I know you'll do what you want. We do need a replacement for Elizabeth at the store. And I guess it isn't all that far to Fort Morgan; since we wouldn't be heavily loaded down, we can travel at a fast pace.

But what are you going to tell Tommy about our going off? And, Abby, it will be us going, not just me!"

Abby thought for a minute or two, and then smiled a purely feminine smile. "Most men seem to think that women are always looking for a new dress or a trinket, or something frivolous like that, so you just tell Tommy that I heard there was a new shipment to Fort Morgan that I wanted to see about. He won't think anything at all about our trip!"

And, sure enough, Tommy didn't give their sudden trip a second thought.

Jim and Abby left the next morning, taking enough luggage for a few days' visit, and driving Tommy's nicest buggy, pulled by his fastest team. Jim felt a bit uncertain about it all, but determined to see it through, while Abby felt excited, and very interested in meeting Laurie Burdock.

Chapter Thirteen

The widow Donavan's late husband had been a successful freight operator, and some folks around Fort Morgan gossiped that he had amassed a huge fortune, and left it all to his widow (since those rumor-mongers hadn't seen the couple throwing large amounts of money around while he was alive).

Those tales, in turn, had led to another rumor, this one being that Mrs. Donavan had secret caches of money hidden all throughout her house (since she hadn't been seen spending a lot of cash since her husband had died).

The widow Donavan had hired Laurie Burdock to clean her home weekly, and to wash her clothing as needed. Laurie cleaned Mrs. Donavan's home one Friday morning, and then left for the Prairie Kitchen. The following day, Saturday, an elderly friend of the widow Donavan came over for a visit and to discuss the Sunday school lesson for the following morning.

(Mrs. Donavan had a standard routine of meeting her friend at the woman's house on Friday afternoons, and had been doing so for years, a fact well known around town, but that particular Friday her friend had arranged to have a dress fitting with Mrs. Arthur, so their meeting had been rescheduled to Saturday morning at Mrs. Donavan's house.)

When the visitor received no answer to her knocking, she thought maybe Mrs. Donavan was doing some chore, and was unable to hear the knock. After all, the visitor was a slightly-built elderly woman, and she knew she didn't make hardly any noise pecking on the door. So, not receiving a reply, she pushed open the unlocked door and went in, calling out, "Sarah! Are you home, Sarah? Yoohoo, where are you?"

When the visitor rounded the corner off of the hallway, and could see into the kitchen, she was stunned and horrified by the sight before her. She felt sick to her stomach, and almost fainted; she had come upon a macabre crime scene. Mrs. Donavan lay on the floor, not moving, and there was blood everywhere (or so it seemed to her friend).

After turning away from the terrible scene, and taking several deep breaths, the elderly woman was able to force the nausea down. She then quickly left the house, and scurried as fast as her old legs would carry her directly to the Marshal's office. It was, in fact, the fastest she had moved in decades!

The Marshal sprung into action. He told the elderly woman to lie down in one of the jail cells, and he'd be back to question her later. He sent his deputy to fetch the local doctor and bring him to the Donavan house to examine the body. He himself raced to the house, pausing only long enough to ask the preacher (who he fortuitously passed on the street) to go to the jail to comfort the elderly woman, not even spending the time to explain why.

Soon, the Marshal was examining the worst crime scene he had ever visited. Even to an experienced lawman, it was a truly nauseating sight.

Meanwhile, on his way to fetch the local doctor, the deputy (of course) told every citizen he saw on the way to the doctor's office why he was going for the doctor, and (of course) those people told everyone they saw what the deputy had said, and thus the story spread like wildfire within the town.

By the time the doctor arrived, there was a crowd of on-lookers gathered, eagerly trying to see some gore. The Marshal had just barely managed to keep everyone out of the house (although he did have to threaten to shoot a couple of people if they didn't comply with his orders; and, after one look at his expression, those people believed him – and they were right to believe he'd do it).

Once his deputy got back, the Marshal gave him strict orders to keep everyone outside (including informing the deputy exactly what he'd do to him if anyone got in, since he knew that it must have been through the deputy's loose talk that the town folks had learned about the crime).

The doctor examined the body of poor Mrs. Donavan, and told the Marshal that she had been stabbed multiple times. He told the Marshal that she had fought fiercely for her life. After some witnesses had been sworn in, and looked at poor Mrs. Donavan, her body was removed to the Undertaker. The house was locked up, so no nosy folks could get in, and the evidence could be undisturbed and viewed again later.

Now, almost everyone in town knew that Laurie Burdock was working for Mrs. Donavan. They also knew that Laurie was working several jobs; some knew she was saving money to search for her unknown father, but most people just knew she was trying to get as much money as she could as fast as she could.

In addition, they all knew that Laurie was at least half Indian. The Indian Wars were still going on, and some folks in town had lost family members or friends in battles with Indians. Also, many in the town simply didn't trust any Indian, half-breed or full blood.

Therefore, some people, in their small minds, put these circumstances together and decided that Laurie must have killed the poor woman, since almost everyone thought they knew for certain that Mrs. Donavan had lots of money stashed around her house.

The Marshal was inundated with questions about why he wasn't immediately arresting Laurie for the murder, or at least investigating Laurie. Finally, he gave in to the pressure, and, not ready to arrest her, went to interview Laurie. Those people with a serious bias against Indians saw this as more proof that Laurie was, in fact, guilty.

On the day after the murder, around noon on Sunday, Jim and Abby Watson rolled into town. They proceeded to the Prairie Kitchen, and were surprised to see that the restaurant was only about a third of the way full. Surely, the only restaurant in town would have a big crowd after church let out? It always had before, according to Tommy.

Teresa Jacobs greeted them, and, after reciting the day's menu to them, asked what they would like to eat. Jim and Abby ordered their food, and then followed up with what they considered to be a fairly innocuous inquiry about Laurie Burdock.

Teresa gave them a very tired, but very sharp look, and, after Abby had quickly explained that they had been told about Laurie by Tommy, Mrs. Jacobs said that Laurie and the Marshal were in the back searching Laurie's belongings.

Both Jim and Abby had such shocked looks on their faces that Teresa realized that they weren't just seeking gossip, and she explained about the murder, and the assumption by some of the local citizens that Laurie MUST be guilty; after all, she was an Indian.

About that time, the Marshal and Laurie emerged from the back. The Marshal was carrying a small box, and Laurie's shoulders were slumped and she looked very dejected. When the Marshal left, Laurie told Teresa that the Marshal had taken all of the money she had saved up since coming to Fort Morgan. Before leaving, he had instructed Laurie to try to come up with a list of how much money she had received from each of her employers, and a list of everything she had bought, so as to be able to prove the money belonged to her.

Jim had overheard most of this conversation, and he was appalled. He ate his dinner quietly and thoughtfully. Afterwards, Jim told Abby to have another cup of coffee and wait at the restaurant, while he went to the Marshal's office.

The Marshal wasn't at all pleased to have yet another person come to talk to him about the murder, but he patiently listened to Jim Watson, as he introduced himself, and explained to the Marshal how he had heard about Laurie.

Then Jim started telling the Marshal about the French policeman and his efforts to create a positive identification system. When he mentioned that Alphonse Bertillon had discovered that everyone's fingerprints were unique, as well as the bones in their hands, the Marshal, who had been listening politely, but not enthusiastically, began to show some real interest. He asked Jim a lot of questions, and Jim told him everything he could remember about the newspaper article.

After they had discussed the Frenchman's findings, the Marshal asked Jim to accompany him to the site of the murder. The two men walked down the dry and dusty streets until they came to the Widow Donavan's house. The deputy, who had been stationed on duty there, with strict orders to keep any would-be visitors out of the house, opened the door, and the two men entered the crime scene.

Jim and the Marshal examined each and every bloody mark on the walls and cabinets, looking for the most complete and well-defined hand print. Just when it began to look as if this was an exercise in futility, they found one that was ideal for their purpose on a door frame.

The print must have been left very soon after the crime was committed, and before the search for money had begun, because it was the complete imprint of a bloody hand. It looked as if the murderer had leaned up against a door frame to rest, and then pushed away with an

94

open right hand which was still covered in then-fresh blood. It was obviously a large hand which had made that print.

The Marshal found a piece of unmarked paper, and began to draw a picture of the size of the hand print (as he measured it with a length of string along each side, across, and up and down each finger, including the thumb, to be totally certain that he got the measurements right on the drawing).

Meanwhile, Jim excused himself and went outside to the fresh air, where he promptly threw up his meal from the Prairie Kitchen. It puzzled Jim a bit that this situation would have such an impact upon him, a veteran of the so-called Civil War. He knew he had seen far worse, and bloodier, scenes, during the war, and even afterwards, as when he had helped bind up the injuries of the fellow miner some years ago.

Then it struck him what that meant, and Jim realized that he had finally been healed of the awful mental trauma he had suffered in the war. There had been no mental images resurfacing in his mind of the men he himself had killed, or of the dismembered bodies of his fellow soldiers, just a deep compassion for the elderly victim, and a deep disgust for the criminal.

Shortly thereafter, the Marshal called both Jim and his deputy in, to witness the comparison of his drawing to the size of the actual hand print on the door frame. After duly watching the Marshall compare the size of the hand print to the size of his drawing (again using the length of string), both men wrote their names on the sheet of paper, and signed and dated it as witnesses. The Marshal wrote the exact location of the hand print, the address of the house, the name of the victim, and also signed and dated the paper. The evidence was then secured, and the Marshal and Jim walked back to the Marshal's office, leaving the deputy to continue guarding the house.

The Marshal opened his safe and put the witnessed drawing of the hand print in it. He then removed the same small box he had been carrying when he left the Prairie Kitchen less than two hours earlier, and locked the safe.

After that, Jim and the Marshal walked back those same dry and dusty streets, this time to the Prairie Kitchen, and entered. There were no customers in the restaurant, just Teresa Jacobs, Abby Watson, and Laurie Burdock, all sitting at a table together, drinking coffee (or just holding the cup and looking at it, in Laurie's case).

When the women heard the door open, and Laurie looked up and saw the Marshal, fear showed in her eyes, thinking she was going to be arrested.

But, when the Marshal looked down at her with a wide smile on his face, she relaxed a trifle. And, when he handed her the small box containing her savings, she looked both astonished and thrilled, and appeared to be struck dumb.

The Marshal addressed her, in a highly respectful tone: "Miss Laurie, I am very pleased to be able to return your money. Please count it, ma'am, to make sure it's all there. I hope that you understand my position, and that you know that I only did what I had to do, based on the information that I had at the time. But I have now discovered proof which clears you completely of having committed the murder."

Chapter Fourteen

After their initial shock, Abby and Teresa were smiling broadly, but Laurie broke down and began crying. The stress of being the prime suspect in a murder case, of losing the sweet friendly Widow Donavan, of having the townspeople's nasty condemnation of her cost Teresa much-needed customers, and, now, having that weight lifted from her had been too much for her nerves, which were usually so steely.

Teresa's automatic response was one which seemed to be built into her very being – feed everyone to make them feel better – so she rose from the table and asked, "Would any of you folks care for something to eat? Maybe some dessert? We've got a nice chocolate cake, almost untouched, and some pie. Or coffee?"

Jim managed a weak smile and replied, "None for me, but is there somewhere I could wash up and get a drink of water?" (He didn't want to even see food yet, after his episode at the crime scene, but he wanted to rinse his mouth out, he was certain of that.)

Teresa showed him where to go.

The Marshal thanked her, but also declined, replying, "I really don't feel like I could eat anything right at the moment; besides, I'd better head back to the office. After all, I have a murderer to find." (But, he thought to himself, at least now I think I've got a pretty good idea about how to start looking for the varmint.)

When Jim returned, with his mouth rinsed out and his face washed, he sat down at the table with the three women. Then, to the surprise of all of them, including Abby (whose eyebrows raised, but who stayed silent), Jim reached over and took Laurie's right hand in his.

He drew her hand toward himself, wrapping his long fingers around her small hand and, looking at it, assessed the overall size of the hand, including the width of it, and the width and length of the individual finger bones and thumb.

Laurie was shocked, but, somehow, she couldn't explain why, even to herself, she wasn't afraid of Jim, nor uncomfortable with him, even after her past experiences.

Jim put her hand back down on the table, and announced, "The Marshal has a real good eye. He didn't even have to look at your hand."

Abby asked, "Whatever are you talking about?" (She trusted Jim with her whole heart, so she didn't add, "And what did you think you were doing, holding that pretty young girl's hand?!")

Jim looked at Abby first, then glanced toward Laurie, and said, "This shouldn't be talked about, beyond the four of us, because the Marshal needs to do his investigating, so I'm asking all of you to keep it secret. We went to the lady's house, and we found a hand print that was left by the murderer. The hand print is too wide, and the fingers are too fat, for it to belong to Laurie. The finger length is almost the same as Laurie's, but it was clearly left by someone else, not her."

The next day, some anonymous gossip reached the Marshal's ears (in the usual roundabout way it did, of his overhearing two people talking without their paying any attention to his being nearby) that Fred Dawson had scratch marks on his face, and that he must have gotten himself into a fight with some woman; the juiciest part of the gossip was all about speculating who it could have been.

The Marshal didn't ordinarily pay much attention to gossip, but he always listened to it if he overheard any. It occasionally helped him do his job better, in furthering his understanding of the nuances of the town's interpersonal relationships. Since he was an excellent Marshal, he appreciated every little bit of information he could glean. In that way, he could better keep track of who in the town was doing what, and particularly to whom; it helped him keep a "finger on the town's pulse," so to speak. (And, since he was also an honorable man, he neither repeated, nor took any unwarranted personal advantage of, any of that gossip.)

But, after hearing that bit of gossip, and after mulling it over (because something about it tugged at his memory), he had an inspiration.

He hurried over to the undertaker's place of business. After telling the undertaker what he was looking for, the undertaker took him to Mrs. Donavan's coffin, and opened it up. Together, they both examined Mrs. Donavan's fingernails. Sure enough, there were tiny bits of human skin under several of her fingernails.

The Marshal was a meticulous lawman. He wrote down all of the relevant information, and the undertaker's name, and had him sign and date the statement of what they had found. The undertaker reclosed Mrs. Donavan's coffin, and just in time. The pastor of the church and a group of mourners had shown up to give Mrs. Donavan a Christian funeral and burial.

The Marshal returned to his office, instructed a deputy to come with him (and bring a loaded shotgun), and they went up that dusty street yet once again, this time to the saloon. It was common knowledge that Mr. Fred Dawson spent a great deal of time at the saloon.

When the Marshal and the deputy, armed with a shotgun, entered the saloon, they headed directly for Fred Dawson. The suspect looked nervously around, not unlike a cornered rat seeking an exit hole. He was clearly trying to decide on a path of retreat, but there was no place for him to go. So he decided to bluff it out. "Howdy, Marshal!

Have you arrested that Injun gal for the murder of old Mrs. Donavan yet?"

"To tell you the truth, Fred, I haven't arrested Laurie Burdock," replied the Marshal. "The plain fact is, we've proved, beyond any shadow of a doubt, that Laurie Burdock is completely innocent." The Marshal paused at that point, to let that information sink in for everyone in the saloon, who were all listening avidly – but none so avidly as Fred Dawson.

"You sure have been busy telling everyone that Laurie Burdock done it, since she's an Indian.

"But, you see, Fred, instead of going along with it being Laurie Burdock just because she's got Indian blood, I've been conducting an investigation, and I've discovered some additional information about the murder. I've found out that poor Mrs. Donavan fought her murderer as hard as she could. In fact, she managed to scratch someone pretty deep before she was so brutally stabbed to death." Once again, the Marshal paused briefly.

"Oh, by the way, Fred. I can't help but notice … you've got some mighty bad scratches on your face. Now, would you mind telling me exactly when and where did you get those scratches on your face, and who did it?"

"It was a lady friend; she scratched me. You don't know her, Marshal; she don't live in Fort Morgan, she was just passing through. It was a day or two ago. Just a little disagreement. Nothin' you need to arrest her for or nothin' like that. Anyway, how would you know the widow scratched someone? She sure didn't tell you."

The Marshal smoothly and confidently continued, in a slow deliberative manner. "Well, Fred, in a way, yes, Mrs. Donavan did tell me."

The Marshal paused again, having noticed that, with each pause, Fred Dawson got more and more agitated. A cat with a cornered mouse couldn't have been more focused than the Marshal was on Fred.

"I just got to thinking, Fred, and then I went over to the undertaker's place,. You know, where poor old Widow Donavan was taken. And the undertaker opened her coffin, and, well,we looked under Mrs. Donavan's fingernails, and what do you think we found? We found human skin, where poor old Widow Donavan had scratched the face of her wicked attacker, as he was stabbing her to death."

Another strategic pause by the Marshall, and you could have heard a pin drop in the saloon.

"So I've been looking for someone with scratches on his face, probably someone local, who might have heard rumors about lots of cash kept in the Donavan house, and who would know that the Widow Donavan is usually gone from her house on Friday afternoons." A shorter pause from the Marshal followed those remarks.

"Fred, you have scratches on your face. And, Fred, you've been around here plenty long enough to have heard the rumors about the supposed Donavan cash, and you knew the Widow Donavan was usually over at her friend's house on Friday afternoons, same as everybody in this saloon knew that. I reckon if anyone else shows up with scratches, I'll have two suspects, but right now we just have one, and it's you, Fred Dawson.

"Oh, and by the way, who's this lady friend you talked about, anyway?"

"I cain't say her name; she's married," whined Fred.

"Dawson, you keep sticking to that story, and you'll hang for sure," the Marshal said contemptuously (thinking that hanging would be too good for the evil murderer, but trusting in God to deliver His ultimate judgment, and appropriate punishment).

"Deputy, take this man into custody and lock him up. I'll tell the judge that we need to have a murder trial, and real soon!" The Marshal spoke with authority, and no one in the saloon (including Fred Dawson) doubted it would happen.

Jim and Abby Watson sat in the Prairie Kitchen talking to Laurie Burdock and Teresa Jacobs all the rest of the afternoon.

Teresa was afraid that, guilty or not, Laurie would become a liability for the restaurant rather than an asset, and she couldn't afford to lose so many customers. She felt comfortable enough with Jim and Abby that, in front of them, she finally found the courage to tell Laurie, regretfully, that, starting on the following day, Laurie could no longer work at the restaurant, because, although Teresa was very fond of her, her presence working there would ultimately result in bankrupting the business. Teresa told Laurie she'd pay her for the entire week, and she could keep the two dresses.

So abruptly losing her job at the restaurant was earth-shattering for Laurie; she was still feeling the loss of her other employer, Mrs. Donavan.

Just as Laurie was feeling more lost and abandoned than she had ever felt before, since this time she was being thrown out by someone she both respected and liked, and someone she thought of as a friend, Jim spoke up. "Laurie, I guess you've been told that I'm here because of Tommy."

Jim intended his comment to be reassuring, but, since Laurie hadn't been told anything of the kind, she didn't understand Jim's statement at all, and she found it confusing. She was in such a fog that she was unable to grasp who "Tommy" was, not connecting the name to the cowboy she had met just the week before.

Then, suddenly, it dawned on her who the Tommy was that Jim was talking about. "NO! How can that be? How could you know anything about Tommy?"

Abby saw Laurie's confusion, and spoke up to try to straighten out the matter. "Laurie, my dear, as to how we learned about you, it's a simple enough story. Davie, a man who works for Tommy – you might remember Davie, he was one of the two men who were here with Tommy -- was teasing Tommy one day about how attracted he was to you, and I overheard it.

"So later, Jim and I asked Tommy about the young woman he was being teased about, and he told us about you. I can assure you, Laurie, that Tommy has never spoken with such admiration about any woman the way he talked about you. You made a very good impression on him!"

Jim picked up the story then, saying, "And now, as it happens, Elizabeth, one of our best employees in the General Store, has told me that she intends to leave, and move to Indiana. But she said that won't be for several weeks, so I have time to hire a replacement and for Elizabeth to train the new employee.

"The problem is that, although there's a lot of folks looking for work in Denver, most all of them just want to work for a short while, and only until they've earned enough money to go on to California.

"Tommy told us about your search for your real father. Now, I've gonna be honest with you -- we believe that your chances of finding him are very slim, and that eventually you'll have to give up the search.

"But, in the meantime, I have a problem, since I need someone to replace Elizabeth in the store. She knows all about that General Store -- where everything is located, and how much it costs, and how to

103

figure out exactly what it is a customer is looking for even if that person doesn't know the right name to call it.

"Plainly, it's a job for a smart person, and Tommy said you were smart, and he also said you wanted to go to Denver. So I'm offering you that job in our General Store, Laurie."

Laurie had sat silently, trying hard to absorb everything she was hearing, but still somewhat befuddled. "But the store's in Denver. How would I get to Denver? I have some money saved, but I know it's not nearly enough for the stagecoach."

Abby smiled at her, and said, "There's room in the buggy for you to go with us, when we go back to Denver. Luckily, we borrowed one of Tommy's best buggies to come here."

Laurie, still trying to grasp everything that had happened, including what she'd just been told, frowned and said, "This is all happening too fast. I need some time to think about all of this."

Teresa had been listening to Jim and Abby, and her spirits lifted a bit at Jim's offer, since she had been extremely worried about Laurie's future. She knew she had no real choice about having to fire Laurie, in order to keep her restaurant going, but she also knew that Laurie wouldn't be able to find other work in Fort Morgan – at least, not any respectable work.

So Teresa spoke up, and said, with great earnestness, "Laurie, I'll always be sorry I had to fire you, and, if I thought it'd work out for you, I'd beg you to stay in Fort Morgan. You're a good person, and Heaven knows I'll miss you, but you probably need to take this offer.

"Not only are you going to have a real tough time finding another job, but pretty young woman such as yourself is always at risk here on the frontier, what with its shortage of women and too many wicked men. You really need family – or a strong man – to protect you, unless you are real good with a firearm and carry it with you all the time."

Laurie had never before really considered her personal safety as being a serious issue, since she had managed to get this far without suffering any physical harm. She thought about it now, though, including what might have happened when she was with the Porter wagon. She realized that she had been extremely fortunate so far, and was intelligent enough to know that such good luck might not continue.

She said, in a thoughtful tone, "I don't have a firearm. In fact, I've never even fired any kind of gun in my whole life. Any huntin' was always done by the boys."

Jim let her muse on that for a few moments, then gently prodded her. "Laurie, you can take this evening to think about our offer. If you decide to take us up on it, you can use that time to say good-bye to whatever folks you know in town who you care about. Abby and I will be here for breakfast in the morning, and we'll be leaving for Denver after that, with you or without you."

Since it was already almost supper time, and no meal preparations had been made, Laurie and Teresa went to the kitchen to work on the meal. Abby volunteered to help them, telling Teresa she was used to feeding large numbers of people, and Teresa gratefully accepted.

While the three women worked on the evening meal, Jim went to see the Marshal.

At the Marshal's office, Jim was just in time to see Fred Dawson's hand being compared to the Marshal's drawing of the bloody hand print on the wall of Mrs. Donavan's house.

Fred had strenuously objected at first, and started putting up a struggle, even though he knew he was no match for the Marshal and his deputy. But the Marshal wasn't inclined to get into any fight with Fred, so he didn't bother trying to physically subdue him.

He simply drew his revolver and told Fred that his hand would be put on the drawing whether Fred was conscious or unconscious, or whether he was alive or dead. Either way, it was all the same to him, the Marshal told Fred, and it was up to Fred to choose which way it would be be. After hearing that, Fred quickly decided to cooperate.

Fred's hand was a perfect match.

There were hardly any customers in the Prairie Kitchen that evening, and Laurie saw the truth of what Teresa had said about the restaurant's not being able to stay in business very much longer if Laurie remained working there. Already leaning towards going with the Watsons to Denver, that helped Laurie finally make up her mind.

Teresa told her she needn't stay to help with the cleaning up, as she had it well in hand, so, after serving the last customer, Laurie walked to Colonel and Mrs. Davenport's house and filled them in with all the news.

She told them about Fred Dawson being arrested for the murder of Mrs. Donavan, and that she was leaving the following morning for Denver.

"Colonel Davenport, I want to thank you again for all of your help, and all of your wise counsel. I still haven't received an answer to the letter I wrote to the War Department. If a reply comes here, please have it forwarded to me at this address in Denver." She had gotten the address from Abby, and she handed the elderly gentleman a piece of paper with the address written on it.

Colonel Davenport, with a tear in his eye, said, "Laurie, dear child, we've enjoyed your sweet company, and we appreciate your kindness in helping to care for two old pioneers. I'll watch for the reply to your letter, and, if it's all right with you, I'll also write once in a while myself, especially if I think of anything further of benefit to you. Good-bye, and good fortune, young lady, in finding your family! You'll be in our prayers."

The next morning, after breakfast at the Prairie Kitchen, Jim, Abby, and Laurie loaded up their personal things and departed for Denver. Laurie didn't have much, but her belongings now included two almost-new dresses and her savings.

Just before dark, on the second day, they pulled into the barn of Tommy's Livery Stable. Jim remained to care for the team while Abby and Laurie walked the short distance to the Boarding House to deposit their small amount of luggage, Abby showing Laurie to the room she had made ready for her (just in case she came with them). After freshening up a bit, the two ladies then made their way into the dining room to wait for Jim and enjoy their supper.

Jim unhitched the team and pushed the buggy into its usual parking place near the large door. It was a popular piece of equipment, and Tommy had been happy with the investment he made in purchasing the nice, extra-large buggy. Jim then took the harnesses off of the horses and led them to their stalls, where he took off their reins, hanging up the harnesses and reins on the pegs provided. Since there was no one else around, Jim took the large curry brush and began to brush the horses.

Before long, Timmy came into the barn, leading a freshly shod mare, which he placed in an empty stall. Seeing Jim, he said, "Good evening, Mr. Watson! I can take over that chore for you, if you'd like for me to."

Jim smiled and said, "I would be more than happy to give you the work. I'm hungry and I would like to join the others in the dining room."

Young Timmy grinned and replied, "I ate earlier. I will finish this job and give them some oats as well."

Jim said, "Thank you, Timmy." (It was Timmy's job to take care of the animals, but Jim always acted as if the employees were doing him a personal favor when they were just doing their job.)

Everyone thought very highly of Jim Watson, who had started their cluster of businesses.

Chapter Fifteen

Meanwhile, Elizabeth had entered the dining room, so Abby called her over to meet Laurie. "Elizabeth, Laurie here will be your replacement in the General Store. Please teach her as much as you can, before you have to leave, so she knows all she needs to know. Since we want to keep you on as long as you can stay, that should give her a chance to learn a lot from you."

Elizabeth thanked Abby (for reaffirming what Jim had already told her), and immediately extended her hand to Laurie, saying, "Laurie, I'm real pleased to meet you. I'm sure you will love working for these wonderful people. I have."

Laurie only had time to tell Elizabeth that she was pleased to meet her, too, before seeing Tommy enter the room, which caused her to lose her train of thought.

Tommy had, in fact, been day-dreaming about Laurie, as he frequently did when entering any dining room, so he at first almost believed she was a figment of his imagination. After only a second or so, though, he realized she was real, and did a double-take.

He walked directly over to her, and said, "It is you! I'm mighty surprised to see you here, Laurie; pleasantly so, but still mighty surprised. How does it happen that you're here?"

Before a slightly tongue-tied Laurie could manage to respond, Abby decided to take the bull by the horns and confess. "Tommy, you told us Laurie was smart and hard-working and honest. You might not have heard, but Elizabeth here is planning to leave us and move to Indiana when she gets married. So, Jim and I drove out to Fort Morgan and met Laurie, and we convinced her to come work for the General Store."

Tommy's brow furrowed, as he began trying not only to assimilate this new information, but also to understand why they had done it (and without telling him in advance). However, he said merely, "Oh, well, that's great. Nice to see you, Laurie."

Then, still pondering the matter, Tommy went to the table where Davie was sitting, picked up a plate, went to where the supper food was set out family-style on a long table, ladled his food choices onto his plate, and returned to sit beside Davie. As he ate, he began to discuss with Davie the things they would need to do the next day.

After Abby had left the table to go greet Jim, who had just walked into the room, Elizabeth turned to Laurie and asked, "You already know Tommy?"

"Sort of. I met him in Fort Morgan. I was working in a restaurant there, and Tommy and two other fellas stopped in Fort Morgan twice, and ate in that restaurant a couple of times. He said they were on a trip to purchase livestock and feed for his horses, so they passed through Fort Morgan both going and coming."

Wanting to be up-front about it, and be sure that Elizabeth understood about her heritage, Laurie continued. "I was there because I'm half Indian, and I've come West to search for my Indian father. I'm not sure where he is, but I'd stopped in Fort Morgan 'cause it sounded like a place my mother had described to me."

Elizabeth studied for a few moments on what Laurie had told her, then slowly mused, out loud, "It don't really make any sense that they'd go all the way to Fort Morgan to hire an employee for the store here in Denver; no sense at all.

110

"Maybe they wanted to hire you because Tommy liked you and recommended you; or maybe they felt sorry for you, and wanted to help you find your father. I think that's the most likely answer, because, many years ago, I know they adopted a little Indian boy. His name was Johnny, and it hasn't been but a couple of years ago that he went to live among his people, after he got grown.

"I'd been working in the store only about six months when he left. I know that they really loved him, though; that was easy to see.

"In fact, I recall that Tommy gave Johnny a beautiful horse to take with him back to the tribe."

Laurie had been eagerly taking in all of this information, and, having for the first time really considered the Watsons' leap of faith in offering her the position, said, "You're right that it doesn't seem to make much sense at all, for anyone to do what Abby and Jim did. I certainly don't know anyone else who'd do that for someone they'd never even met. And, yes, Tommy had seemed to take an interest in me, for some reason."

Elizabeth grinned at that, and said, "You mean maybe for some reason such as Tommy being a healthy single young man, and you being a very pretty young woman? Maybe lots of other men might not be interested in you, just because you are part Indian, but I know that's not Tommy's way of thinking, 'cause Tommy always thought of Johnny as his real brother, and Johnny was an Indian, and Tommy thinks the world of Johnny. And that's never been my way of thinking, either!"

Laurie smiled, with just a tinge of sadness in it, and said, "Thank you, Elizabeth, for saying that. I confess, I've always thought of myself as being judged unworthy, just for not looking like everyone else around me. But not by Tommy, that's true. And not be Jim and Abby; they're truly the nicest people I have ever met. And, now, I can add you, too, to that list. So, thank you again."

111

After the evening meal was complete, and the dishes and pots were all cleaned up, then came a real treat for Laurie -- Abigail took Laurie to the laundry back room, where the water was heated, and showed Laurie the tubs for the women and how to have a hot bath, that night, and every single day. What a luxury!

Next she introduced Laurie to Jim's cousin Phillip, and Phillip's wife, Susan. Later, she was introduced to Pete and Sarah Elder. It seemed to Laurie to be much like a huge, happy family, and it helped ease, for the first time since she left her mother and half-siblings, her homesickness in missing her own family back in Missouri.

Abigail, Sarah, and Susan all went through their dresses, and each of the women found one or two they were willing to give to Laurie, and several they could share. (A few of the ones given to Laurie needed to be taken it a bit, of course, since Laurie was so slender, but mostly all it took was a belt around the waist to cinch them in.)

Laurie had a warm bath in a real tub after supper, and a "new" (to her, at least) wardrobe of clean clothes to wear; it felt great.

Tommy had only brief glimpses of Laurie at supper times. Their breakfast times were different, as were their lunch times, with Laurie in training at the General Store, and Tommy working at his own Livery Stable business, so he didn't get even a glimpse of her then.

Besides, he and Davie had been working hard, first working to get every one of the buggies repaired, and then a wagon broke down, too. At least they were getting closer to having all the equipment in full working order. Then, following the equipment work, it was inspection day for the horses' hooves. With a herd of forty-some horses, it wasn't surprising that three needed new shoes.

But, eventually, it was Sunday morning, and, although Tommy hadn't been able to speak to Laurie in the preceding days, he had high

112

hopes that going to church would give him an opportunity to talk to her.

Somehow, though, he had missed Laurie at breakfast (she had gotten up very early, ate quickly, and left for church before him). Then, when he got to church, he saw her in deep conversation with the Pastor's son, Irwin Bates, who was a handsome, well-mannered, and articulate young man, and who was obviously delighted to be talking to Laurie. As Tommy watched, he saw Irwin Bates offer his arm to Laurie, to escort her into the church, as they continued their discussion.

Tommy decided that he would come off badly if he tried to join that conversation, so he did what he thought was the next best thing – he stopped to talk to Helen Matthews, a young woman who was clearly on the hunt for a husband. Soon, he and Helen were seated in a pew two rows ahead of Laurie and Irwin Bates. Tommy decided that, even as hard as it was to do, he would show no overt interest in Laurie.

However, Tommy hadn't given up on Laurie; rather, he had come up with a plan to get her attention (he hoped), and get her interest solely focused on him.

He knew Laurie was working at the General Store, and the time when she would be having supper, and that she'd have a little leisure time before going to bed.

Therefore, the following Saturday, Tommy arranged to meet Helen Matthews at the Boarding House for supper. Tommy had arranged for his nicest buggy to be driven to the restaurant, and for the driver to park near the front door and wait. He and Helen would both be dressed very spiffy, and would have their supper at a small table for two, off to the side of the dining room.

Tommy knew he could count on Helen to talk too loudly, to giggle too frequently, and to make a big – and very public – show of letting everyone know that she was going for an evening buggy ride with Tommy.

The fact is, Helen really was a sweet girl, and quite pretty in her own right, but she drove poor Tommy insane, with her almost constant giggling and her flamboyant ways (which was why Tommy hadn't dated her before, and had no interest at all in marrying her).

Tommy entered the dining room after Laurie had started eating. He was dressed up, in the nicest clothes he owned. Tommy walked through the dining room, getting a few comments about his mode of dress, and went to stand at the front door. Sure enough, Helen was already coming up the walkway, dressed perhaps just a bit too formally for the occasion, but all primed and ready for a night out with the handsome Tommy.

Helen didn't disappoint him; she was much too loud, and made lots of overly-broad showy gestures. They ate their supper amid her giggles and raucous laughter. It embarrassed Tommy, but he endured it in the hope of getting Laurie's attention. (It worked. They got the attention of everyone in the dining room, in fact.)

After supper, Tommy and Helen went out to the buggy; all of the bystanders gawked at the fine buggy, which its driver, seeing Tommy coming, had right in front of the door. In short, a person would have to be both blind and deaf to have missed the show that was being put on.

As Tommy helped Helen into the buggy, it occurred to him, for the first time, that it was going to be difficult to suddenly stop seeing Helen without hurting her feelings. He had no wish to hurt or embarrass Helen, and he decided that he should have thought more fully about all of the possible ramifications of his plan before implementing it.

But it was too late to change his plan now. He climbed into the buggy beside Helen; the driver snapped the whip over the horses, and off they went to explore the big city of Denver after dark.

Laurie and Elizabeth were eating supper together again that evening, and they of course saw the entire show. Elizabeth commented, as Tommy and Helen drove away, "Tommy sure looks handsome in that outfit doesn't he?"

Laurie responded, "He does look handsome and dashing. I've only talked to him twice, but it does seem to me as if that lady isn't his style."

"You figured that out after talking to him only twice?" asked Elizabeth, "I was about to come to the same conclusion, but I've known Tommy for almost three years now."

This information caught Laurie's attention. "Really? What kind of a guy is he, anyway?"

"Tommy is really nice," replied Elizabeth. "In fact, just between us, if he\d ever taken an interest in me, I might not be marrying Henry!"

"So, he's that nice, is he?" asked Laurie.

"Oh, yes, he's very polite, even to people he doesn't like. Tommy never curses or speaks crudely -- not that he sounds highfalutin, like he's been to college, but he doesn't use coarse language. He's kind of quiet and humble; why, a person'd never know that he owns that livery stable and all those horses, wagons, and buggies, unless someone else told him."

Laurie recalled Tommy telling her about the livery stable in an off-handed manner, not at all bragging, just trying to answer her question about this trip. "He's awfully young to own such a large business."

Elizabeth nodded, and added, "I was told Tommy's mother died when he was very young. His father owned a livery stable, and was killed in an accidental fall from the hay loft. Jim and Abigail took him in, and helped him keep the business going, until he was old enough to take it over alone. They've been like parents to him."

Laurie said, "Jim and Abigail are truly nice people. They helped me move here from Fort Morgan, you know."

"They'd help anyone," added Elizabeth. "Like they did Phillip and Susan. As I heard the story, Phillip is Jim's cousin from Georgia, and he was coming with Jim and Abby to Denver when they met Susan, her husband, and children, and gave them all a ride in their wagons.

"But then Indians attacked them on their way here, and Susan's husband was killed. Phillip waited for Susan to finish mourning her husband, and then he courted her; they got married several years ago."

Laurie sat, wide-eyed, at hearing the tale. "These people are nothing like the family I left. My mother loved me, but her husband never did. What about Pete and Sarah Elder -- how do they fit into this family?"

"Laurie, I don't know all the details, but the short version of what I've heard is that Jim and Pete were working at some gold mine, and they hauled gold in a wagon, to a bank, I suppose. One day, they were attacked by robbers, Jim was hurt, and Pete refused to leave him to go for help.

"Later, the gold ran out at the mine, and they didn't have that job no more. But, as it turned out, Jim was given a reward for capturing the robbers. Jim insisted on sharing the reward money with Pete and Sarah. They're all really close friends; more like family, really."

"I suppose they took me on because Tommy asked them to. I really pushed Tommy away when I first met him; not that I didn't like him, but I was real unhappy, and felt trapped, and couldn't figure out how to find my father. I don't guess he is interested in me no more since he's taken up with Helen," explained Laurie.

"Whoa! You mean Tommy asked you out?" enthused Elizabeth.

"Well, no, not exactly. After the first time I met him, he went to the house where I worked a couple days a week, and asked the old gentleman I worked for how to get an introduction to me. Then he told me later – after I told him I didn't have time for him -- that he would just make a pest of himself and see how that worked out," added Laurie.

"But, after you got here, what did he say to you?" asked Elizabeth.

"Well, nothing. I didn't see him at all for a couple days, and when I went to church with Jim and Abigail, I saw him with Helen," explained Laurie.

"Was it before or after church? Did he try to speak to you?" inquired Elizabeth.

"I saw him before church, but he was alone then. He didn't come over and he didn't say anything to me. Then, after the preacher's son escorted me into the church, Tommy came in with Helen and sat in a pew in front of us."

"Hmm, I think that explains what happened tonight. Tommy has always avoided Helen. She's like an open book. Helen's ready to get married, and just about any man who's breathing will do. Tommy knows that. If he saw you with Irwin Bates, he must be trying to make you jealous," opined Elizabeth.

Laurie asked, "Do you really think so? If that was his aim, then it sure worked! But, even so, I don't feel like I could possibly deserve someone like Tommy."

Elizabeth practically glowered at her, and said sternly, "Don't even think that! I haven't known you very long, Laurie, but you're plenty worthy, and any man, including Tommy, would be lucky to have you as his wife.

"Woman, you need to put yourself in Tommy's way. Be in front of him as much as you can manage. If it helps, tell yourself you're doing it to save him from Helen, before he carries this too far and he finds himself caught and bagged. See if you can do him some kindness … at least be right friendly. And don't be so hard on yourself."

Chapter Sixteen

Meanwhile, Helen and Tommy were seeing the sights of Denver and talking (mostly by Helen). But every time Helen brought up the subject of marriage or children, Tommy changed the subject quickly (and not always very tactfully). Helen also kept giving Tommy opportunities to kiss her, blatant invitations almost, but he never took the bait.

Finally, Helen just blurted out, "Tommy, I thought you invited me on this ride because you were sweet on me. Why'd you ask me out?"

Tommy had been thinking about that answer for at least thirty minutes before Helen asked it, so he was ready for the question. "Helen, you're mighty sweet, and you'll make some lucky man a great wife...."

He paused then, and Helen interrupted the pause with an exasperated, "BUT...?"

Tommy plunged on, "I know that you're sweet on Irwin Bates, but it didn't look like that was ever going to work out. So, I thought I'd try to cheer you up, and show you a good time, tonight. But I realize I've been distracted and haven't been good company. Truth is, I've got someone else on my mind. I hope I didn't lead you on or anything."

"You might at least have let me know why you were asking me out," snapped Helen.

Tommy added, "I feel awful bad about the misunderstanding. I sure do hope I haven't hurt your feelings, Helen. You really are a sweet girl."

"Tommy, I tried to get you interested in me before, and it didn't work. I should have realized that you didn't just suddenly fall in love with me," admitted Helen (who, indeed, was a sweet girl).

Tommy leaned over and kissed her on the cheek. "Thanks for understanding. You let me know if I can ever do anything for you -- like giving you a buggy for a moon-lit ride with Irwin – or anyone else you take a fancy to."

The second half of the ride was a lot more fun than the first half. Tommy and Helen enjoyed each other's company, and talked about what they wanted the rest of their lives to be like.

The driver pulled up in front of Helen's parents' home, and Tommy jumped down first and then helped Helen descend, lady-like, to the ground. He walked her to her front door, held her hand, and kissed Helen on the forehead. Then he said goodnight and went home.

Back at the boarding house, Tommy found Laurie still up, sitting in the front room. She was reading a book by candle-light. Tommy was a little surprised, and said, "Good evening, Laurie."

Laurie looked up, and replied, "Good evening, Tommy." Then she looked at the clock and exclaimed, "Oh, my, look at the time; it got completely away from me."

"What are you reading that's so good?"

Laurie held the front cover up for Tommy to see. "Macbeth; it's by William Shakespeare," she replied.

"Macbeth is a little too heavy reading for me. I'd be more interested in something like, say, Aesop's Fables," said Tommy.

Laurie thought that over for a few moments, then added, "I've always liked a little dark drama. Even in real life, often times I've enjoyed people saying or doing more-or-less outrageous things."

120

Tommy smiled and replied, "Sometimes a little shock in the conversation can get people to start thinking in a different direction. I know some people use vulgarity that way, but I don't like it – vulgarity, that is."

"Did you and Helen have a good time?"

"Yes, we did. Who told you her name … oh, I guess it was Elizabeth?"

"Yes, it was. Then you saw us eating supper together?"

"I did. Dad told me that she was getting married and moving to Indiana so her husband could work for her Uncle."

"Actually, it's his older brother, I think, not her family. Elizabeth will be with us through the end of the week. They're getting married on Saturday, and starting for Indiana on Monday."

"That's coming quick. Are you having any trouble learning your job at the general store?"

"No, no trouble, though there is an awful lot to learn. But I've made myself a lot of notes about where things are located, and prices and everything. It'll take me a couple more weeks, I'm sure, before I can feel like I'm on sound footing there."

"Then I'm sure you need your sleep as badly as I need mine. I have lots to do tomorrow, so I'll say goodnight," said Tommy.

"Yes, I do need my sleep. I should've gone to bed an hour ago, but I just got so interested in the book. Goodnight, Tommy."

The next Saturday, Tommy went to Elizabeth's wedding, met her new husband, and wished them luck. On Sunday, at church, Tommy saw Irwin Bates alone, dusting the pews and the pulpit before church. Tommy walked up to Irwin and said, "Hello, Irwin. How've you been?"

"Oh. Hi, Tommy. I've been just fine; and you?"

"Fit as a fiddle, old boy," Tommy replied. "I went to the wedding yesterday of Elizabeth, a girl who works in the general store. She and her husband are moving back to Indiana. It set me to wondering when you were going to settle down and get married?"

"I'm not sure, Tommy. Not sure I can find a woman that'll have me."

"Oh, I don't think that could be a problem for you. Why, I remember when I used to see you and Helen Matthews at church together every Sunday -- and Wednesday night, too! Helen's a pretty girl, and sweet, and she'll make someone a good wife."

"I think Helen got mad at me some months ago; she quit talking to me."

"Irwin, are you sure she just didn't get tired of waiting on you to let her know what your true feelings about her were?"

"I hadn't thought about that possibility, Tommy. Maybe I should ask her to go with me to that dance coming up in a couple weeks?"

"You'd better do it soon, or someone else might beat you to it. And you're lucky I can't dance, or I just might be tempted to ask her to go myself!"

The choir came trooping in about that time, and people started settling into their favorite pews, so Tommy went back and sat down by himself. He didn't see Laurie or the Watsons anywhere yet, so they must be coming a little later.

As he turned to look around to see if he could spot Laurie, Helen Matthews came in. She waved at Tommy, then went to another pew and sat down. Irwin Bates walked over to her, and they exchanged a few words, then Irwin sat down beside Helen.

122

Tommy was hopeful.

Chapter Seventeen

In May, 1876, a party of the confederation of Lakota Sioux, Northern Cheyenne, and Arapaho Indians, including some other Great Plains Indians, had visited the Ute Reservation in an attempt to recruit the Utes into the coming war against the US Government.

Johnny Little Bear opposed such a war, and strongly advised against it. He argued, first, that many people on both sides would die, and, second, that the Indians would inevitably lose. Johnny also pointed out that, while there were bad white men, there were also bad Indians, and that all of the transgressions weren't just on one side. He described to the Council the huge waves of white people coming West, and how well prepared they were to change the very structure of the lands. They had plows and other tools for tilling the ground, and planting crops, and different ways to preserve their food, so they didn't have to always be moving around looking for a food source. Johnny pointed out that the white man could be a formidable enemy -- or a valuable ally, if the Indians were willing to learn from the white man's culture, and accept some of its restrictions on their own traditions.

Johnny admitted that was a lot to ask of Indians, but he also pointed out the white man's Government was trying to keep the white man out of their reservations. But he also admitted that was impossible to do completely, simply because there were just so many white men who invaded their reservations, some hunting for animals (for food or for their skins), and others looking for gold or silver, and the Army couldn't constantly patrol the entire boundaries of the reservations.

Those Indians in favor of joining the bands under Sitting Bull, Crazy Horse, and others were quick to point out that Johnny Little Bear had lived with a white family for several years, and that his father, Sam Running Bear had been a Scout for the US Cavalry. That background made Johnny a traitor and a spy in their eyes, and any advice from him was therefore suspect, and against the best interests of the Indians.

Johnny explained that, when he was a young boy, his father became sick, so he tried to steal a horse so he could go for back to the tribe for help. He was caught by two white men; as all the Indians knew, stealing a horse was a hanging offense, but Johnny told them that the white men didn't harm him. Instead, they listened to his story, loaned Johnny a horse, and followed him to where his sick father was, with their only intention to help. There was nothing that could be done for his father; he died shortly, and the white men buried his father according to their customs, in a respectful manner. One of the men adopted Johnny, but they both treated him as a favored son, and they taught him their language and ways. Johnny told how he knew he was different from the white men, and how, after he was older, he wanted to return to his tribe and be among his own people. So the white men accepted his decision and brought him back to his tribe, with many gifts for him and for the tribe.

He also reminded the members of his tribe that a friend of that family, named Billy, came to visit a couple of years before, and brought tools to give to the Utes so they could farm and raise food much easier. In conclusion, Johnny said, "Those people aren't our enemies, and all white people shouldn't be attacked just because some white men are evil." After the tribal members pondered Johnny's words, only a few of the Utes joined with the other tribes to form the enormous army of Indians.

However, even with the large number of Indians in the confederation, and in spite of their fierce fighting, and their triumph in some early battles, in the end, their tribal differences, and lack of sufficiently coordinated strategic skills against numbers and armaments far greater than their own, brought them down.

It so happened that Lt. Colonel Edwards (to whom Laurie had written) had been reassigned to the Seventh Cavalry, to serve as an observer and advisor to Lt. Colonel George Armstrong Custer, because of his extensive experience with Indians. [Of course, as history tells us, both men were killed in the battle of the Little Bighorn.] Only a few of Lt. Colonel Edwards' letters and notes survived, between his reassignment and the subsequent movement of the Army Camp just outside the Ute Reservation where Johnny was now living.

When Laurie's letter arrived in Washington, it was forwarded to the officer who took over Lt. Colonel Edwards' small command. He had the matter looked into, but the only information that could be gleaned from the surviving papers was that Sam Running Bear had died of unknown causes in Montana territory in or about 1870. An otherwise unidentified Indian boy was returned to the Ute Indian tribe in or about 1873. That information was compiled in a formal report, and forwarded to US Army Headquarters in Washington, DC. After the information was finally received and evaluated at Army Headquarters, a reply was prepared and eventually sent to "Laurie Burdock, c/o General Delivery, Fort Morgan, Colorado."

It was only because of the notoriety of Miss Burdock (resulting from the murder investigation) that the letter made its way to Colonel Davenport. Colonel Davenport promptly put the letter in an envelope and forwarded it to "Laurie Burdock, c/o Watson Boarding House, Denver, Colorado," along with a short note from himself and his wife.

Winter was closing in by the time the letter reached Laurie. When the mail was delivered to Abigail, she saw the letter and took it straight away to Laurie at the General Store. Fortunately, Laurie was between customers, and she fell eagerly upon the envelope. Abigail didn't even have time to leave before Laurie had ripped open the envelope and quickly scanned the contents. With great disappointment,

Laurie's arm, holding the letter, fell limply by her side. Abigail became concerned, and asked, "Bad news?"

Laurie, with tears in her eyes, nodded, and said, broken-hearted, "This was my last chance to find my father and my brother; but now this letter says that my father is dead, and that there aren't any records to even tell my brother's name."

"I'm so sorry, Laurie." Abigail put her arm around Laurie, and attempted to console the young woman. Laurie murmured, disjointedly, "It doesn't make sense that I should mourn the loss of my father, and not finding my brother. A year ago, I didn't know either one of them existed."

"Sure it does," Abby disputed stoutly. "It's totally reasonable for you to mourn for your father, because you knew about him, and you wanted to find him and love him, and it doesn't matter a hill of beans how long ago it was that you learned he was your father!"

"That's so sweet, Abby," replied Laurie, "and it's true. My stepfather treated me terribly; when I found out that's all he was, just my stepfather, and that my real father existed somewhere, I wanted to find him and know him, 'cause I believe that surely he would've loved me."

Another customer came in then, and he needed help, so Laurie pulled herself together, put the letter into her pocket, hugged Abigail, and went with the customer to where he could examine the products he was interested in.

Within a few weeks of Tommy's encouraging words to Irwin, word leaked out that Irwin and Helen were going to marry in the Spring. Helen had wanted to marry Irwin ever since they were youngsters, but Irwin had always been too shy to make any romantic overtures to her, and she had finally given up on him. She wanted desperately to leave the smothering atmosphere of her home, where her

127

extremely socially prominent parents – rather snobbish, really -- had constantly bombarded her with directions as to what behavior was acceptable and what she was never to do. She wanted to have her own home, and be a loving wife and mother, and never again have to be so circumscribed in her actions (although her being a nice, sweet, girl wouldn't change). And now all of her dreams were coming true, including those dreams of Irwin.

As for Tommy, he'd never been able to break through that hard shell surrounding Laurie; the best he could manage to get from her was a civil conversation from time to time. It seemed to him as if she was obsessed, with something preying on her mind. Laurie seemed to retreat further back into her shell after receiving the letter. Tommy was unaware of the letter, but he saw that Laurie was less talkative, and seemed less happy than she had become after she first arrived at the boarding house.

Tommy decided to try again to talk more to Laurie, deeper than he'd been able to thus far. One night after supper, he noticed that Laurie had gone off with a book to the sitting room. He already knew she like to read, and, with Winter coming on, it was too cold and dark to go outside. Tommy picked up a book himself, and selected a chair that wasn't too close to Laurie's, so he wouldn't be obviously encroaching, but was still close enough to talk. After reading for about fifteen minutes, Tommy asked, "Hi, Laurie. Are you still reading that Shakespeare book?"

Laurie looked up, marked her place, and replied, "No, I'm reading Louisa May Alcott's Little Women. What about you? What are you reading?"

"Leaves of Grass, by Walt Whitman," he replied.

"I must say, I'm a little surprised that you're reading poetry – especially, THAT poetry. I had you figured as liking adventure stories.

128

And, as I understand it, that poetry is a bit unchristian in its devotion to worldly and fleshly ideas."

Tommy considered what she'd said. "It actually does seem to be emphasizing attitudes contrary to teachings in the Bible. I don't fully appreciate his way of looking at things, but it is interesting. I've sure never read anything quite like this before. But, you know, the store hasn't received any new books in a couple of months, so choices are limited. They'd sell many more books if everyone could read. And, while we're talking about reading choices, from what I've heard about Little Women, I'm surprised to hear that you're reading that book. You don't seem to me to be the type of woman who'd accept others deciding for her how she should spend her life."

Laurie cocked her head to one side at hearing that, looked at him a bit differently, and said, "Thank you ... I think. However, we do have to face reality. Since women bear the children and the men don't, there's very little we can do to alter the roles society has laid out for us. After all, you can't expect a pregnant woman to do the hard work a man must do to provide for his family, and you can't expect a man who has to work in the mine or herding cattle all day to come home and wash clothing and change diapers. Of course, I suppose one could expect that, but it wouldn't be very realistic, would it? Anyway, I guess I'm more like Jo than Amy."

Tommy nodded his head thoughtfully, and said, "You were right about my taste in books. I much prefer something like Moby Dick to poetry. I think I've read most of the books we have here at the boarding house; at least all of them that sounded interesting to me. I hear the Adventures of Tom Sawyer is really good, and I'm anxious to read that one, but I haven't been able to find a copy of it."

Laurie was beginning to like Tommy; not that she had disliked him, but she was seeing him in a new light. Upon reflecting on her

129

feelings toward Tommy, she began to realize that her unhappiness about the letter had maybe unfairly colored her conversations with Tommy. He really did seem nice enough, and friendly but not pushy.

Laurie changed the subject a little bit, ready to keep the conversation flowing. "When I first came here, I was expecting something kind of like what I left back in Missouri. It's a lot different here. Everyone seems happy, or at least content, with their life. Jim and Abigail are wonderful people, and, while I don't know the others as well, they seem awfully nice, too."

Tommy smiled, and said, "Yes, they're really great! They raised me as their son when my father died, and they've always been there for me."

Laurie stared off into the distance, and spoke in a small, sad voice that Tommy had never heard come from her before. "My father died, too. I never knew him, but I still miss him. Maybe I just miss having a father."

Tommy felt instantly sympathetic. "Laurie, I'm sorry that you never knew your father. My own father died when I was young, but I have many good memories of him. I can well imagine that, never having had a father, there would be a hole in your heart and in your life."

Laurie looked back at Tommy, and said, with great bitterness, "Humph. My mother had a husband, and I didn't know he wasn't my father until after he fell off his horse drunk and broke his neck and died. That's when my mother told me about my real father. When I learned that her husband wasn't my actual father, it made me happy.

"I came West to find my real father. But I received a letter recently that my real father is dead. Not only that, but the writer of the letter didn't even know how he died, or even where he's buried. So now I'll never know him, and he'll never love me."

130

Tommy said, gently, "There are lots of people here in the West who died and are buried in unmarked graves. Graves of would-be settlers headed for California are scattered all across this country. Much like it is in wars, preserving the remaining life takes priority over everything else. Even mourning is a luxury that many don't have."

"I know you're right, Tommy," agreed Laurie, sorrowfully, "but it still hurts."

"It'll get better with time. Honest, it will. It took a long time for me to get over losing my Dad," added Tommy. "Especially since I was running his business after he died, everything I did reminded me of him. I've never forgotten him, of course, and I still miss him, but the sharpest pain is gone. And I'm comforted knowing that he is safe and well now, at his new home in Heaven."

Laurie felt much better, with some of the her raw emotions soothed a bit, after listening to Tommy. She wished him a good night, put up her book, and went up to bed, where she slept the most undisturbed sleep she'd had since receiving the letter from the Army.

Tommy felt sad for her, but relieved to learn that he wasn't responsible for her withdrawal; making a resolution to keep talking to Laurie as regularly as he could, he, too, went up to bed.

Chapter Eighteen

In an effort to lay in sufficient supplies before the worst of the Winter snows, Tommy, Davie, and Timmy once again set out to buy hay and grain for the livery stable and the general store.

When Laurie found out they were going, she asked Tommy if they would be stopping in Fort Morgan. Tommy assured her that they were, so Laurie sent a package to Colonel Davenport, along with a letter. It included some perfumed soap for Mrs. Davenport and a package of special tobacco for the Colonel. The letter thanked them again for their help when she needed it most, and a brief summary of how thing had been going for her.

Tommy decided they should take three wagons this time, and try to buy more grain than in the past. There were no other employees who could be spared to be gone so long, so it was decided to use gun shots to signal each other if necessary. One shot was "Lead wagon, stop and wait," two shots was "Turn back to the wagon behind," and three shots was "Circle the wagons, there's trouble."

The early snow had just about all melted off, but there was a heavy frost on the ground as they steered their teams out onto the street. Denver had grown so much in the few years since their business had been established that it took them the better part of an hour just to get out of town. There were lots of local buggies and wagons, together with covered wagons full of families headed further West looking for a better life, plus pedestrians going to and fro.

After a few days, Fort Morgan lay directly ahead. It was a bit early in the day, but Tommy decided to stop there in spite of that. He left Davie and Timmy to care for the animals and set up their camp while he went to see the Davenports. Mrs. Davenport met him at the door and invited him into the parlor while she went to fetch the Colonel.

When the Colonel and his wife reappeared, the Colonel (even more so than his wife) was very anxious to hear all the news he had of Laurie. Tommy explained that Laurie was doing well, but was still preoccupied by news that her father was deceased. The Colonel was somewhat distressed to learn that her father was dead; he hadn't opened the letter (since it wasn't addressed to him) before forwarding it on to Laurie.

Then Tommy gave Colonel Davenport the letter from Laurie, and handed the package to Mrs. Davenport. Mrs. Davenport was delighted with the perfumed soap. (Obviously, Laurie had noticed that the only soap they used was homemade lye soap, molded into large rectangular bars.) The Colonel was quite happy with fresh tobacco for his pipe; it was the flavored kind he had always preferred, but which was hard to get.

The Davenports also enjoyed reading the letter from Laurie, which was full of heart-felt gratitude for their help. The Colonel asked Tommy if he could stay long enough for them to write a reply back to Laurie. Tommy explained that he couldn't, but that he'd be coming back through Fort Morgan, and it was agreed the Davenports would have a reply ready then and he'd take it to Laurie.

After dinner at the hotel, Tommy and his men went back to their wagons and animals and bedded down for the night, covered in blankets against the cold prairie wind.

The next morning, they got up before daylight, hitched up their teams, and began their journey toward Nebraska. They had identified several farms where they would likely find hay and grain. They fully expected a longer trip this time, but not as long as in early Spring, when everyone's hay and grain would be getting low.

Three weeks went by, during which they encountered two snow storms. The three wagons were almost full of hay and grain, and they hoped they could start back for Denver soon. Up ahead of them, they knew, lay another farm, only a few miles away, and that fellow always seemed to have hay for sale, so, since the daylight was almost gone, they camped for the night, their hopes high to complete the buying part of their trip the next day.

In the morning, the horizon was clear, with just a few high clouds, and they hitched up and set out for the farm, moving slowly due to their heavy loads. However, by early afternoon, they could detect a column of smoke in the distance. The men exchanged worried glances, and Tommy retrieved his rifle and checked to be sure it was loaded. The other men did likewise. Even the normally playful Davie was solemn.

An hour later, they came upon their first view of the farm – it was a shocking sight. The farm had been burned, and was still smoldering. The house and the barns were smoking shells. There were many tracks of horses, none of which were wearing shoes; obviously, to the three men, those had been Indian horses.

The men stopped their wagons in front of the house, and went inside what was left of it to investigate. Unfortunately, they found five burned bodies in the house. The bodies appeared to be the approximate size of three adults and two larger children. They remembered that the family had a grown son and two teenage girls. No one wanted to look too closely at the bodies.

Tommy looked around outside, and the unshod horses seemed to head off toward the North and seemed to have arrived from the South. He found a not-completely burned tool shed, in which was contained several hand tools, including two long handled shovels (they being of no use to a war party). He and Davie began digging graves;

Timmy served as their relief, by spelling each of the other two men from time to time.

After digging the five graves came the worst part. Moving the bodies made everyone sick to their stomachs, especially young Timmy. None of the men tried to identify which body was who; they couldn't bear to do that. They didn't know the right names anyway. They just put a body in each shallow grave, covered it up with dirt, and made a cross of rocks on top of each. After burying them, Tommy conducted an impromptu funeral service over the graves, quoting the twenty-third Psalm from memory. "Yea, though I walk through the Valley of the shadow of death, I will fear no evil…." Then Tommy picked up the shovels and put them into the wagon. He looked straight at the other men, and said, in a warning tone, "I sure hope we don't need these again, but we might. We all need to be extra watchful from now on."

Since the Indians had apparently headed North, Tommy and his men headed South. As much as they would like to find another farm to get all of their wagons full, at the same time they were all in total, unspoken but clear, agreement to head generally in the direction of Denver. They also, again by mutual unspoken agreement, kept all three wagons as close together as they could.

When it was around time to stop for the night, Davie said, "Tommy, let's keep on going. I couldn't possibly sleep, and I doubt either of you two could either. Let's put as much distance between us and that place as we can." Timmy nodded quickly in agreement, but Tommy said, "First, we see to the horses. We're dependent on them, and they've been pulling these heavy wagons all day."

They fed the horses grain, gave them water, and allowed them to rest. A few hours later, they were moving again. Tommy took the lead. In the early hours of the morning, they came to another farm. There was no evidence of fire, but the house was still dark. It must

135

have been about 3:30 or 4:00 am, almost time to expect someone to get up anyway, so Tommy walked up to the front door and knocked hard -- nothing. Next, he pounded on the door with his fist.

He could hear some moving inside, and, in just a minute or two, Tommy could see the light of a kerosene lamp as it came slowly to the front door. Someone inside shouted, "Who's there, and what do you want?"

"Morning, sir, my name is Tommy Thompson; there are three of us out here. We're on a trip from Denver, buying hay and grain."

"Well, Tommy, if that's your name, I don't generally open my door to anyone who comes knocking in the middle of the night, no matter what they might be buying or selling, so come back after it gets to be daylight and I can see you."

"Yes, sir, I understand, but this is important. We just came from the Bradshaw farm. We buried the Bradshaw family yesterday afternoon." Tommy's statement was met by a long silence, then, "What happened?"

"We figure it was Indians. We found lots of horse tracks with no horseshoes. Both the house and the barn were burned. We found the bodies in the house; there were five of them. We gave them a Christian burial, and been traveling all night to get as far away from there as we could."

They could hear the latch moving in the door; then the door opened, very slowly, revealing a man in a nightshirt, holding a big pistol. The man held up his lantern so he could see who was there. The young men didn't appear to be wearing pistols, and didn't have any weapon in their hands. "I'm sorry, boys. Living out here on the prairie is lonesome, and we don't never expect anyone this early. And lots of times them that do come this early ain't welcome. My name is John Walker. Please come inside. I'll make us all some coffee."

As they entered the front room, a woman came in from a back room, wearing a housecoat and inquiring what the problem was. Her husband said to her, "It sounds like there's hostile Indians around these parts, Martha." Her mouth dropped open, and fear showed in her eyes. "Oh, John, surely you're mistaken?"

Tommy explained, "Ma am, we came upon the Bradshaw farm yesterday. We went there to buy some hay and grain, but we found the house and barn had been burned. We buried five bodies before we left, and then we headed in the opposite direction from the unshod tracks we saw." He continued, "We couldn't eat or sleep, so we've been driving our teams all night. We stopped here to alert you folks to the Indian raid. And, maybe, buy some hay and grain from you."

John Walker welcomed the change in subject, which served to divert their minds, at least for the moment, from the recent tragedy. "I have both, but mostly grain."

"We have almost a full load of hay, but we really need as much grain as we can haul," Tommy explained, "so if you can sell us some of that grain at a price we can agree on, we got us a deal made."

John Walker named a price that sounded good, so he and Tommy shook on it. Mrs. Walker had been busy cooking, and she fed everyone a nice breakfast, after which Tommy, Davie, and Timmy loaded as much grain as possible, and topped off the two wagon-loads of hay as well. It was just barely daylight when they had finished the loading. Tommy paid Mr. Walker, and noticed Mrs. Walker busy packing up clothing and various other belongings. By the time they said goodbye to Mr. Walker, he had began hitching up his team. They never asked the Walkers where they were going, but Tommy decided it was definitely not to the Bradshaw farm, nor even in that direction.

Several days later, they met a column of soldiers. The officer leading the soldiers asked them if they had had any contact with

Indians. Tommy truthfully told them, "No, sir, we haven't seen any Indians; but we did see their horse's tracks, and we sure saw the devastation they left behind."

The officer was very interested in what they'd seen, exactly where they'd seen it, and when. Tommy gave the soldiers all of the information he could, including that it was the Bradshaw farm, and telling about burying the victims. He also explained that it looked to him like the Indians had come from the South and it looked like they left headed North, so he had decided to head Southwest toward Denver. The Army officer told him that sounded reasonable, thanked Tommy, and the soldiers departed, heading to the North.

Seeing the US Army column headed after the Indians, even though they were nearly a week behind the Indians, gave Tommy and his men more confidence, and they weren't as afraid.

Chapter Nineteen

Unbeknownst to Tommy and his men, the contingent of the 5th US Cavalry Regiment, which was led by Colonel Nelson Miles, followed the Indians to the Tongue River region, where those Indians joined other bands of Indians under the Lakota leader, Crazy Horse. No doubt the Indians were planning another victory, like the Battle of the Little Bighorn River. Crazy Horse wasn't crazy, though most people would consider him very reckless. His reckless bravery in battle was an inspiration to his warriors. (As an example, Crazy Horse and his men always volunteered to be the bait when trying to trap the US Army soldiers in an ambush.) However, the Indians were unaware that the different contingents of the 5th Cavalry were also consolidating their forces. Colonel Miles was slowly, methodically, pulling his patrols back, in order to be prepared for another battle.

The Montana Winter of 1876-1877 was harsher than normal. The US Army troops which were camped near the Tongue River awoke to a heavy snowfall on one particular January day. The forces of Crazy Horse and Two Moons, about five hundred Indian warriors in all, attacked the soldiers at 7 am on January 8th, 1877.

Colonel Miles swiftly set up defensive positions, and the battle of Wolf Mountain (or, as it is sometimes called, of Tongue River) ensued. It was a hard-fought battle on both sides, but didn't result in huge numbers of casualties on either side. However, the soldiers gained the strategic advantage of capturing most of the high ground, and the Indians chose to withdraw. At first, it seemed like the battle had been fought to a draw, but in actuality it left the Indians in a hard place, without their normal supply of buffalo meat.

Tommy and his men's journey back to Fort Morgan was uneventful after leaving the Walker farm. Almost immediately upon their arrival there (after first taking care of the horses), the young men all went to see Colonel Davenport and share the story of what they'd seen with him. After hearing it, Colonel Davenport took them to see the Mayor, so the Mayor could hear the story directly from them; Tommy was the main narrator. Colonel Davenport and the Mayor had already been working on plans to defend the town if it came under Indian attack, but not with the same impetus or level of haste that they now had.

After one night in a warm bed, a hot bath, and a hot breakfast, the men continued on their way to Denver. With three heavily loaded wagons, it took the better part of five days to get home from Fort Morgan.

The story that the young men had to tell was riveting. Every man and boy in Denver, it seemed, wanted to come by the livery stable and hear about the exciting experience from one or more of them. The reactions from their families were more sober. The Watsons called a family meeting, in fact, which took place shortly after Tommy's return. All of the extended family was present. It was decided that all future trips such as this one would include at least two armed men per wagon, and that there would be a minimum of three wagons.

Unfortunately, but understandably, all three men suffered nightmares for a while, with young Timmy having the most problems. Tommy assured him that he wouldn't be asked to go again.

At supper one evening, after they had been back a few days, Laurie came over to the table where Tommy was eating, and said, smiling mysteriously, "I have a surprise for you, Tommy."

"Really? What is it?" Tommy felt happy, both to find out he had a surprise coming, and to see Laurie being so friendly towards him. Laurie who had one arm behind her back, drew her arm out; in her hand was a book, with the cover facing away from Tommy. She gave

Tommy the book, and he turned it over to read its title. "The Adventures of Tom Sawyer! However did you find this?" Tommy asked excitedly.

"Some fella was trying to trade it for one night's board. Abigail wasn't interested in that kind of book trading, so after she left, I paid him the amount of one night's board, and I got the book," she beamed. "Oh, thank you, Laurie. That was really nice of you," gushed Tommy. Laurie shrugged, "Oh, I got my money's worth already. I read it while you were gone. You'll like that book!"

In mock concern, Tommy got a very serious look on his face, and said, "Actually, this doesn't look too good. It's against all the social rules. Men are supposed to give gifts to women, not the other way around." Laurie was ready for him, though. "It isn't a gift; I'm just going to let you read my book."

"Oh, well, then, that's perfectly acceptable etiquette, I'm sure. And I really appreciate the opportunity to read your book, Miss Burdock," said Tommy, with a huge grin. Then suddenly Tommy remembered. "Oh, I forgot to tell you. Colonel and Mrs. Davenport loved your letter and your gifts! The Colonel was smoking that tobacco when I last saw him, and I reckon Mrs. Davenport is still sniffing that soap!"

Laurie smiled and replied, "Oh, that's nice. Thank you for delivering them for me. And thanks, too, for bringing their reply back to me; Abby gave it to me. I expected thanks in the reply, because they're both so nice, but it's good to hear that you saw that they really truly did like what I sent them."

Light chatter went on between them for a while longer, and then Tommy went off to read about Tom Sawyer's Adventures, convinced that the exchange between him and Laurie would set the tone for an easy, growing friendship between them.

In mid-December, Laurie received another letter from her source in the US Army. It read:

"Dear Miss Burdock, Upon further inquiry of the Army Scout known as Sam Running Bear, I have discovered the names and whereabouts of John and James Reed. I came upon this information due to inquiries about the late Colonel George Armstrong Custer. I am sure you are familiar with his death last summer fighting the Indians. Colonel Custer was part owner in a Silver Mine on Whale Peak in Colorado. John and James Reed are two brothers who were trading with various Indian groups for furs. The Reed brothers were friends of Sam Running Bear and received information from him about the location of Indian groups who might be open to trade. They also provided the Army with information about Indian movements. The fur trading became unprofitable due to the scarcity of buffalo. It is said these brothers gave up trading and became miners. Their last known location was the Whale Silver Mine near Whale Peak in Colorado. The nearest town is Grant, Colorado. I pray this information will be of some value to you." The letter was signed by a Captain Jamison.

That evening, Laurie began trying to determine where Grant, Colorado was located. She had little luck with those she asked. Then she saw Tommy, and asked him if he knew; but Tommy, instead of replying directly to her question, asked, "Why? Did you plan to visit Grant?" With her patience growing thin after getting so many "I dunno" answers, Laurie's response was somewhat curt. "Two men who knew my father may be working at the Whale Mine near Grant."

Tommy, now familiar with Laurie's great desire to find information about her brother (and possibly more family members), said, "I don't know where those places are located, but you've got plenty of time. It's Winter, and, even if we knew exactly where they were located, it'd be dangerous to start out for mining country until Spring." Laurie was crestfallen. Tommy looked at her sad face, and added, "However, Denver is the state capital, and I'm sure the state has some sort of Bureau of Mines or something similar. I'll go inquire about locations of mines, and routes to get there, so we can be ready in the Spring."

Laurie perked up at that, and said, smiling with gratitude, "Thank you so much, Tommy. I'd really appreciate it. I know this whole search sounds futile, but I so want to have my own family." Tommy smiled, nodded, and then went back to the stable to help a customer; but he was whistling.

Chapter Twenty

In mid-March, Tommy once again interrupted Laurie's reading. "Excuse me, Laurie, but I understand a couple of the passes through the Rockies are open now. They tell me there's still some snow, but there's bare ground in many places. Do you think we could start for the Whale Mine as early as April? I know you're anxious to learn all you can as quick as you can."

"Oh, Tommy, that would be great! You've been so sweet and considerate to me, "answered Laurie, fairly glowing with happiness. But, then, her expression changed, like quicksilver. "And here I've been rude and even mean to you in the past, yet you've always been kind, and somehow still seem interested in helping me. But, believe me, I'm not worth your attention."

"Laurie, it takes a tough woman to make it in the West these days. I know you've had some really rough times, but I've seen you overcoming all that, every day. I don't know everything you've been through, but, if you ever want to talk to me about it, or about anything, I promise I'll lend you a very sympathetic ear," offered the young man.

Laurie looked up at him, and saw his sincerity. She decided that she could unburden her heart to him, and that he wouldn't judge her harshly. So she told him, without any noticeable inflection in her voice, about the ridicule she'd endured, about her stepfather and his disgusting actions, about how her mother had told her about her real father, and about the awful choice she had faced from Mr. Porter. Tommy was horrified, and wanted, more than he ever had about anyone, to shield her and protect her to the utmost of his ability from any and all future unpleasantness; but he dared not interrupt her, believing that she needed to let it all out so she could move forward.

"Then I met some people who were real nice, and good to me," Laurie said, almost in awe. "You know some of them; you've met Colonel and Mrs. Davenport, and, of course, you know Jim and Abigail. Since I've been here, they, and the whole family, have treated me so kindly; you have, too, Tommy. And I can tell that I've begun to heal. I realize there are real Christians in the world. Oh, if only I had grown up in a loving family like the one you have here," Laurie lamented.

Tommy could stand the pressure no longer. "Laurie, oh, my dear, sweet Laurie, I'm so sorry to learn of your travails. I had no idea just how bad it had been for you. But it's over now, and you've many friends to make sure you never have to go through any such awfulness again. And, now that you are healing, it helps to understand that hatred is a very harmful emotion, harmful to yourself, so you're only hurting yourself by hating. Besides, Laurie, if your life had been comfortable and pleasant, you'd never have come here and I'd never have known you, and that would've been a great loss for me."

"I don't see how that could be so bad. You would've eventually read Tom Sawyer anyway," Laurie replied, in a flat, off-handed manner, now a bit embarrassed that she'd told him so much about herself. Tommy looked at her intently with a serious, very probing look on his face, but said nothing. "What?" asked the dense young woman.

Tommy began to search for words, and he started turning red. "Laurie Burdock, surely you must know that I've been in love with you ever since I first saw you in Fort Morgan?"

Laurie's mouth dropped open, and it was her turn to search for something to say. She blurted out, "NO! That's impossible!" Seeing Tommy's expression, she tried to recover her equilibrium. "Uhhh, I mean, no, I never suspected anything like that. I'm so sorry. You've

145

been so nice to me, but you can't be in love with me; you just can't. I'm not ready for anybody to be in love with me, and I'm certainly not ready to be in love with anybody." Laurie sounded as if she were in a total panic, and she looked ready to flee.

"That's all right," soothed Tommy, "I'll wait 'til you are ready. Don't worry, Laurie, it'll be all right; there's no rush. I just thought maybe I should tell you, that's all. In the meantime, do you want to go up to Whale Mine in early April, if, of course, we don't get any late blizzards?"

Laurie, still taken aback, thought it over for a minute, and replied, "Please understand, Tommy, I don't want to take advantage of any feelings that you might have for me. But I can't deny that I really would like to go to that mine." Tommy assured her that he understood, and so they agreed to plan on leaving in April for the Rocky Mountain area where the mine was located.

By mid-March, Denver itself was clear of snow, and Tommy's inquiries indicated that most of the mountain roads were passable. Therefore, the first Monday in April, Tommy asked Laurie if she was ready to travel to Grant in a day or so. Laurie enthusiastically answered, "Absolutely!"

Tommy had to arrange for Davie and Timmy to run things in his absence, and he gave them clear instructions on what to do if anything went wrong – basically, they should go talk to his Dad (Jim Watson) or to Pete Elder, if Jim wasn't available. Laurie spoke to Jim and Abby about taking off about a week, and explained the purpose of the trip. After a little discussion with other employees and Abby, a week's worth of time off was arranged, and Laurie would just have to repay the work to the people who would fill in for her.

Supplies were loaded into one of Tommy's enclosed buggies, including an ample number of quilts and blankets. Then Laurie got

146

inside while Tommy climbed into the driver's seat. Tommy was wearing two pair of pants, the heaviest coat he owned, and fur-lined gloves. Laurie, too, even though she was riding inside, was bundled up.

At the end of the first day, Tommy and Laurie stopped for the night at a small public house in Georgetown. It wasn't terribly cold, but Tommy was glad he had on heavy clothing. After the animals were stabled, given food and water, and blankets placed on their backs, Tommy and Laurie went into the kitchen for supper. (Laurie wasn't convinced the public house was much better than spending the night in the buggy, but the family who lived there were pleasant, happy to have company, not just for money but also for conversation.)

After serving them a nourishing, but plain, meal of beans and corn tortillas, the woman of the house asked, "What brings you folks out this way?"

Feeling reticent to share her situation, Laurie rather reluctantly replied, "We're headed up to Whale Silver Mine to meet some family friends."

The woman's face went from smiling to expressionless, and her forehead wrinkled up into almost a frown, as she tried hard to look merely sympathetic, and not just plain nosy. "Is it about that avalanche up there this past Winter that you're going? Did you have kinfolk in it?" Sudden panic showed on Laurie's face, and Tommy got very concerned. "No," answered Laurie, "we never heard anything about one of those, what did you call it, avalanche?"

Tommy spoke up then, both to explain to Laurie and to seek more information from the woman. "An avalanche is when a lot of snow up on the mountain gets so deep and heavy that it breaks loose and slides down the mountain. What was it that happened, ma'am, and where was it?"

147

The woman furrowed her brow, seemed to be trying to remember something, and then finally said, "They was several folk kilt, I know. I heard some names, but, Lordy, I cain't remember what they were. There was a woman and a child killed, as I recollect, and some men, too, but I didn't know none of them. It was somewhere around the mine, or at the mine -- I disremember which."

"I sure hope it didn't involve any of the people we'd planned to meet up with, but we've come all this way, I guess we need to go up there and find out for ourselves," replied Tommy.

The man of the house, who had been sitting silently listening, spoke up, "Wall, if'n you want to know who was kilt, you won't be havin' to go all the way to the mine. Fella came by here a week or two ago and said that last month, when the snow started a meltin', that's when they found the bodies. They buried 'em all at Grant. A'course, the ground still being froze, they couldn't be buried reg'lar like, so they piled rocks on top of the bodies." After hearing that, Tommy didn't ask anything else. He and Laurie excused themselves and went to their rooms to try to sleep.

The next day, Tommy and Laurie set out early, and, in the afternoon, they came to Grant. There they received the whole gruesome story.

They asked the first person they met in Grant about the disaster. He was a wiry old man, and he was happy to tell the story. "On January 7th last, the snow slid off of the mountain and crushed the bunkhouse at the Whale Silver Mine. Originally, the victims were believed to have been swept into the valley, but when the snow began to melt, they found the bodies."

Tommy was aghast, "Oh, no. Do you have their names?" The old man replied, "Well, some of them. There were some that nobody knew who they were. We do know for sure that James, John, and

148

Matthew Reed were all killed, as well as a Reed child and a Mr. J.H. Ralph. There was also an unidentified woman, and there were two unidentified men. No one claimed the bodies, so they wuz all sent here to Grant for burial."

Tommy dropped his head, and turned away. "Young man, wuz some a them kin?" Tommy turned back to old man, and said, "We just wanted to talk to James and John Reed. Thank you for your information." Then Tommy turned and walked back to his buggy. Laurie had climbed down, but the quiet conversation had been too far away for her to hear.

Laurie quickly asked, "Does he know the details? Was it really at the mine? Did the Reed brothers escape from it?" Tommy looked at her with mournful eyes, and her spirit fell. "I'm sorry, Laurie. Last January, there was an avalanche at the mine, and the entire Reed family was killed."

"Oh, no, how horrible! The entire family? What do you mean by the entire family?"

"The man said it included John, James, Matthew, and a Reed child, as well as another man whose name I can't remember. There was also an unidentified woman, and two unidentified men."

Laurie was shocked at the possibility of an entire generation of a family's lives being snuffed out. "I wonder if there's any more of their family somewhere. There may be cousins, uncles, aunts, or other relatives, who'll never know what became of their Colorado kin; certainly those that weren't identified will be just be lost forever. It seems kind of selfish that my first thought wasn't of them, but of myself, that the information I was seeking had slipped away from me once again."

The fact that Laurie's priorities were changing wasn't lost on Tommy. While he was sad about the deaths, and about the loss of the

149

information which Laurie sought so desperately, Tommy could see and appreciate the changes being made in the woman he loved, changes being made by love.

Chapter Twenty-one

Crazy Horse's people were on the edge of starvation; there were no buffalo any where near for them to harvest, nor wild berries or other edible vegetation, leaving very little food for the families. Crazy Horse faced the reality of his situation. Therefore, on May 4th, 1877, Crazy Horse, leading a ragtag band of starving Indians, arrived at the Red Cloud Agency near Fort Robinson, Nebraska, intending to surrender to the Army and stop fighting.

The next morning, Crazy Horse, accompanied by a group of Indian scouts and Indian Agency people, as well as a Lieutenant Lee, went to Fort Robinson, where he attempted to effect a surrender, so that then he'd be able to return to the reservation with his people so they could get food. But surrender was refused, and Crazy Horse was arrested and imprisoned. [The following September, in what has been variously called an escape attempt or an assassination, Crazy Horse was stabbed by an Indian Agency guard, and died.]

Meanwhile, Tommy still kept trying to woo the reluctant Laurie, but it seemed as if she was much too distracted, never able to get her mind off of her past unhappy experiences, nor free from her quest to find her Indian family (primarily, now, her brother), and consequently she showed no interest in pursuing any romantic involvement.

Laurie had, at least, begun writing fairly regularly to her mother, whose letters she received in return (along with occasional notes from her sister). Those letters should have helped satisfy her intense longing for familial love, but they never seemed to be sufficient to fill the hole left in her heart by learning her real father was dead and no one knew even the name of her missing brother.

Laurie had become an excellent employee of the General Store, and the owners (partners Jim Watson and Phillip Smith, two first cousins from Griffin, Georgia) thought very highly of her. Laurie was the first to open the store in the morning, and the last to close and lock it in the evening. She knew the location of every piece of merchandise in the store, and its price, and was fairly well versed in what everything was used for (and so she could suggest alternatives, if the exact item being sought was unavailable). Since she was also a pretty woman, that also attracted the male customers; but they all soon learned that, while Laurie was pleasant, she was all business.

Laurie clearly was a Christian, with a good background of Biblical learning, and she could quote many of the more familiar verses from memory; but she only attended the local church sporadically. Tommy, on the other hand, attended church regularly, and it distressed him that Laurie would often spend Sundays reading whatever book she could get her hands on, or attending her personal chores, such as sewing, instead of attending church services.

Laurie often used her free time to make dresses and other articles of clothing from flour sacks (the ones which were printed with floral patterns were her favorites) which she obtained from the boarding house. She also made some clothing from bolts of cloth she purchased (on credit, mostly) from the general store. Her salary wasn't large (in fact, it was rather small), but she didn't need much money, since her pay from the general store included, as an extra benefit, her room and board at the Watson Boarding House. Most of the articles of clothing which Laurie made, she sold through the general store, and she used those proceeds to pay off her debt for the cloth.

She was still saving as much money as she could, more out of habit now than for financing the search for her family, since she had all but given up on continuing the search, having run out of all her known options (although still feeling the longing, deeply and almost as a constant companion).

One day, in late Winter, Laurie was leafing through one of the several catalogs that were sent to the general store. She was looking for merchandise that might sell well, to perhaps recommend to Jim or Phillip, when she came across an advertisement for a pair of earrings.

The picture wasn't very good; it was only a drawing in black and white -- but the description of the earrings sounded absolutely stunning. They were 24k gold, and set with dark blue Sapphires. Laurie fell in love with them instantly. Even though these were for pierced ears, and her ears weren't pierced, she didn't care; they were lovely. She had never had any jewelry before, but, somehow, those particular earrings called to her.

Jim saw her pouring over that one page for such a long time, that he came over and asked what she was looking at. At first, Laurie tried to turn the page, and brush off the question, embarrassed that he'd seen her staring at something so frivolous; but Jim didn't tease her, he was sincerely interested, so she finally confessed that she thought those were the most beautiful earrings she'd ever seen. Jim glanced down at the page and saw that they cost fifteen dollars. He told Laurie that he would order the earrings right away, and, if she made two nice Easter dresses, he would trade the earrings for the dresses. Laurie readily agreed! Jim told her the approximate size of each dress, but, other than that, didn't make any requests about them.

Laurie selected two fabrics, after Jim had left and the store was closed, and wrote the cost down in the ledger against her account. As soon as she got back to the boarding house that evening, Laurie began immediately working on the two Easter dresses. To quiet her frugal conscience, she kept telling herself that fifteen dollars was a lot of money, true, but she really didn't have anything else she needed to do with her free time. Besides, she had read all the books she could find (except Moby Dick).

At supper time, Laurie went over to see Phillip's wife, Susan, who had pierced ears, and asked Susan how to go about getting her ears pierced. Susan asked her about what earrings she'd be wearing , and Laurie explained about the earrings that had been ordered. When Susan heard that, she counseled Laurie that she should wait until she actually had the gold earrings in hand, so she could put the earrings on immediately, in order to keep the holes in her ears from closing up.

Susan also suggested she talk to the doctor who was boarding with them for suggestions, and pointed out where he was sitting. Laurie went over immediately, introduced herself, apologized for interrupting his meal, and asked if he had time to talk to her after he'd eaten. He recognized her from some prior dealings with her at the general store, and said he certainly had time after supper, and they arranged to meet in the sitting room.

When they met later, Laurie explained about wanting to get her ears pierced. The doctor asked her about the earrings she was proposing to wear, and approved of their being real gold. He told her that cheap earrings could cause a serious infection in newly pierced ears. He went into some detail about the importance of ensuring the cleanliness, not only of the earrings, but also of her ears and the needle to be used, to prevent infection. He told her that continued cleanliness was important after the piercing, too, as the site would still be vulnerable.

Laurie thanked him for all of his advice, and offered to pay him a fee, but he refused, saying he was glad he was able to pay her back for all of the assistance she had given him in getting the items he needed at the general store. (He was quite happy that she didn't have a serious medical problem.)

From the sizes Jim had given her, it sounded to Laurie as if the dresses were for his wife Abby and for Sarah Elder. When Laurie told Jim on the Saturday morning before Easter that the two dresses were ready, her guess was proven to be correct. Jim asked her to deliver them to Abby and to Sarah, which Laurie did promptly. Both Abby and Sarah loved their new dresses. Abby's dress was a deep rich rosy pink, while Sarah's was a cheerful red and white gingham, and both had full skirts and lots of ruffles (and large pockets, which were handy and appreciated).

At the same time, Laurie delivered a dress to Susan Smith, Phillip's wife. Phillip had already made a deal for Laurie to make the dress for Susan before Jim's arrangement with Laurie. Susan's dress was soft golden brown, made of fine cloth which Phillip had gotten specially for her, so Phillip only paid Laurie for the sewing. (After Phillip had ordered the cloth, he had told Jim what he was doing, and Jim had gotten the idea to get Laurie to also make dresses for Abby and Sarah, but he didn't order any special cloth, preferring to let Laurie chose the material.) Susan was really happy with her new dress, too

Laurie's new earrings arrived just in time for Easter. Susan had done the honor of piercing Laurie's ears; she had held a piece of ice on each of Laurie's earlobe's until it became almost numb, and then quickly ran a needle through the lobe. (Laurie grimaced noticeably, but didn't cry out.) The earrings were promptly inserted into the new holes. Susan told her to rotate the earrings regularly, so the skin didn't grow back across them.

Laurie wore the new earrings, and a new dress that she had made for herself, to Easter Sunday Service. It was blue and white gingham (to complement her dark blue sapphire earrings), with a border of blue lace, which she had salvaged from an old dress, around the neck and the sleeves. She had also fashioned herself a belt, using the same fabric and decorated with the same blue lace. She was

155

beautiful; more importantly, she looked happy. Tommy was very pleased to take Laurie to church that Easter Sunday morning. He was pleased that she was going to church, and that she was beginning to finally be convinced that she had value. Laurie was slowly coming the realization that several people, whom she admired, thought highly of her.

Jim Watson admired Laurie's drive, and her thrifty ways, and had asked her once, in a joking manner, what she did with all of her money, since she never seemed to spend any of it. (He was also concerned that maybe someone was operating some scheme or fraud against her, causing her to "invest" her money unwisely.) Laurie replied that she put it in the bank, her only explanation being that, one day, she might need it.

In May of 1877, the news reached Denver that Crazy Horse had been captured. Hope was beginning to blossom that the Plains Indian Wars were coming to an end. From this time on, until about 1890, attacks decreased, and conflict with the Indians became rare.

A few nights after they'd heard the news about Crazy Horse, Tommy found Laurie in her usual chair in the sitting room, after almost everyone else had gone to bed; she was reading. "Hello, Laurie; what are you reading tonight?"

Laurie grinned at him. "I finally worked my way down through the books to Moby Dick. I put it off 'til last, 'cause I didn't think I would like it -- but I do. Though I think I'm more on the side of Moby Dick than the whalers." Tommy laughed, and said, fondly, "Leave it to you to see the huge fish as the hero."

Laurie frowned and retorted, "He isn't a fish; he's a warm blooded animal. Whales can think and even communicate with other whales. I read all about that in a newspaper that was at the general store."

Tommy ignored her correction, not sure he believed it (having not seen the newspaper article himself, he wasn't sure she wasn't kidding him, and he didn't want to look ignorant). He said, instead, "I don't think I'd like going to sea, but it would be interesting to actually see one of those whales up close ... IF it wasn't mad at me, that is."

Laurie considered such a meeting, and said, "I don't know if they're normally peaceful or not. Most of their contact with humans seems to be humans trying to kill them -- for their meat or their oil or both. They might view that as showing all humans to be unfriendly."

Tommy mused, "Well, injured land animals, which people hunt for food, do fight back when they're hurt but not dead. It would seem reasonable that sea creatures would do the same."

Laurie looked at Tommy intently, as though trying to read his thoughts, and asked abruptly, "Can we change the subject?"

A surprised Tommy nodded his head and said, "Sure, what do you want to talk about?"

"Going to visit the Indians."

"Oh. Laurie, I don't think that makes much sense. There are many Indians tribes and a whole lot of them don't like us. Besides, many of the tribes are nomadic; they move around a lot, and you can't be sure where they are. You would need a lot more information than I think you have, or, otherwise, it could be a long and an expensive waste of time."

"Well, I know my father was a Ute," Laurie ventured, "so that should help, shouldn't it?"

"Some," reasoned Tommy, "since it does cut down the number of possibilities. There are two Ute reservations that I know of, one in the south and one in the north."

"Colonel Davenport told me that, and he said he thought my father was from the northern group," replied Laurie.

"How could he know that unless he had your father's name, and unless he knew something about him to base that information on? It's not easy to know which reservation a particular Ute might be on, unless you know him. Like me, for instance … I know that my adopted brother lives on that northern reservation with his tribe."

"Oh, but I do know my father's name. I thought you knew that!"

Tommy perked up at hearing that, and said, "Well, no, I never heard you say a name, you've always just referred to him as your father."

"Why, you're right. I haven't ever called him by name, have I? I guess I just assumed that saying his name wouldn't mean anything to anyone but me, 'cause I thought that no white people would have any knowledge of the Indians. So I just never mentioned his name at all," Laurie responded. "Just like you, maybe, never bothering to tell me the name of your adopted brother who's a Ute!"

Chapter Twenty-two

Tommy said, "You're right; I wouldn't expect many white people to know many Indians; and, you're also right, I never thought about mentioning that my adopted brother was a Ute, either." Curious, Tommy asked, "What was your father's name?"

Laurie replied, "Oh, My mother told me his name was Sam, and Colonel Davenport told me that he was probably Sam Running Bear."

Tommy's mouth fell open, and he stared at Laurie. The shock on his face wasn't lost on Laurie. "Tommy? What is it? You know something! You've heard of him!"

Tommy pulled up a chair and sat down next to Laurie. "I was there when he died. I helped to bury Sam Running Bear. Up in Montana, north of Bannack, Montana."

Laurie was the one now in shock. "It can't be. Don't you dare make fun of me! Or tell me some lie just to make me feel better!"

Tommy was shaking his head the whole time she was talking. "No, I would never do either of those things. MY adopted brother is YOUR half-brother! His name is Johnny Little Bear!"

"Are you sure that what you're telling me is the truth? The Army said they didn't know where my father died, or what killed him."

Tommy was starting to get annoyed that Laurie kept refusing to believe him, questioning and doubting everything he said; here he had the information the woman he loved had been looking for, and she wouldn't believe him. "We don't know what killed him either. Dad and I were two or three days' ride north of Bannack, in a snow storm. Johnny tried to steal a horse from us, but, thankfully, the horse threw him off and we caught him. After Dad heard him tell why he needed the horse, Johnny took us to his father, who died soon after we got there. We buried his father, and took Johnny back to Bannack with us. It was sure hard burying him too. The snow was several inches deep except under that overhanging cliff. Fortunately, we found enough stones, since the ground was frozen.   All his ... your father said was something about going to the Great Spirit. My Dad will tell you the same thing. It was several years ago, I must have been twelve or thirteen, and Johnny was about ten or eleven."

Laurie was trying to grasp what he was saying, but felt confused and somewhat disoriented at hearing all of this information from what was to her the most unlikely of sources. "But then why did you send him away later? Back to the Indians? Didn't you like him any more?"

"We didn't send him; he wanted to go," Tommy explained gently. "Johnny knew he was different from us, and, though he had lived around white people a lot, he was treated differently by some of them, and he realized that he also looked at things differently than white folks. He wanted to be a real Indian, true to the traditions of his father and mother, and learn their ways, and he knew the only way he could do that was to live with their tribe. We've heard from him a time or two since he left, but nothing in months."

Laurie finally realized that Tommy was being truthful, and that he had given her the answers to her questions and the solution to her search. Joyfully, she threw her arms around his neck and hugged him enthusiastically. Keeping his own arms at his side, mindful of her past experiences, Tommy asked, "Is it all right for me to hug back?"

Laurie smiled at him, a wide, full smile. Although she had removed her arms from his neck before he finished asking his question, she promptly threw her arms around him again, and said, "Sure, it is!"

Laurie rested her head on Tommy's shoulder, feeling something she had never known before -- a warm and tender hug that transmitted a genuine wish to care for her. Laurie didn't understand this new feeling, but she definitely knew she liked it. She tilted her head back a little bit from Tommy's shoulder, in order to look him in the eyes, and asked, in a wondering, awed tone, "Is that what love feels like?"

Tommy, who at first had thought her movement back was going to be an outright rejection, smiled in relief, and said, "Absolutely! I want to hug you like this the rest of my life."

Laurie grinned playfully, and replied, "I don't know about that. I have to think on that for a while." But she didn't dismiss the idea.

The next day was a Saturday, and Laurie and Tommy attended the wedding of Helen Matthews and Irwin Bates. It was a beautiful wedding, with the groom's father officiating, and his brother as Best Man. Helen's cousin was Maid of Honor.

Laurie had taken the lead some months before to help Helen find exactly the right dresses for the wedding party; she had even sewn some extra touches on the bridesmaids' dresses and hats herself, after ordering those items. She had also ordered the wedding dress, which came all the way from San Francisco.

Helen, always nice, was so grateful for such competent and thoughtful assistance in the planning that she had even asked Laurie to be one of her bridesmaids; but Laurie declined, with thanks (realizing that she didn't really fit into that circle, and not wanting to be any distraction from the bride).

The men all wore formal suits, all black coats with tails, fancy striped trousers, and white bow ties. The bridesmaids all wore lovely yellow silk taffeta dresses, with a trim of yellow rosebud-print silk ribbon, and broad brimmed white silk-covered hats with yellow silk hatbands and dangling yellow silk ribbons. The bride's dress was white silk, covered with a white lace overlay, and had fancy tucks on the bodice decorated with small pearls. She wore a long white lace veil flowing from a white velvet hat. Her dress had only a short train. Helen looked radiant, and Irwin had never looked happier.

Tommy provided his fanciest buggy, and a driver dressed in a red coat, to drive them to a lovely hotel in the mountains above Denver. To Laurie, it seemed like a wedding from a fairy tale book she had leafed through at the general store. (In fact, it was the illustrations in that fairy tale book that gave her the inspiration for the wedding attire.)

Although the clothing was expensive (Helen was the only daughter of the most successful banker in Denver, and Irwin's father was the Pastor of the largest church in Denver, so cost wasn't an obstacle), it really wasn't a costly wedding at all. Helen and Irwin had insisted on not "showing off" by holding an expensive reception at any upscale hotel ballroom, where some of their friends might feel uncomfortable, so the reception was held at the Boarding House with an open buffet and coffee or tea to drink.

It was the biggest and fanciest wedding any of the Watsons, Elders, or Smiths had ever seen. Neither Tommy nor Laurie had ever seen anything like it, and they were impressed. However, Laurie told Tommy, "I can't imagine spending all that money on just one day."

Tommy replied, "People in business, that is to say, big business, and other people who live their lives in the public eye, have to be different than other folks. The men in that wedding party already had at least one black formal suit. They probably didn't buy anything new. Yes, Mr. Matthews spent a lot of money on silk dresses, but all of his business associates got invitations to the wedding, and just about everybody in town will know about it, 'cause he also invited the local newspapermen. In short, spending the money on those dresses was probably very good for business; it established the bank as a thriving operation, and thus encouraged people to do business – get bank accounts, make deposits, arrange financing, get loans, and so forth – at that bank instead of any other in town. I think the net result was the wedding cost him very little, and he even may have made money on it."

Laurie could hardly believe it, but, as she looked over the church full of people, most of whom she didn't know, she could see lots of silk top hats and loads of expensive clothing. "I suppose you're right, Tommy, but it doesn't feel right to use a wedding that way."

Tommy added, "Being in business for yourself, and buying supplies regularly, and getting to know the people who sell those supplies and who also utilize your services from time to time, then their friendship makes the unpleasant parts of business much better, and makes the pleasant even feel like fun. They know what you use, and sometimes, if they have a need to get rid of something, and they know you can use it, then you get a better deal. Everyone needs to make money, and being fair and friendly makes it go better for everyone."

After the wedding reception was over, Tommy and Laurie joined Jim and Abigail Watson back at the boarding house kitchen for some cool, refreshing tea.

"Dad, I have some really interesting news for you and Mom," began Tommy. Jim arched his eyebrows, and inquired, "Do we need to sit down first?"

"Not yet," grinned Tommy. "Laurie told me some information she learned last year about her father. He was an Army Scout, and he was a Ute Indian, and his name was Sam Running Bear,"

Jim was shocked. "Maybe I should've sat down. I guess you told her all about Sam and Johnny?"

"I did," answered Tommy, "all that I could remember."

Jim had still not recovered. "It's incredible that Laurie is Johnny's half-sister. This is too amazing. It can only be the hand of God at work here."

Abigail injected, "Yes, it is amazing, but it isn't really all that strange,. Just think about it. Compared to the folks back East, there's a lot more folks out here who know each other, or at least know about each other. And how many white people know Ute Indians? Not that many. But, any way you look at, and I do thank God for His grace, it's wonderful news. Laurie now has family out here in the West, and she can get on with the business of healing."

Jim stammered, looking bewildered, "Healing?"

"Laurie suffered greatly at the hands of some ungodly people, and now she can work at learning how to forgive and get on with her life," explained Abigail (not wanting to get Jim all fired up about the precise nature of that suffering, not real sure that he wouldn't saddle up and go after Mr. Porter right then). "Since her suffering has stopped, and now she knows about her brother, it'll no longer be one step forward and one step backward – it'll all be moving forward."

"I do already feel a sense of relief, Abigail," added Laurie; "or maybe it's a release."

"Does this mean you will marry me now, Laurie?" asked Tommy eagerly.

"Maybe," replied Laurie, "just not right now, but maybe."

Everyone laughed, even Jim and Abigail who weren't quite sure why they were laughing!

Chapter Twenty-three

The following week, planning began for a trip to Utah, to visit Johnny Little Bear at the Ute reservation. Tommy and Laurie were going, of course, and also Jim and Abigail Watkins. It was decided that they would take three wagons, with Tommy and Laurie in one and Jim and Abby in another, and the third one loaded down with supplies. They would carry plenty of supplies (for the people and the horses) and lots of water. They had previously discussed having at least two armed men per wagon for safety, but, with the Indian attacks less of a problem, decided that they would be sufficiently protected with Jim and Tommy; so they just needed one more good shooter.

As their good luck continued, Philip, Jim's cousin, had a chance meeting with a photographer traveling the West taking photos of Indians, soldiers, trappers, miners, and any other group of people that would look foreign or exotic to the people back East. The photographer was an unheard-of man by the name of Jones, but he had a camera and all the materials for him to make tintypes and develop the images. He also claimed to be a decent shot with a rifle, so he was allowed to go along, in the third wagon.

And, so equipped, they began the journey North, up along the edge of the Rocky Mountains. After several weeks, the travelers entered Wyoming. No Indians had been seen, and, indeed, few humans either. Jim was called upon to shoot a Prong Horn Antelope for fresh meat to add to their diet. Jim killed the animal with one shot, but admitted he was grateful it had been much nearer than the one he killed on the overland trip from Montana a few years before. All of the travelers enjoyed fresh roasted meat for their supper.

Once they had passed the higher elevations of the mountains, they crossed back into Colorado, and headed southwest toward the Ute Indian reservation.

People were a little more plentiful in this area, away from the higher mountains, and they saw several small groups of Indians, but those Indians never approached them, or seemed to pay any attention to them either.

After two more weeks, the party came to the outskirts of an Indian village. Jim had learned how to ask for Little Bear in the Ute language, so he saddled one of the horses and went into the village to inquire. It was, in fact, a Ute village, and the Indians were friendly toward the white man who spoke some of their language and who knew one of their tribe.

An older man indicated that he knew Little Bear, and, when he was unable to communicate enough to help the white people further, he got his horse and motioned for the party to follow. No one in the party knew where they were going, nor how long the trip would be, but they felt that it was their best choice to find Johnny.

They camped overnight that evening, and, the next day, after several hours of traveling, the older man showed them another Indian village, and indicated that they were to wait where they were. He then mounted his horse and rode into the village. When he came back, he brought Little Bear with him, and, after seeing that Little Bear recognized the white man who'd asked about him, he rode back to his own village.

Johnny Little Bear was happy to see Jim and Abigail and Tommy, but he wasn't so sure about all the extra people in the wagons. Jim shook Johnny's hand, and Abigail hugged him; then the three of them stood talking out of hearing range for a few minutes. Clearly, they were explaining about why they were there – and, possibly, about

Laurie. Then the three returned to the wagons, where Tommy and Laurie stood waiting. Tommy ran and embraced his adopted brother.

Then Jim introduced Laurie to Johnny Little Bear. Johnny was understandably confused, and didn't understand at all how he could have a half-sister that he had never known about. Consequently, he didn't approach Laurie, but just stared uncomprehendingly at her. Laurie could easily emphasize with his reaction, remembering her own shock at hearing about a half-brother, and so she decided to take it slower than she really wanted to. She started by asking him if he had an aunt who was about twelve years older than Johnny.

Johnny, puzzled by the question, replied, almost seeming to weigh each word, "Yes, my father had a sister who is older than me, by about that much. But what does my aunt have to do with this?"

Laurie replied, "Your aunt has met my mother. My mother was caring for you temporarily at the Army fort when your mother died of fever. My mother's parents had died of the same fever, so my mother and your father became close over their shared grief. Your father sent for his younger sister to take over the care of you. After his sister arrived, your father had to leave the fort on a mission, guiding a mapping patrol, and was gone several months. While he was gone, my mother's brother came to Colorado and took my mother back to Missouri. My mother didn't know it then, but she was pregnant with me … and your father was my father."

Johnny stood looking at Laurie for a few moments, and then he asked her to wait right there. He went back into the village, and soon returned with a woman ten to fifteen years older than himself. In the company of Jim, Abigail, Tommy, and Laurie, and in the Ute language, Johnny Little Bear asked his aunt about a white woman who was living with his father when Johnny was small. The aunt confirmed the story told by Laurie's mother.

Johnny felt awkward, unsure how to proceed, and tried to put his feelings into words: "I have been living back here with my tribe long enough that the way I react to women is different than the way I was taught when I lived with Jim and Abigail. It feels strange to have a sister; I have never had a sister before. Indian men treat women differently than white men treat their women. I have a wife, and I have a young son. I would be pleased to introduce you to them." The news of his marriage, and that he was a father now, came as a happy surprise to Jim, Abby, and Tommy, and they all took turns congratulating him.

Johnny then took Laurie into the village, and Laurie greatly enjoyed meeting her Indian relatives, especially her new sister-in-law, Wanekia, and her nephew. The rest of the travelers let Laurie have separate time with her new-found family members, and they set up their camp close to the village. They had, of course, brought gifts for Johnny, as well as some for his tribe, which they gave to him to distribute appropriately.

They stayed for a week, and had planned to stay another week, but word came that Crazy Horse had been murdered. When Johnny learned of this, he told Jim that they should go, immediately, and that he would accompany them to help prevent any problems along their journey. He feared that angry Indians would take out their anger on any white people they found. Besides, it was getting cold at night, and they should return to Denver before the heavier snow fell.

Laurie bid her Indian family goodbye, after posing for some photographs taken by Mr. Jones. The entire party intended to sort of retrace its steps, except it turned out that Johnny had a little different route. It was somewhat distressing to Jim and Tommy, since Johnny was taking them along trails made by Indians, rather than by wagons and teams, and those trails weren't as well-defined. But Johnny assured them that he knew exactly where he was going, and that it was a much safer route.

The nights were getting cold now, and a chill was in the air even on bright sunny days. The mountains were stunningly beautiful, and Johnny knew exactly where to stop so the animals could feed on lush tall green grass and where there was plenty of clear fresh water. Some fishing was done whenever they had the opportunity, to improve their diet, which was heavy on beans and bacon. (Beans and bacon were preferred travel provisions, because they are high energy foods, with lots of calories, and easy to keep without refrigeration, and easy to pack for a trip – although monotonous to eat, day after day.)

After about a week, Johnny killed a deer, and everyone enjoyed the fresh roasted meat.

Well into the second week, Johnny became uncharacteristically quiet, and he kept watching a ridgeline to the west. Finally, a worried Jim Watson asked Johnny what he was looking for so intently. Jim was concerned that they might be in danger from some hazard or attack which only Johnny knew about. Johnny gave a slight smile, and told Jim not to worry, it was a surprise for his newly discovered sister.

Then, one day, suddenly, Johnny told Jim to turn the wagons toward the ridgeline; it was easy to see that in front of them was an excellent place to camp, but it was just a bit earlier than they usually stopped. Soon, Johnny instructed Jim to halt the wagons, and start setting up camp for the evening. Johnny next brought his horse alongside Tommy's wagon and called for Laurie. Laurie came to the opening in the cover, and said, "Yes, my dear brother?" (She liked calling him "brother" and did it often.)

Johnny edged his horse right up against the front of the wagon, and asked, "Laurie, do you think you can climb over onto my horse, behind me?"

"Sure," replied the dark-haired beauty. And, putting her words into actions, she proceeded to easily join Johnny on his horse, and put her arms around his waist. Jim was beginning to understand, so he climbed down from the wagon and followed the horse. Tommy also rode his horse alongside of Johnny and Laurie. About fifty yards further, they came to a cleft in the ridge, which could easily provide shelter from a storm, and Johnny pointed down at the ground to a pile of rocks about four feet wide and about eight feet long. "Laurie, here is the grave of our father, Sam Running Bear."

Of all the things her imagination could conjure up, she had had no idea Johnny was taking her to her father's gravesite. Laurie, who was surprised, to say the least, suddenly started crying. Johnny became upset, and looked perplexed. "But I thought you wanted to find him?"

"I did," sniffed Laurie, between sobs. "It's just that I never knew him, and he didn't even know I existed, but I know he would have loved me and I would have loved him. I feel such a sense of loss, but, at the same time, I feel relief that he isn't really lost any longer."

Johnny was relieved, and said, "Then it is good. But you shouldn't cry. Indians don't deal with death the same way as white people. We aren't so likely to look back, and, once someone has died, we don't usually speak of them again. They have gone to the Great Spirit, and are no longer of us. Maybe we live more in the present because our lives require us to keep looking for food and preparing to live with the elements. I suppose that is why people who call themselves 'Civilized,' tend to call us 'Savages.'"

Camp was set up, and everyone enjoyed each other's company. The next morning, Johnny told Jim, "I am sure you know the way home from here, since Bannack is about three hours that way," and pointed toward the southwest.

"Yes, I know the way from here, Johnny," was the reply, and then Jim Watson hugged his adopted son, understanding that Johnny needed to get back to his own son and his wife in the Ute village.

170

Camp was broken, and Johnny said a long good-bye to Laurie, and shorter (but nonetheless meaningful) good-byes to Abigail and Tommy. Finally, Johnny turned back toward his village, and the Watson party headed south for Denver. About an hour was spent in Bannack, reminiscing, and showing Laurie where Abigail and Jim were married, and where Tommy father had owned a livery stable. They visited his grave for a short while, and then continued on their journey south. Fortunately, they only experienced one small snowfall before returning to their home.

Tommy wasn't the only one who had noticed that Laurie was slowly changing. She seemed happier and more relaxed than she had ever been since Tommy had known her. She hadn't said a sharp word to anyone during the entire trip, nor retreated into some private place that made her seem remote and sad (as she often used to). Laurie also had a smile on her face almost all of the time.

Though she never addressed Tommy with intimate words, she did act in a manner consistent with someone who cared a lot about him. Laurie went to great effort to take Tommy food when it was served, and seemed to enjoy letting Tommy help her up on to the wagon when she was clearly athletic enough to do it without Tommy's assistance.

"Dearest Mother,

"I have the information about Sam Running Bear and his son. It really is extraordinary! Sam and his son, Little Bear, now called Johnny Little Bear, were in Montana when Sam became ill. Jim Watson, one of the owners of the general store where I have been working, and Tommy found him and talked to him before he died. Jim took Little Bear into his family. Tommy is just a little older than Johnny. Tommy is the young man who has

asked me to marry him. I think I will, but I'm not ready to tell him that yet."

"Since the Indian Wars have quieted down somewhat, we took a long journey to the Unitah Reservation to look for Johnny Little Bear. We found him and his family. I met his aunt who took care of Johnny after Uncle Bob took you back to Missouri. She still remembers you. Johnny doesn't remember you, but he was just a baby. His aunt never talked to Johnny about you at all. We visited my father's grave on the return trip from the reservation. Johnny took us there through lovely valleys and scenic mountains."

"Johnny has a wife and a young son. We had a wonderful time visiting. Because of his time with the Watson family, Johnny speaks very good English. Better than many people in Missouri! Mother, it is wonderful to have an older brother, even if he is only a half-brother."

"Mother, I wish that you could meet Tommy and all the rest of the household. How are my Missouri half-brothers and sisters? I miss seeing them."

"I love you and miss you, Mother."

"Laurie"

Chapter Twenty-four

Maysville County Farm circa 1873

"Laurie, it was heartwarming to get your letter. I am so happy that your life is taking a much happier turn out west."

"I never wanted to worry you, but after Jasper died, we couldn't pay the rent or grow enough food in the garden. We moved into the Maysville Poor House with the other people of like circumstances. We had to work very hard, but at least there was a roof over our heads. Your brother, Ted, went to live with and work for your Uncle Bob on his farm since his son, David, had left home."

"You might remember old John Morton, his wife died about the same time as Jasper. He needed someone to cook and clean, so he gave me a job and a place to live earlier this year, it is a lot to do, but it keeps your two sisters out of that Poorhouse! His children are mostly all

grown, though he has one son still living at home. John owns his house and farm, but he is old enough to start having trouble with rheumatism. He asked me to marry him and we had a long talk about it. He is lonesome as I am. John is a quiet man, but just as sweet as he can be. His sons are not opposed to the marriage. I still miss Jasper, except when he was drinking."

"We plan to get married in the winter, so we might be married by the time you receive this letter."

"Your loving Mother, Evelyne"

After the return from Utah and Montana, everyone had to catch up on their jobs, and there was little time for group discussions about the trip. A few days after Laurie received the letter from her mother, Tommy again saw Laurie reading in the Boarding House sitting room, and he went over and sat down beside her on the bench seat. "Hello, Laurie, are you reading something new?"

"No, Tommy, I'm just rereading something I had read before … the Bible."

"Hmmm, that's a far cry from Macbeth."

"Well, if you must know, I was reading the Love chapter of Corinthians."

Tommy was a bit surprised to hear Laurie say she was reading the Bible, but the Love chapter gave him courage. "Does that mean you have a love question?"

She looked at him for a long minute before replying. "I'm trying to decide if someone really loves me or not. I didn't have any daisy to pluck petals from to find out."

"You don't need the Bible to find out if I love you, Laurie. I've been in love with you ever since I saw you pick up that little child in the street in Fort Morgan and return him to his mother's side. You asked for no thanks, you just did it. Not to mention that you are the most beautiful woman in the world."

Laurie's mouth dropped open slightly, and she gasped, "You did tell me once that you had seen that, but I'd forgotten all about it."

"Yes, I first saw you walking down the street and was admiring your outside beauty. Then I realized that you were sweet and caring, and just as beautiful inside. I've gone to church with many pretty young women, and picnicked with a few, but never felt any pull on my heart from any of them. Then, that day, when I saw you going down the street, well, I felt that pull, for the first time ever, and something told me that you were the one for me.

"And to learn that you're the half-sister of my best friend and adopted brother, that just adds more proof that I was right and that it was meant to be."

Laurie regarded him in silence, as she thought about him, and what it might be like to be married to Tommy; then she said, "Tommy Thompson, I will marry you." Tommy's whole face lit up at that, but, before he could speak, she continued, "I do have a request for a wedding present from you. I know we have obligations and work to attend to here, so I don't ask for it to be soon, but I really would like for you to take me back to Missouri to see my mother and my half-brothers and half-sisters there. Now, if you think that's an unreasonable thing to ask, tell me so, and I won't ask it of you."

Tommy looked into her eyes and said, "That's not unreasonable at all, Laurie. I'd like to meet your other family. But we have one other small problem. What if you're a terrible kisser, or you think I'm a terrible kisser? It's my firm opinion that we need to remove all doubt."

Laurie grinned, took his face in her hands, and gave him the warmest, gentlest, kiss he had ever received. Tommy looked into her and said, "I think this is going to work just fine."

Tommy put his arms around Laurie and held her so tightly that it was hard to tell where Tommy ended and Laurie began. They were so engrossed in each other that they both jumped a little when they heard Abigail Watson speak, "Hey, what's going on here?"

Hearing that, Tommy and Laurie dropped their arms from each other and turned toward Abby, who was standing in the doorway. Tommy, his embarrassment shown by his bright red face, said, "Mom, Laurie just agreed to marry me!"

"Oh, that's wonderful. I'm so happy for both of you. I can't wait to tell your father! Have you talked about a date yet? Weddings take some time to plan. We need to start thinking about all of the details involved. And, of course, now that you're going to get married, you need to go see Pastor Selby Bates and get counseling."

Chapter Twenty-five

The next morning, Tommy and Laurie walked hand in hand over to the Methodist Church. Pastor Bates wasn't at the church, so they proceeded to his home, which was just a few houses away. When Mrs. Bates came to the door, Tommy asked if they could speak to the Pastor. Mrs. Bates led them into the study, and went to get her husband. In a few minutes, the Pastor came into the room and, being an experienced clergyman, closed the door behind him. "Good morning, Laurie, and good morning, Tommy. Is there something I can help you good folks with?"

Tommy replied, "Yes, sir, Pastor. We'd like to seek your counsel, with a view toward you performing a Wedding Ceremony for the two of us." Laurie nodded her head in agreement.

Pastor Bates took his seat in a large overstuffed chair and laid his hand upon a well-worn Bible. He asked, "Are you both Believers in Jesus Christ, and that He died for our sins, and that then on the third day, He was resurrected from the dead?"

Both Tommy and Laurie nodded their heads, and said, "Yes."

Pastor Bates hesitated, briefly, and said, "I need a truthful answer here. Please be assured that I will NEVER speak a word of your answer to anyone, other than maybe the Holy Spirit." (His hesitation was longer this time.) "Are you obedient?"

Tommy replied in the affirmative, but Laurie was silent -- she looked puzzled. Pastor Bates asked again, this time a little differently. "Laurie, have you committed Adultery?"

Laurie smiled, relieved, and answered, "Oh. No, I haven't. I thought you were talking about any violation of any of the Ten Commandments."

177

Pastor Bates seemed even more hesitant at hearing that, but he plowed on. "Your answer leads me to the conclusion that you might have done something we need to talk about, my dear. Perhaps we need to talk privately?"

Laurie looked very serious, and replied, "No, I can talk about it here in front of Tommy. He knows about it. I hated two men, really hated them a lot, for a long time, but then you talked one Sunday about the 'sermon on the mount,' and I got to feeling bad about the way I felt about those two men, so I forgave them."

Pastor Bates didn't seem to be all that reassured. "Laurie, would you tell me something a little more about that hatred you felt?"

"Well, Pastor, when my step-father fell from his horse in a drunken stupor and broke his neck, I gave up plotting to kill him."

Pastor Bates seemed quite worried at hearing that. "Hmm, and what about the second person of whom you spoke?"

Laurie again replied, "When I was trying to go West to find my father, I was working for a family, taking care of their children, when the Missus up and died. Didn't really seem to bother her husband much and he decided that I'd be a good substitute for his wife, with or without matrimony. He tried to make me agree by saying if I didn't agree, then I could just leave the wagon out in the middle of the open plains. So I packed my flour sack and set out on foot. Fortunately, some Christians folk found me a couple of days later and gave me a ride."

Tommy decided he could help the Pastor and Laurie, and injected, "You see, Pastor, Laurie's step-father kept trying to force her to sleep with him, so she ran away."

The Pastor was relieved that Tommy understood and accepted Laurie's past, and also that it wasn't a reflection upon her character (as he had feared). "My dear, I am so sorry to learn of your experiences.

I'm pleased to learn that you have forgiven both men. I'm sure that experiences like this can be very trying for a young woman, but I'm pleased that you appear to have overcome the sins against you."

Tommy had a tear in his eye when he spoke. "Oh, Laurie, it's dreadful to hear of what you went through, and, if you will marry me, I'll do my very best to love you, and protect you, the rest of my life."

Laurie slid over next to Tommy, put her arm around his waist, and her head on his shoulder, and said, "I've already given you my answer to that question. I'm ready to make wedding plans."

Pastor Bates looked at the young couple in front of him, and said, "You young people go and make your plans. Just let me know the date of the wedding, so we can make sure the sanctuary is available when you need it! I'll be pleased to officiate." With that, he rose from his chair, opened the door, and called out to his wife, "Ona, see if you can fix this lovely couple a cup of coffee, and give them a piece of that very tasty cake you made yesterday, too!"

Laurie and Tommy returned to the boarding house and, that night at supper, everyone was talking about the coming wedding. The family women -- Abby Watson, Sarah Elder, Susan Temple, and Laurie -- were all huddled around a table, talking about wedding dresses, hats, veils, trains, dates, groomsmen, and bridesmaids. Laurie explained that, since it was already late in September, she and Tommy didn't want to wait until the following June, so she thought Christmas would work out better. Everyone agreed that Christmas would be a fine time for the wedding. That night, Laurie wrote her mother another letter:

Dearest mother,

Tommy and I plan to marry at Christmas time, though since it is really snowy around here that time of year, the date might get moved around.

179

Tommy is willing to bring me back to Missouri to visit you in the summer. We would come in the spring, but it will be very busy here with his business in the spring.

I am so happy that you have found someone. Yes, I remember John Morton, but I never met him. His farm was about halfway between ours and Maysville. I went by his place whenever I went into town.

Mother, I wish you could meet all of these wonderful Christian people here in Denver; Jim and Abby Watson own a boarding house, Jim and his cousin, Phillip and Susan Smith own a general store, while Pete and Sarah Elder have some financial interest in all of that, but mainly they both serve as assistant manager of all three businesses. Oh, the third business is the livery stable which is owned by Tommy. Everyone works together and helps everyone else when needed. Even the paid employees are more like family than workers.

They do so much business, it is amazing. The boarding house has the best food in Denver and the general store has more things in stock than any other store in the same area.

Take good care of my sisters and tell Uncle Bob and Teddy that I said Hello!

Your loving daughter,

Laurie"

Chapter Twenty-six

Abby Watson, Sarah Elder, and Susan Temple all became heavily involved with helping Laurie plan her wedding. In fact, they were so heavily involved that it almost reached the point where Laurie felt like objecting to the constant attention focused on her, and all of the suggestions, but the women were all so sweet, what could she do?

Abby took her young daughters over to the general store, because she recalled seeing a Wedding Dress catalogue from a New York City store; she found it and gave it to Laurie, who was quick to proclaim her inability to afford anything from that catalog. Abby pointed out that it would still be valuable for ideas about how to make the dress, including what kind of material to use, and what accessories went with it. Anxious to see if any of the wedding dresses appealed to Laurie, and since Sarah and Susan were taking care of things at the boarding house, Abby decided to stay at the general store while she waited for her to look through the catalog.

After about an hour of carefully scrutinizing each page of the Wedding Dress Catalog, Laurie called out excitedly to Abby, who was feeding her youngest child: "Oh, Abby, I found a beautiful dress!" Then, after looking at it even more closely, she added, with resignation in her voice, "But I can't imagine how I could afford even the fabrics to make it."

Wiping food from the chin of the little girl, who had just learned to walk, Abby asked, "What kind of fabrics is it made of?"

"Silk," responded Laurie, "and lace, lots of lace."

"Hmm," mused Abby, "I've been told that there's an old widow lady, on the other side of town, who makes lovely lace. I remember that someone at church bought some lace from her a year or two ago, for a wedding veil; I think it was the mother of the bride. She said they were thrilled with the lace, and very happy with the price, too."

"I wonder if she's still doing it, and if she's still in town. I'd like to talk to her, but how would we ever find her?" asked Laurie.

Abby filled the tiny spoon once more, and tried unsuccessfully to interest the child in some more food, as she thought about Laurie's question. Then she put the spoon down, and said, "Jenkins; that's the family name, I think, of the bride. That's the problem of attending a large church. There's too many people to ever get to know them all; besides, there are so many just passing through on their way farther West. I'll ask Pastor if he knows how to find the Jenkins family."

By now the possibility of a wedding dress like the one in the catalog was making Laurie eager to learn if it was just a pipe dream, or if it could become a reality. Laurie coaxed, "You know, if we wait until Sunday, the pastor will be too busy, and, besides, he'll have other things on his mind then. Abby, I can watch the baby and wait on customers, if you could go talk to him right now."

Abigail smiled fondly, remembering her own excitement when preparing for her first wedding to Henry Johnson. It had been so long ago; she had been so young, and so happy. (Her memories also included how it had been so difficult for her, both emotionally and financially, when Henry died back there in Montana, and how lucky she was to have found Jim Watson.) "Hmm, I was just thinking, Laurie. We both are very lucky. Yes, I'll go see the pastor now. Here, take the baby. If you should get too many customers, call her big sister, Sally. She's very mature for six years old, and she'll be glad to play with the baby if you need her help."

As soon as Laurie had taken control of the situation with feeding the baby, Abby pulled on her sweater and headed straight for Pastor Bates' home.

Abby realized she should have worn a rain coat about the time she started knocking on the Bates' front door.

"Why, Abigail Watson! Come in here, right now! You'll catch your death of cold out there in the freezing rain!" exclaimed Sophronia Bates.

"Oh, I rushed right over here to ask the Pastor something. I didn't even notice it was raining when I left; it isn't raining all that much, and I wasn't outside more than a few minutes," replied Abby.

"That may very well be," chided Sophronia Bates ('Ona' to her husband and her friends), "but if you get wet out there, and there's a wind blowing, you'll take a chill and there's no tellin' what you might come down with! Come into the kitchen, where it's warm."

"Is Pastor around this afternoon, Ona?" asked Abby, as she rubbed her wet hands on her skirt to dry them.

"Well, he has gone off, and he didn't say where he was going either, so I don't know when he'll get back. But, you're in luck, I just made a fresh pot of coffee; that'll warm your innards. I don't remember, do you take cream and sugar?" Ona was already starting to pour a cup of steaming coffee, without waiting for an answer.

"Oh, yes, cream, and one lump of sugar, please. You're always the perfect hostess, Ona. You should've married a politician!"

"Hee hee, don't ever say anything like that in front of Selby!" Ona giggled. "He knows that, before I met him, I was sweet on a fella that became a Senator. That man left his wife here in Colorado every time he went to Washington. The poor woman was worried half to death every time he left home. I think she worried more about all the hussies they must have up in Washington than him getting injured or killed on the way!"

183

"I don't think I'd worry about Jim going off for long periods of time, but I know I like it a lot better when he's at home every day," said Abby. "What I wanted to ask the Pastor about was a wedding he performed about a year ago. But maybe you know the answer. The bride's name was Jenkins, as I recall. They found some old lady here in Denver that made lace at a very reasonable price."

"Oh, my, yes, what a beautiful veil Sally Jenkins made with that lovely lace she bought from that lady. Sally was such a pretty bride, but all brides seem to glow at such a wonderful time in their life. Sally and her new husband moved to California, I think. He'd just gotten a job with a big bank, as an auditor, I think it was. The bank sent him out there to look after their financial interests in a couple of businesses they had acquired. You know, I can't imagine how much work that would be. I was never any good with numbers myself; Selby does all the finances. He just gives me the money that I need to buy food, and whatever else I need to take care of the house."

Ona was well known by her friends to ramble on and on, but she was also appreciated for her discretion when it came to steering clear of passing on any gossip, or any congregate secrets which might have been told to her by the pastor. Indeed, no one ever knew whether he told her about any confidences he'd received (although he almost always did, valuing her input and trusting her to keep them secret).

"Now, what was it you wanted to know, Abby?"

"I especially want to know how to contact that lady who made the lace for that veil … what her name is, and where she lives."

"Oh, silly me, of course, what with Laurie getting married, and now you asking about lace, I should have known. I declare, Abby, I get so sidetracked sometimes. I see you need some more coffee." Ona poured Abby more coffee without waiting for an answer. She asked Abby if she didn't want a piece of cake, too, but Abby politely declined.

184

"Let me think now, Abby. It was a widow named Mrs. 'Day-Are', but you spell it kind of funny. It's spelled d-e-a-r, so lots of people think her name is 'Dear' when they see it wrote out. Seems like she was from France or Spain or somewhere over there in Europe. You know those people over there talk funny, and write funny, too."

"Ona, you've been a lot of help. Do you know if she's still in Denver, and where she lives? Oh, your coffee is quite nice; thank you for both cups. It's really warming me up."

"Oh, Abby dear, I'm so glad you like the coffee; here, have some more – these cups are so small. Selby bought them several years ago when a man came around selling china. Selby had to convince him that we didn't have enough money to pay the price he was asking, and then the man sold them to us at a very reasonable price. Oh, yes, where did Mrs. Dear live? Let me see, we live on the west side of town, and I was told she lived thataway from the church" (Ona pointed), "so I think she lived on the south side. There's an area of houses down there where the houses are smaller and cheaper looking; they're quite close together, too. There's lots of poorer people down there. I don't remember the street name, but if you found that area, I'm sure you could find someone who knows Mrs. Dear. Remember, the spelling doesn't look like how you say it, so some folks might know her by the name 'dear' if they've not been told different."

"Ona, I think I know the area. There's a couple areas around Denver where people seemed to be in too big a hurry when they built their houses, and the houses look like it. I'll talk to Jim about that area, and see if we can find her. Laurie wanted a dress with a lot of lace on it, but that would be too expensive if we ordered it from New York or even New Orleans." Then Abby rose to leave, not wanting to give Ona a chance to pour her any more coffee.

"Oh, Abby, do you really have to go so soon? We've just got started on this pot of coffee, and it's been such a lovely conversation, too. And you haven't had any cake."

"I really do need to go, Ona. I left the baby with Laurie, and she was supposed to be helping customers at the same time. Thank you, again, for the lovely coffee and the information. Give my best to the Pastor when he returns." Abigail was steadily moving to the door and had her hand on the door knob by the time she finished speaking.

"Well, dear Abby, if you really must run. Please come back and visit me again, real soon, now, you hear!"

"Bye-bye, Ona," Abby called, seconds before she closed the door behind her and started hurriedly toward the General Store.

Abby took a quick second to make sure Laurie and the baby were doing all right, and then went to Jim's office. Fortunately, Jim was there, digging through a small pile of invoices and bills. "Hello, Darlin'! What have you been up to? Why are you so wet? You're fairly dripping all over the floor."

Abby stopped and rubbed her hands on her skirt again. They were wet and cold; that storm only had ice -cold rain in it. Abby hadn't heard any thunder, but often rain storms in the Denver had ice in them, either hail in the summer or sleet in the winter. She took a quick peek into the mirror in Jim's office, and, indeed, her cheeks were red from exposure to that raw Colorado wind. "Oh, I guess I am all red-faced and wet. I just came back from a quick visit with Ona Bates. It's really hard to get away from that woman! Ona was telling me that a lady who lives in one of those poorer areas here in Denver makes beautiful lace, and at a reasonable price. She said the woman's name was Mrs. Dear, spelled d-e-a-r. Do you think you could find her for us?"

Jim wrinkled his brow, and quizzed, "Who is 'us'?"

Abby quickly added, "Me, Laurie, and the rest of the wedding dress team."

Jim smiled his knowing smile, and said, "If you'll get me my raincoat, I'll go ask some people at the saloon in that area of town."

Abby never bothered to answer, but turned and scurried away to get Jim's coat for him as he found what he had been looking for, and laid it aside to finish when he returned.

Tommy was just as quick in saddling a horse for Jim, and off he went looking for lace. When Jim rode out into the street, he understood why Abby was red-faced and wet. The wind was really blowing very hard, and, as Jim held his head down to keep the rain from blowing into his face, the horse's mane stung his face. Jim was glad to have his raincoat on over a heavy winter coat!

As he rode, going through Jim's mind was the possibility of trading merchandise with the lace maker, and selling her lace in the store. He accepted nice homemade clothing items from women (often widows and spinsters) to sell in the store, and he usually paid them in merchandise (which was mutually beneficial to both the store and the maker of the clothing); it was well-known he was always scrupulous in ensuring that the exchange was fair to the women. Often, he would order a bolt of fabric for someone, who would make several outfits from it and then pay for the fabric with a dress or suit of clothes.

Jim had some difficulty finding Mrs. Dear, but, when he finally did find the widow lady, her name turned out to be Mrs. Michele de Armas. She was very enthusiastic about trading her handmade lace for fabric and thread. In fact, it was an absolute blessing. She sold very little lace, and her situation bordered on desperate. Jim asked the price, and then agreed to purchase all the lace the lady had on hand. She hugged him, with tears in her eyes, when he paid her in cash. She was already tasting, in her mind, the good food she could now afford, and rejoicing in the fuel she could buy for her stove.

Jim loaded all the lace into a carpet bag (which she gladly loaned him) to take it to the store. Jim invited her to come to his General Store when the weather was better, and they would discuss how much lace would pay for any of the items Mrs. de Armas wanted.

It was starting to get dark by the time Jim returned the horse to Tommy. They chatted a few minutes, and then Jim hurried into the store with his treasure of handmade lace.

Abby and Laurie peeked into the carpet bag, and were ecstatic. After the store closed, Laurie brought the carpet bag to the boarding house, where she, Abby, Sarah Elder, and Susan Smith could examine all of it. They were very much like children in a candy store, as they sorted through the lace, and discussed how each piece could be used to make a wedding dress. They all seem to agree that each of them had perfectly wonderful ideas, and that it was going to be difficult deciding on just a single one. (Since Laurie was an independent young woman, it did occur to her that SHE should be THE ultimate decision-maker, but, unless and until it became absolutely necessary, she didn't want to spoil the excitement of the others by so declaring.)

After much discussion, the ladies finally settled on a white cotton silk for the dress. When Abby first suggested the fabric, everyone looked at her as if she was crazy.

Abby began to explain, "Jim sells it here in the General Store. I found it so interesting that I wrote to the supplier, and asked how it was made. It seems that an Englishman named John Mercer invented it in 1844. Silk was too expensive for anyone but the very richest people in Europe, and Mr. Mercer discovered a process called Mercerizing. In this process, the cotton is soaked in sodium hydroxide, and then neutralized in an acid bath. This causes the cotton fibers to swell up,

188

and get silky. Soon after, they started calling the fabric Sateen, since the purpose was to substitute for the expensive fabric Silk Satin. The treated yarns were then woven the same way as Satin, making a shiny, soft, and flexible fabric."

Laurie exclaimed, "Abby, you are so smart!"

The rest of the women readily agreed with Laurie, and they all exclaimed about such a wonderful fabric. When the excitement settled down, Abby quietly explained, "When you run a General Store, it helps if you can explain about products to your customers." (The very next morning, the first thing that Laurie did after opening the store was to rush to find that bolt of white cotton silk! She immediately put it aside, underneath the counter, wrapped in brown paper, with her name on it.)

The final dress had a high neck and elbow length sleeves. (Several discussions were had over designing it with such short sleeves for a wedding in December, but, here, Laurie stood firm, and prevailed. She stated, with great conviction, that this design looked better; besides, since the dress was covered in lace, it would cost less to make, not to mention that the design used all of the lace which was available! The other women couldn't contest any of those points.) The dress was nipped in at the waist, but not tightly so, and the waist was circled by a wide white ribbon, tied in a bow at the back, with the ribbon ends flowing softly down almost to the floor. It was gorgeous, looking even more glamorous than the dress advertised in the wedding dress catalog.

In fact, Laurie loved the dress so much that it was only reluctantly that she decided to resell the lace, or, if she could, the entire dress, after the wedding. It was the right decision, since Laurie didn't have enough money to pay for all that lace and fabric. She understood that, sometimes, going into debt temporarily in order to make money could be a smart decision (hence her purchasing fabric on credit to make dresses to sell), but she didn't like being in debt for any longer than about one month maximum (and she definitely didn't want to start her married life in debt); she was a very intelligent young woman.

Hearing about Laurie's plan for the dress, Jim suggested to Abby and his partner Phillip that the general store might buy the wedding dress back from Laurie, and use it for a display, for advertising not only their bolts of various fabrics but also the local dressmakers. Abby was very enthusiastic about doing that, as was Phillip. Jim assured them that it was strictly a good business deal. (And, he thought to himself, if, as a result of the store's buying the dress, Laurie just happened to get a fair amount of money for it, and quickly, well, that was all to the good. But, as it happened, Abby and Phillip were thinking along the same lines themselves.)

The exact date of the wedding was the subject of much discussion among everyone in the family, in coordination with the pastor, and it was finally set for Christmas Eve, Monday, at seven pm. On the Saturday, December 22nd, before the wedding, twelve inches of snow fell on Denver, Colorado. The temperature hovered between 10 and 15 degrees Fahrenheit during the day, and dropped to zero (and a little below) at night, for about a week.

The wagons, buggies, and especially the numerous horses making their way around town kept the snow from being much of an issue on the streets. Tommy and Davie spent a great deal of time clearing a walk-way from the boarding house to the Methodist church over that week. Fortunately, it wasn't far, only about two blocks; however, the blocks were long ones, and the wind kept blowing the snow back across the path, particularly in several troublesome places.

The plan was that the wedding party would get dressed at the church, so they wouldn't have to face the elements in their fancy clothes (and, as a side benefit, the groom would get his first glimpse of the magnificent wedding gown at the ceremony, as would the guests).

Then, after the ceremony, the bride and groom would be driven by buggy back to the boarding house.

A reception would be held in the day room at the boarding house, and a full meal would be provided for the wedding party and wedding guests. The regular end of supper at the boarding house was at 7:30 pm, so the boarders would be exiting about the time the wedding party would be arriving from the church (with the wedding guests close behind them). Since the entire family would be at the wedding, it was necessary to hire some local women to cook and serve both the regular boarders and then, later, the wedding party.

After the wedding dinner, the bride and groom would be whisked away by buggy to the Charpiot's Delmonico Hotel and Restaurant at 386 Larimer Street (it was also known as "the Delmonico of the West"), where the bride and groom would enjoy the luxury accommodations for an entire week. Their suite was one of the most expensive rooms available in the hotel, and was a real extravagance at two dollars per day. Tommy had insisted upon splurging on the room, telling everyone that they would be, after all, just-married newlyweds, and neither of them should have to lift a finger to do any mundane chores as they got used to each other. (He also told Laurie, in private, that going to the Delmonico was the only way for them to have that time all to themselves, away from the family; she acknowledged the truth of that, which persuaded her to agree.)

At about 6:00 pm on Christmas Eve, Tommy went to the church and got dressed in one of the Sunday School rooms; afterwards, he went directly to the Pastor's office to wait for the ceremony to begin. Tommy wore black freshly shined boots, black trousers, a black coat with tails, and a collarless bibbed white shirt (which had a button-on collar and button-on cuffs). Tommy's tie was tied with a four-in-hand knot, and was deep red in color. Jim Watson did the honors with tying the tie, since Tommy normally wore a simple string tie when he went to church and had never tied any other type of tie.

After what seemed like hours, the piano started playing, and, on their cue, the Pastor, the Bridegroom, and the Best Man left their hiding place and slipped into the sanctuary in front of the pulpit. But their "slipping" was unnecessary, as all eyes were on the rear of the room as the wedding party entered. Then came the blushing, slender, and beautiful bride; her long dark hair was arranged in a soft coil, with white ribbons woven through it, and she wore her blue sapphire earrings, which sparkled like stars. She carried a Bible covered in white leather, and she was wearing the loveliest, most expensive-looking wedding dress which anyone in the church had ever seen. Gasps of delight arose from the guests, while Tommy was almost as awe-struck as if an angel had descended from Heaven and was walking toward him; he was mesmerized by the vision coming toward him.

Pete and Sarah Elder's little boy was serving as the ring bearer. Pete would also give away the bride, since Laurie had no parents or other relatives locally to do the honors. (One the reasons why Pete had been chosen to walk her down the aisle was so that he might be available to prevent his son from running amuck with the ring.) The toddler was so adorable that he nearly stole the show from the beautiful bride -- but not quite. The little boy stopped almost exactly where he was supposed to stop, in response to his Uncle Jim's hand signal.

When Laurie, holding fast to Pete's arm, stopped in front of Pastor Bates, the Pastor asked, "Who gives this woman to be joined in Holy Matrimony?"

Pete Elder spoke his lines eloquently: "I do, as a substitute for her father, who cannot be present at this joyous occasion."

Then Pete stepped back, and the handsome bridegroom stepped forward, and Laurie transferred her dainty hand from Pete's sturdy arm to Tommy's. Pete joined his wife, Sarah, on the front pew facing the Pastor and the wedding party (except, of course, for the bride and groom, whose backs were to them).

Pastor Bates' resonant voice, perfect for such occasions, and tempered by years of long sermons, filled the Sanctuary: "Dearly Beloved, we are gathered here today, in the presence of this company, to join Thomas Leonard Thompson and Laura Edith Burdock in Holy Matrimony.

"What God has joined together, let no man cast asunder. Does anyone have cause to object to this marriage? If so, let them speak now, or, forever, hold their peace."

Silence filled the church house, and, after about ten seconds, Pastor Bates continued: "Hearing no objection, I would like to remind everyone here of the words of the apostle Paul in his first Epistle to the church at Corinth. In chapter thirteen, starting in verse one, Paul explains, 'Though I speak with the tongues of men and of angels, but have not love, I have become sounding brass or a clanging cymbal. And though I have the gift of prophecy, and understand all mysteries and all knowledge, and though I have all faith, so that I could remove mountains, but have not love, I am nothing. And though I bestow all my goods to feed the poor, and though I give my body to be burned, but have not love, it profits me nothing.'"

Pastor Bates paused to let the people consider the wisdom thus expressed, and then continued: "Paul went further saying, 'Love suffers long and is kind; love does not envy; love does not parade itself, is not puffed up; does not behave rudely, does not seek its own, is not provoked, thinks no evil; does not rejoice in iniquity, but rejoices in the truth; bears all things, believes all things, hopes all things, endures all things.' I would counsel any married couple to carefully consider these things, remembering that the Lord commanded that we should Love one another as ourselves."

Pastor Bates paused again, to also let the people ponder those words, and then added: "'Love never fails.' The author of the largest portion of the New Testament finished his description of love by saying, 'And now abide faith, hope, love, these three; but the greatest of these is love.' We have a God who loves us and desires that we strive to be like Him. The message which Paul sent to the church of Corinth is both a description of His love for us and His desire for us to love others in the same manner.

"Love changes as we mature in it. But that doesn't mean this description of love changes. As we learn more about our husband or wife, that enables us to find more meaningful ways of expressing our love for them. This strengthens a marriage, and makes the union happier, and that pleases God.

"Now, Thomas Leonard Thompson, do you take Laura Edith Burdock to be your lawfully wedded wife, to love her in sickness and in health?"

Tommy replied, "I do."

"And, Laura Edith Burdock, do you take Thomas Leonard Thompson to be your lawfully wedded husband, to love him in sickness and in health?"

Laurie replied, "I do."

Pastor Bates then asked, "Is there a ring?"

Jim Watson bent down to retrieve the ring from the little pillow carried by the youngest child of Pete and Sarah's children. However, the little boy had been distracted by activity of his sisters, and had started to move in their direction, so he was out of his assigned place. Jim simply took a step forward, picked up the little boy (who was well known to him, and thus perfectly comfortable with Jim's action), and held him on one arm. Jim then calmly loosened the pin which held the ring, and handed the ring to Tommy, as the congregation chuckled at the toddler' antics.

When Tommy finally had possession of the ring, Pastor Bates said, "Place the ring on her finger, Tommy."

Tommy fumbled around a tiny bit, but succeeded in getting the ring on Laurie's finger.

Pastor Bates then said, "Repeat after me, Tommy: Laurie, I give you this ring as a symbol of my love for you..."

Tommy dutifully responded, while gazing into Laurie's eyes, with great earnestness, "Laurie, I give you this ring as a symbol of my love for you..."

Pastor Bates continued, "... and as a token of my commitment to you and to our marriage."

Again, Tommy responded, "...and as a token of my commitment to you and to our marriage."

Pastor Bates then turned and addressed Laurie: "Laurie, repeat after me: Tommy, I accept this ring and will wear it as a symbol of my love for you..."

Laurie, who had practiced these words for days, was still fearful that she might forget what to say; she swallowed hard, and said, gazing directly into her groom's eyes, "Tommy, I accept this ring and will wear it as a symbol of my love for you..."

Pastor Bates continued on: "...and as a token of my commitment to you and to our marriage."

Laurie responded, more confidently, "...and as a token of my commitment to you and to our marriage."

Pastor Bates then lifted his eyes from the couple and looked out at the congregation. "Now, by the authority of the God of Creation and of the State of Colorado, I pronounce you Man and Wife. May God bless your union, and bless you both.

"Tommy, you may kiss your Bride."

Tommy readily reached his arms out to Laurie, who stepped into them, and wrapped her own arms around Tommy, and they embraced in a long, tender kiss. (As far as Tommy and Laurie were concerned, there was no one else in the church – there were just the two of them. So they weren't self-conscious at all, which was obvious to everyone.) The congregation roared its approval!

Chapter Twenty-seven

Pastor Bates injected, "Well, if you two can break away for a little while longer...."

Tommy and Laurie, a little embarrassed, ended their kiss, but they didn't completely remove their arms from each other.

Pastor Bates said to the congregation, "Please allow me to introduce to you, Mr. and Mrs. Thomas Thompson!"

The congregation rose to its feet at that, and a few strategically located young people opened their bags of rice and passed them around as Tommy and Laurie ran down the aisle, which had turned into a gauntlet of family and friends throwing rice.

Upon emerging from the church, Timmy Elliott handed Tommy a heavy coat, and, at the same time, Helen Matthews Bates helped Laurie into an equally heavy coat for the ride to the boarding house for the reception. Davie Barton was seated in the driver's seat, and he snapped the reins on the matched team of white horses as soon as Tommy and Laurie were safely in their seats, and away they went in a clatter of hoof beats the two blocks to the front of the boarding house.

After the reception and wedding dinner, Tommy and Laurie changed clothes (getting into not-quite-as formal attire), put their heavy coats back on, and picked up their several pieces of luggage. After running another gauntlet of family and friends, they went back out to the buggy, again driven by Davie, and he drove them up town to the Delmonico of the West where the newly-weds were treated like royalty (at least on their arrival).

When Tommy and Laurie returned from their week-long, blissful honeymoon, they came back in a buggy which Davie had left for them at the hotel that morning. As soon as the buggy arrived at the boarding house, Laurie took her lovely wedding dress, carefully hung on a padded hanger, and covered with paper to keep it clean, to the general store. She didn't know how else she could sell it, except through the store, and she wanted to talk to Jim Watson about it right away.

As Laurie walked into the store, she was greeted by several female employees, who insisted on hugging her and telling her what a lovely wedding it had been, and how lovely she was, and bombarding her with excited questions about the Delmonico Hotel.. Jim heard the commotion, and came out of his office to add his congratulations as well. "Hello, Laurie! My my, you look simply radiant today."

Laurie started to speak, then frowned, "Goodness me. I don't know now whether I should call you Boss, Sir, Jim, or Dad."

Jim grinned at hearing that, and replied, "Laurie, I'm fine with any of those titles; you just use whichever one you feel comfortable with … except Sir! And I do want to tell you that Abby and I are absolutely thrilled to have you in our little family."

With a lump in her throat, Laurie came to a quick decision on what she wanted to call Jim. "Thank you, DAD! That means so much to me." Never having been able to know her real father, Laurie felt a flood of what was almost relief at finally having a true father figure in her life. The demons which had chased her were being conquered.

"Oh, I almost forgot. As much as I simply love my wedding dress, the fact is that it is just much too expensive for me and Tommy to pay the cost of the material, since I'm never gonna wear it again. It'd be terribly wasteful for me to keep it around just for a memento, so I've brought it to you to see if maybe you might sell it -- either the entire dress or the material it's made from."

Laurie held onto the paper-wrapped hanger while she waited for Jim's decision.

198

Jim smiled, and said, "I know what an emotional attachment brides have for their wedding dress, and, as it turns out, I have a plan for that dress, a plan which I think you will approve. Some of the most influential people in Denver – and even Colorado -- attend that church, and they also regularly do business with our store. I've been asked by numerous mothers of brides-to-be about that dress, and about the material it's made from. So my plan is to place your dress on display in the front window of the store; we'll put signs beside it, which provide information about the cost of the Cotton Silk and of the lace. I feel the attention which you and this dress have already brought to our business will make a good impact on our bottom line profit. And, in return for our being able to use the dress as advertising, the general store will cancel your debt for the material. Do you think that's a fair exchange?"

Laurie handed the dress to Jim, exclaiming, "Oh, Dad, that's wonderful! I won't mind not owning it at all, not when I can see it every day to remind me of just how lucky I am to be married to Tommy, and to have such a wonderful adopted family!"

Jim smiled his characteristic smile, and said, "Laurie, we certainly do love you, and I mean ALL of us love you."

At that, Laurie threw her arms around Jim, who could neither resist nor respond with his hands full of wedding dress, but became embarrassed when Laurie hugged him tight. Although the extended family was close, his wife Abby was the only one who hugged him.

Tommy came upon the scene, and said, "I was wondering why you didn't come back to the boarding house yet. You didn't even go inside, you just picked up your wedding dress and told me you were taking it to the general store; you said you wouldn't be long."

Laurie took her arms from around Jim and turned to her husband, explaining, "Oh, Tommy, everyone has been so eager to find out about the hotel, and to tell me how beautiful our wedding was, that I just couldn't tear myself away from all the attention."

Tommy barely heard her explanation; he was too excited. He told her, "While we were gone, Abby and Susan moved all of our things out of our individual rooms, and moved them to the new wing they had built, the one with the larger suites, and they moved us into a suite on the ground floor on the end. That gives us more room, and more privacy, since the bedroom is near the outside wall."

Laurie was clearly overjoyed about that. "Oh, that's wonderful! I've wondered how we'd be able to make-do, since our individual rooms were so far apart and couldn't be linked, and I just assumed we'd both have to fit into one room. But a big suite … that's perfect!"

The two of them left Jim and their friends, and returned to the buggy. After carrying the rest of their luggage to the new suite, Laurie began arranging their things and the suite's furniture to suit her, humming happily all the time, while Tommy went to the boarding house kitchen for coffee. In just a few minutes, Tommy returned, carrying a steaming coffee pot and two cups. Since it was still over two hours before supper would be served, they sat down to talk, over a cup of hot coffee, about the location of the furniture, and about other items they needed to make the new suite feel more like home.

After they had agreed on the layout of their new abode, Tommy changed the subject. "Laurie, I spoke to Jim a few minutes ago, while I was waiting on the coffee to brew, about how we might work in the visit to your mother in Missouri. He's always thinking, and he has some really good ideas. Jim suggested that, instead of waiting for Summer to travel, we should go in early Spring. He thought that we could make it a business trip that way. He said it'd be worthwhile to take the train, and stop ever so often in some of the smaller cities, and see if we could contract with local farmers in those places for hay, grain, and even the purchase of horses. So many settlers are passing through Denver; we always sell out of horses, and saddles and wagons, too. Many folks come this far by train, or several to a wagon, and then leave for other territories, some of which don't have rail service, so they need horses.

"I think Jim has a really good idea, since, when we drive the buggies along the trails, we always seem to spend a lot of time traveling to outlying farms along the way, trying to find hay and grain and horses, and some of those side trips never work out with us getting anything so they're just a waste of our time. It'd be much easier if we knew ahead of time where we were going.

"So, we could leave here in March, and return before the end of growing season. What do you think?"

Laurie quickly replied, "Oh, my, Tommy, I don't know anything about your business or what it takes to keep it going. Whatever you think best is all right with me. So I'd be very happy to start whenever you wanted to go, but March does sound good to me, and so does the train. Should I write to my mother today, saying we might be visiting her around the Spring, or should I wait a while?"

It was decided between them that Laurie should write immediately, since there was always something of a delay in the mail.

Dearest Mother,

Tommy and I were married on the Monday before Christmas. We had a lovely stay in a nice Denver hotel for our Honeymoon. Tommy is so sweet, I can't understand why it took me so long to make up my mind.

We are going to start for Missouri in mid-February and we will stop several times during the trip so Tommy can try to arrange contracts with farmers for food for his animals, both hay and grain. I am so anxious to see you and my brother and sisters.

Love, Laura

Planning for the trip was hectic. Tommy decided that Davie should take over the day-to-day operations while he was gone, but, again, he should rely on Jim and Pete for advice if he had any questions.

As the early winter days crept by, Laurie and Tommy settled into an extremely happy married life; they both continued to work, and to finalize their travel plans, buying their train tickets with planned stops in cities where Tommy had previously had the most success in purchasing grain and hay.

Based on her mother's marriage, which, after all, was the one example she'd seen the most closely before, Laurie had never even dreamed that a marriage could be so happy, and two people could be so compatible, that she could really feel as if the two had become as one. (She had seen the Davenport marriage, and the marriages of Jim and Abby, of Susan and Phillip, and of Sarah and Pete, of course, but from more of a distance.) She herself had never expected to marry, but, now, she thanked God every day for guiding her to Tommy.

Laurie had also taken her new Bible (which Susan and Phillip had ordered, in its white leather cover, for her and Tommy as a wedding gift) and, very carefully and painstakingly, wrote in its Family History page the date of their wedding. Susan had shown her that page, and she was eager to start recording their Family History.

The first day of February dawned cold and clear. The sky was a deep cloudless blue, and a brisk wind from the northwest drove chills through the body – even those wearing the heaviest coats, and even through those coats backed up by the otherwise warmest long-handled underwear.

Tommy and Davie were busy repairing one of their oldest wagons, trying to get another few years of service from it before turning it into a pile of spare parts. It was late in the afternoon, and the sun was getting low in the West, casting long shadows into the barn where they worked.

One of those long shadows moved, and that movement wasn't lost on Tommy. He looked up toward the open barn door and saw the silhouette of a man coming toward them. Tommy laid down the wheel which he and Davie had just successfully reassembled, and straightened up as he faced the dark shape against the low sun in the West. "Good afternoon; may we help you?"

The man approached several more steps before asking, in a virtual monotone, "Is one of you Mr. Thomas Leonard Thompson, or could you direct me to where I might find him?"

Tommy had never before in his life been addressed by his whole name, except during the recent wedding ceremony, so he was surprised to hear the stranger recite it in its entirety. "Yes, I'm Tommy Thompson; what can I do for you?"

The man then asked, still virtually expressionless in his voice and in his facial expression, "Are you the Proprietor of this establishment and the son of the late Ethel Benson Thompson?"

Chapter Twenty-eight

A puzzled Tommy replied that he was indeed that person, although he had heard no one speak his mother's name in many years.

The man spoke again, in the same rather mechanical manner, "I have a special communication for you from the offices of Baker, Baker, and Miller, attorneys at law. I will need your signature showing that you have received it, and, if the gentleman with you would be so kind, his signature as a witness that you have received the document."

"What's this all about?" asked a surprised and alarmed Tommy. The man was rather nondescript, dressed neatly but not fancy, and in no way confrontational, or scary, but the situation was rather unnerving.

The answer wasn't at all helpful. "Sir, I have no idea what this communication contains. My job is strictly a delivery service. I deliver documents, and obtain proof that the correct person received them. Would you please sign here? And write today's date in the space provided? And if the other gentleman would do likewise?"

Tommy took the envelope and turned away from the sun so it would illuminate the writing on the outside. Sure enough, it was addressed to him, in his full name, and neatly printed in the upper left corner was inscribed "Baker, Baker, and Miller," with a downtown Denver address below the name of the firm. Still unsure what it was about, Tommy took the pad from the man, and wrote his name on the line by the X, and then added the day's date beside it.

Tommy next handed the pad to Davie, who wrote his name beside the word Witness , and also wrote the date beside his signature.

The man examined the signatures and dates, said, "Thank you very much, and good day," then turned and quickly departed.

Tommy looked at Davie, and said, "I need to take this envelope into some better light to read what's in it, and I think I'll probably need to talk to Dad about whatever it is. So I need to ask you to put the tools away and close everything up here, and then go to the office and watch for any late customers until six."

Davie nodded, and said, "Sure, Boss. I hope it's nothing bad."

"Thanks, Davie, but I have a mighty uneasy feeling about this."

Tommy took the strangely delivered envelope into Jim's office. Jim wasn't there, but someone had already lit the gas lights, so Jim was probably expected to be there sometime soon. It was a good place to read this document without interruption. Tommy carefully used Jim's letter opener to open the envelope as neatly as possible, then pulled the contents out and began to read:

To whom it may concern:

The Law Firm of Baker, Baker, and Miller of Denver, Colorado, representing the interests of Lawrence D. Thompson of Springfield, Illinois, in the matter of Thompson vs. Thompson, doth hereby declare that:

Whereas, Lawrence D. Thompson is the only close living relative of the late Josiah L. Thompson; and

Whereas, Thomas L. Thompson, the son of Mrs. Ethel Benson Thompson and Mr. Henry G. Benson, is not entitled to inherit from the Estate of the late Josiah L. Thompson, absent legal adoption; and

Whereas, Lawrence D. Thompson is willing to recognize that Thomas L. Thompson might have some investment in the business, arising strictly from the standpoint of labor possibly exerted in excess of financial benefits already derived from said Partnership;

Now, therefore, Lawrence D. Thompson is willing to sell and convey to Thomas L. Thompson his ownership and interest in said business for the sum of Four Thousand Dollars ($4000.00).

Otherwise, the Law Firm of Baker, Baker, and Miller is authorized to represent Lawrence D. Thompson by filing suit in the Superior Court of Denver, Colorado, to claim his rightful inheritance of full ownership of Thompson Livery Stable.

Respectfully submitted:

George Anthony Miller, Attorney at Law

Tommy was reading through the letter, for the third time, when Jim walked into the room, and said, jovially, "Why, hello, Tommy. Were you looking for me, or just taking advantage of the light?"

Tommy looked up with a grimace on his face. "Dad, I think I have a really big problem here."

"What's the problem?" asked Jim, instantly serious.

Tommy hesitated a moment, collecting his thoughts, and then said, "It appears there's this fellow, Lawrence Thompson, who claims to own my Livery Stable business. He seems to be saying that I'm not really Tommy Thompson, that I'm actually Tommy Benson, and that my real father is a man named Henry Benson. His lawyer says that this Lawrence Thompson is the closest living relative to my Dad, so he should have inherited Dad's business, not me. He says he's willing to sell me his rights in it for four thousand dollars. I haven't got that kind of money. Why, probably all of the assets of the entire livery stable would be hard pressed to reach that amount of money. Do you think he could really take my business away from me if he goes to court?"

Tommy handed Jim the letter, and Jim read the letter carefully, twice. Then he sighed deeply, and answered. "As it happens, I've talked over inheritance with my attorney, since I wanted to make sure that Abby would be protected if anything happened to me. As I understand it, if there is no will, the law in most states would pass a husband's estate to his wife, or, if there is a wife and children, half to the wife and the other half to be divided among the children; if there is neither wife nor child, then the estate would go to the closest relative of the deceased. Your mother died before your father did, so, if the man can prove that this Henry Benson is actually your father, and that you were never adopted by Jake – although, in some states, even adopted children can't inherit unless they're named in a Will -- then it looks like he might be the heir and able to take your business away from you!"

Chapter Twenty-nine

Jim paused, thinking about what to do next. "One of the deacons is an attorney. Before we do anything rash, we need to let him read it, and I'm sure he'll have questions for you. Do you have any legal documents belonging to your parents?"

Tommy thought long and hard. "I don't know that I have any legal documents. I have my Mom's Bible, which I put away so it'd be safe. I've also got a collection of old receipts for horses, wagons, and such from the business when my Dad was alive, and maybe a few letters, I'm not real sure; but I haven't looked at them in years."

Jim had only been half listening, but replied, "You go and find any papers you can; I suppose they'd be in the old trunk up in the attic. I'll go talk to Sam Schaeffer, and show him this letter. I probably won't accomplish any more today than make an appointment for us to see him in his office. I should be back before supper."

Jim jerked on his coat, grabbed his hat, and hurried out the door. Jim was in such a rush that he almost ran over Abby and Laurie talking as they rounded the corner. "Oh, sorry, ladies. I ought to be back by supper, but, if I'm not ,save me something, Abby." And, with that, out the door he flew.

"Where are you going in such a hurry?" asked Abby even though the door closed behind Jim before she had finished asking. "My goodness, Laurie, I haven't seen Jim in such a hurry in a long time!"

Before they could do or say anything else, Tommy came out of the same doorway, in almost as big a hurry. The look on his face, combined with Jim's rushing out, told both of the women that there was some sort of major problem involved.

"Tommy! What's wrong?" asked a concerned Laurie.

Tommy stopped, and responded, dolefully, "It looks like I'm being sued. A fellow in Springfield, Illinois, is claiming that he owns our Livery business. He says that my father, Jake Thompson, wasn't my real father. He says that, since I was never adopted, that makes him the closest living heir, not me. But, he says, he's willing to sell me the business for four thousand dollars. We aren't broke, but we don't have nearly that much money. So you may have married a pauper."

The shock showed immediately on Laurie's face, but she quickly replied, with great firmness, almost angrily, "Tommy Thompson! I've been poor, 'most all my life, and it don't matter one bit to me being poor again. There's no shame in being poor, and I didn't marry you for your money, or because you owned a livery stable. I married you because you're sweet, decent, and kind – and because I love you. We're both strong and healthy, so we can work, like so many other folks do, and we'll be just fine!"

Tommy had a stunned look on his face at her vehemence; but, then, after Laurie's words sunk in, he said, equally firmly, feeling a deep gratitude that he had been so blessed as to have such a loving wife, "You're right, Laurie. We'll just do whatever we have to do. And we will be just fine, no matter what happens."

Meanwhile, Abby stood quietly and unobtrusively nearby, awe-struck by the dramatic situations taking place in front of her, and was deeply moved.

"Now, I've got to go look for my father's papers." Then Tommy embraced and kissed Laurie, before hurrying away.

Tommy found an oil lamp, lit the wick, and climbed the steps into the attic. As he cleared the top step, the rafters and underside of the roof lit up from the lamp light, and the shadows retreated quickly to hide behind boxes, crates, pieces of furniture, and an occasional carpet bag. Various personal items, including important heirlooms and keepsakes, belonging to the several families allied together in the boarding house (Jim and Abby, Philip and Susan, Pete and Sarah, and Tommy and Laurie) were nested in different parts of the attic.

Tommy soon found his own personal cache of belongings. There was a tin-type photograph of his Mom and Dad, who were now both deceased; it was the only picture he had of them. Tommy was drawn to study it with wonder, as he always did when he saw it. If only the fever hadn't come and his mother hadn't gone over to a neighbor's to help nurse another sick child, if only his father hadn't gotten in too big a hurry while throwing down hay for the animals ... if only, if only, if only. Always IF ONLY loomed. Tommy missed his parents, even though he only had a few faint memories of his mother, who died when he was quite young, and those of his father were almost always of him working and working. Tommy had no memories of them being a family, and he sometimes felt cheated a bit.

Finally, he put down the old tin-type, and found an old cigar box full of papers, and his mother's Bible. He grabbed the cigar box to take it to show Jim and the deacon-attorney. Tommy first thought he'd just leave the Bible safely stored away, since he had a Bible of his own and Laurie had her wedding gift Bible, but then he thought it would be nice to show Laurie his mother's Bible.

After climbing down from the attic, Tommy returned the oil lamp to its place on the shelf by the stairs, turned the wick down, and blew his breath into the chimney; only when the light went completely out did he turn his gaze from the lamp (being ever mindful of the danger of leaving any potential fire starter unsupervised).

Tommy passed by the little two-room suite where he and Laurie lived, and left his mother's Bible on a small shelf by the bed. Then he turned on his heel and left the room, hurrying down the hallway toward Jim's office, where the light was better.

On top was a letter from his Aunt Geraldine, in Minnesota. Jim Watson had replied to her letter telling her about Jake's accident. Tommy briefly looked over the letter, since it was from his father's sister expressing her grief on hearing that her younger brother had died in the fall. Tommy had received the letter himself, so he was sure there was nothing helpful in it, but he thought he ought to re-read it to confirm that.

Next was a letter to his father from Tommy's grandmother, Louisa Ball Thompson, informing her son (Tommy's father) that his dad had died, and she was going to live with her brother, Josiah Ball. (Clearly, Tommy's grandmother had named his father for her brother.) She also mentioned, rather cryptically, the need for her son to repent of his sins, since the return of Jesus would be like a thief in the night. Tommy puzzled over that reference for a while, since he didn't understand its meaning, before going on to the next piece of paper.

Next in the cigar box was a letter from a Preacher in Illinois, telling Tommy's mother that Henry Benson had asked for forgiveness before he died; but there was no explanation as to why Henry Benson needed to be forgiven. The Preacher's signature was so hard to read that Tommy couldn't figure out his name, but the Preacher's address showed that it came from a church in Joliet, Illinois. The letter was dated April 1857, about a year after Tommy was born in 1856.

There was little else in the box, other than a receipt for some horses which his father had purchased from the Army in 1866. Nothing in the box appeared to Tommy to be of any help to him; if anything, it seemed to possibly even contribute to confirming what Lawrence Thompson had claimed.

Tommy was still sitting at Jim's desk, thinking dismally about his situation, when Jim came back to the boarding house. Jim went directly to his office, and told Tommy that the attorney, whom he had spoken to briefly, told him that Lawrence Thompson might very well have a valid claim to Tommy's business. He had explained to Jim that more information was needed, of course, and they should try to learn as much as they could, but, at that point, it appeared the best course of action might be to negotiate with this Lawrence Thompson fellow.

Tommy seemed awfully depressed, but Jim tried to encourage him as much as he could. "You'll still have your family, you know, and you're young enough to start over."

Tommy looked up at Jim, with a tear in his eye, and replied, "I've worked so hard for so long, and, now, it seems, for nothing."

Jim was already shaking his head before Tommy had finished speaking. "No, not for nothing; maybe you were just in training. I know that I'm very proud of the young man you've become. I've got a lot of confidence that you'll still be successful in all you do."

Tommy, not feeling much buoyed up, said, with regret, "I don't suppose now that I can afford the trip which I promised Laurie. I need to break it to her tonight that we're not going to visit her family in Missouri, and then see if I can't get my money back from having bought those train tickets."

Again, Jim shook his head. "Right now, you own that livery stable; no one's taken it away from you yet, so you need to keep running it just as you always have. I think you should still go on the trip. Consider that, if you come through this still owning the livery stable, you don't want to have wasted time by not having done what you wanted to do. Laurie is anxious to see her mother and the rest of her family again, and to introduce you to them. Although I'm sure that she'd fully understand if you decided to cancel the trip, I don't see that you need to. And there's one other important reason to go ahead and take the trip; after you visit her family, I really think you should go on up to Illinois. It's not much further, and you need to see if you can

212

learn all of the facts about your parents, and about this Henry Benson. Remember – if Lawrence Thompson does manage to acquire your business, then he'll have paid for your trip back East."

Tommy went to see the attorney, Mr. Miller, and explained what a shock it was to receive Mr. Miller's letter. Tommy asked the attorney for some time to try to verify Lawrence Thompson's relationship and claim, Tommy's own family history, and to raise money to pay Mr. Lawrence Thompson assuming Tommy found no evidence to prove something other than the claim.

Mr. Miller suggested thirty days, but Tommy insisted that it would take him at least two months since he plan to return to Illinois to speak to relatives. Mr. Miller agreed to sixty days.

Chapter Thirty

A week later, Tommy and Laurie were on a train headed for Maysville, Missouri. The train was a bit more expensive than driving their team, but it was a lot quicker. The original plan, for making contracts with farmers to supply their hay and grain needs, was put on hold until it was determined exactly who was going to be the owner of Thompson Livery Stable.

The closest train station to Maysville was Osborn. When the train chugged into Osborn's little station, Laurie was surprised to see a small crowd of people waiting there; the Osborn station was always virtually empty. As she looked out the window of the train, the faces became more distinct, and she recognized almost every one of the group: her mother (with an older man, obviously John Morton, Laurie's new step-father, standing by her side); her mother's brother, Uncle Bob; her brother,Ted; and her three younger sisters, Mildred, Cynthia, and Sophie.

Laurie climbed down the steps of the railroad car and ran to hug her mother. Tommy went back to the baggage car, and unloaded their luggage. There were two carpet bags and a small trunk, and soon it was all sitting on the train platform, and Laurie got happily busy introducing her husband to her mother, her new step-father, her uncle, her brother, and her three sisters. Frankly, the sisters all nearly swooned to see the tall, handsome, gentlemanly Tommy with their sister, who they had feared would never come back home.

Ted was only two years younger than Laurie, and her three sisters were all roughly two years apart, with the youngest, Sophie, being thirteen years old. They all had light brown or slightly blonde hair and fair pinkish skins, which was quite a contrast to Laurie's dark, almost black hair and smooth tan complexion.

214

It was a good three-quarters of an hour before any effort was made to leave the train platform, and, indeed, they might have stayed there all day, if the train hadn't finished loading its passengers and cargo, and began chugging away with so much noise that no one could understand what anyone else was saying.

Osborn was a stop on the Hannibal and St. Joseph Railroad, and was about twenty miles South of Maysville, so it took a good two hours for the family to reach Maysville, but the time passed very quickly with everyone talking almost at once. There were so many of them that they had to be spread out over several conveyances, and there had been a fierce competition to decide who got to get in which; there had even been a loud push by Laurie's siblings to crowd them all into a single buggy with Tommy and Laurie, but their plea was sensibly ignored.

The final decision was that Laurie would ride with her mother and Tommy in one buggy, driven by her new step-father, Mr. Morton; her sisters would ride in the other buggy, driven by Uncle Bob; and Ted would drive the wagon containing the luggage and some supplies which the family had picked up in Osborn.

After an initial thorough scrutiny of Tommy, and making a decision that he was as good a man as her daughter's letters had said, Laurie's mother devoted most of her attention to her beloved daughter. Tommy and Mr. Morton talked, and they quickly decided that they liked each other. Tommy hit it off very well with Mr. Morton, who really appreciated having gained such an industrious and hardworking young man in the family, and Tommy saw that Mr. Morton was an intelligent, caring man who loved his new wife and family.

Laurie's Uncle Bob was very well pleased to see that Laurie had apparently married so well, and had to frequently hide his grins on the trip back to Maysville as he listened to her sisters discussing the handsome Tommy, how lucky their sister was to have married him, and

215

how sophisticated and well-dressed she was now. (They had made special notice of her blue sapphire earrings in her pierced ears, too.)

As the wagon and buggies passed through Maysville, Laurie noticed a familiar face emerge from the barbershop. It was the Reverend Silas Jones, the preacher with whom Laurie had engaged in a shouting match over two years before.

Laurie reached over, grabbed Mr. Morton's arm, and asked him to please stop. No one else in the buggy knew what was up, but Mr. Morton obliged his step-daughter by stopping the buggy. Before anyone could ask what was on Laurie's mind, she vaulted from the buggy and ran to the sidewalk in front of the barbershop.

Reverend Jones stopped, and his mouth dropped open at the sight of Laurie. His mouth started moving, but nothing came out.

Laurie went up to Reverend Jones, and said, contritely, "I'm so glad to see you, Preacher. We last parted, I'm afraid, on unfriendly terms, and I wanted to apologize, and to ask you if we could put that all behind us. I'm so sorry for all the awful things I said to you. Please forgive me."

Reverend Jones looked Laurie right in the eye, and responded, his voice ringing with sincerity, "Miss Burdock, I was convinced that you would never forgive ME. I'm so glad that you have mercy in your heart for an old man, who suffers from the weaknesses of the flesh."

Laurie smiled with relief, and replied, "The Apostle Paul said, 'When I would do good, evil is present with me.' I dare say that the Devil was having a wonderful time exploiting all our human emotions the day they buried my step-father!"

The old Preacher grinned at that, and said, "I know you're quite correct about the old Devil! Fight him as we will, he's always with us."

Laurie put her arms around Reverend Jones and gave him a short gentle hug, then corrected him. "Oh, it's not Miss Burdock any more; it's Mrs. Thompson these days."

"I'm so glad for you, Laurie. I can see that the Lord is with you, and with your husband as well, for you to be so happy. I wish the two of you every Happiness and Blessing from our Lord and Savior!"

Laurie smiled and said, "Thank you, Reverend Jones. I really must run now. We're on our way to my mother's house. My husband Tommy and I have only just arrived back here in Maysville. Good-bye, and may the good Lord bless you and your work on His behalf!"

"Good-bye, Mrs. Thompson! It was so good to see you!" Deeply moved, Reverend Jones stood there watching as the buggies and wagon rolled on out of sight.

In another hour, the three horse-drawn vehicles pulled up in front of the house belonging to John Morton, and the unloading, of people as well as luggage and cargo, was quickly accomplished.

It was pure bedlam for the next hour or so; but, finally, Laurie finally had some time alone with her mother. She hadn't wanted to bring up the subject in front of anyone else, but she wanted her mother's guidance. "Momma, a man is suing for ownership of Tommy's business. Tommy inherited the business from his father, but this man claims that Tommy's father wasn't really his father, that Tommy had another father, and this man claims to be the closest living relative to Tommy's father. We don't know what to do. Can you help me think of something to help Tommy? I love Tommy, and I don't care if he owns a business or not, but it really means a lot to him."

Laurie's mother, Evelyne, instantly replied, "Doesn't he have a family Bible?"

Laurie said, "Well, Tommy has his mother's Bible. But what good does that do him?"

Evelyne Morton began to laugh softly. "Honey, don't you know that mothers always write in the Bible when their children were born, and when they got married? Births and weddings and deaths in the family are always written there."

"No, I never knew that. My friend Susan did give me a Bible, and she showed me a Family History page in it and told me to write down me and Tommy's wedding date in it, but I thought that was just something she did. Did you do that?"

Evelyne quietly got up and went into her bedroom, coming back out with an old well-worn Bible. "This was my grandmother's Bible, and it has in it the dates of my mother's birth and of her marriage to my father. It also tells the dates when Bob and I were born, as well as our brother, Edward, and his death when he was five years old."

Mother and daughter pored over the old Bible for a long time, reminiscing about the births and deaths and other details recorded in it which Laurie had never heard about before. Laurie discovered that she had been named for her mother's sister, who had died before her mother was even born, a fact she hadn't previously known.

About this time, Tommy came by with John Morton; they had been discussing a problem with the health of one of Mr. Morton's horses. Tommy had examined the animal, and determined the problem was Rain Scald, or Rot; he had seen it one particularly wet winter in Colorado, so he was familiar with it. Tommy told Mr. Morton that the Horse Doctor had suggested to him to feed the animal some particular herbs, such as Burdock, Marigold, Cleavers, and Nettles. The Horse Doctor had also suggested that these same herbs could be ground up into a powder, and placed on the affected area (after it had first been cleaned well). Tommy commented that he had taken that advice, and it had cured his horse, so maybe it would work for Mr. Morton's horse.

When Tommy had finished relaying the veterinarian's advice on treating Rain Scald, Laurie got his attention. She motioned him over, saying, "Tommy, I think you need to see this. Momma, would you show the Bible to Tommy, and tell him what you told me about the dates written down?" Laurie then got up and gave her chair to Tommy, while she went off to talk to her new stepfather.

After John Morton and Laurie had made small talk for a few minutes, John stated, "Laurie, I'm real impressed with your husband. It's hard to find a man of that age these days who knows anything about horses, other than how to drive them hard!"

"Oh, Mr. Morton, Tommy's mother died when he was a baby, and his father didn't marry anyone else, and he didn't have any help in the livery stable either, so he took Tommy to work with him every day. Tommy grew up seeing how to handle horses right, and how to fix wagons and buggies," Laurie explained, "and he kept on working and learning about it all when he took over his father's business after his father died. Tommy's not afraid of hard work!"

When Tommy and his mother-in-law finished talking about the Bible, Tommy got up and went over to where Laurie and Mr. Morton were standing. "Laurie, I think you were right. There may be something helpful. When we get to Illinois, we need to search for some family Bibles. I should have looked in Mom's Bible back in Denver, after I got it out of the attic, and I sure would've if I'd understood what it might contain, but I suspect that it'll be my grandmother's or my great-grandmother's Bible which will give us the answer that we need."

During Laurie and Tommy's three-week stay in Maysville, they had a great time. Tommy spent a good deal of time with the menfolk -- Mr. Morton, Uncle Bob, and Ted. They all enjoyed each other's company, and, thanks to Tommy's expertise, they repaired two wagons and an old buggy.

Tommy and Ted even had time to go fishing at the natural lake which they had passed on the way from Osborn to Maysville; the lake was part of the Little Platte River. They were successful, and everyone enjoyed a fish dinner that evening.

Laurie, her mother, and her sisters had a great time visiting, too. Their time together centered around discussions of Laurie's difficulties before she met Tommy, and her duties at her job at the General Store back in Denver. (Laurie had made up her mind to be very forthcoming about her experiences, deciding that hearing about them might help her sisters be better prepared in their own lives if they ever encountered such situations.) Laurie's sisters and her mother were all thrilled to hear all about Abby, Sarah, and Susan working so hard to make the beautiful wedding dress which Laurie described in great detail.

At the evening meals, everyone was spellbound by Laurie's stories of meeting her half-brother, visiting her natural father's grave, and meeting her Ute Indian relatives. They were equally awe-struck by Tommy's stories about Johnny Little Bear. (Tommy didn't tell them about the corpses which he, Davie, and Timmy found on one of their trips; he tried not to think about it, ever, and most definitely didn't want to talk about it, ever.)

After the three-week visit, Laurie and Tommy bid their farewells. (They explained to Laurie's mother and step-father, in private, that they had to go on to Illinois to search for evidence which could save his business. They saw no need to worry the rest of the family about that.) There was much crying and hugging, and many promises to write, and an abundance of expressions of love.

Tommy had bought a nice buggy and two horses while in Missouri, rather than attempting to continue by train. The scattered nature of the existing train service made it extremely difficult to board from anywhere near Maysville, Missouri, and then make all of the necessary connections to get to Springfield, Illinois.

Oddly, there was railroad service into Springfield, and into many other cities, but problem was that the railroad wasn't a single connected system, but rather a motley collection of small three-city and four-city lines, at that time. It was some years (and several bankruptcies) later before the railroad became a workable system for anyone other than relatively local travelers just going to a nearby city.

It was only about a hundred miles or so to Springfield, but to get there they had to cross the Mississippi River. A railroad bridge had been built across the river, so a lot of business had been taken away from the river ferry, which used to control all crossings, of persons and of cargo. The result was that better prices were available on the river ferry than before, so the Thompsons crossed the Mississippi River on the river ferry operating out of Hannibal, Missouri. Late the second day, they arrived in Springfield, Illinois.

Upon their arrival, Tommy inquired of a man on the street for the name of a good hotel. The answer was a long, confusing list of names, until the man finished by saying, "In my opinion, the best hotel in town is the Revere House; it's run by old Mr. Joel Johnson. He's been in the business for a long time, and he makes sure the place is clean and pleasant. It isn't the cheapest, but it sure is the nicest."

Tommy and Laurie registered at the Revere Hotel, had their luggage taken to their room, and then asked around the hotel if anyone knew of a family named Thompson. No progress was made, and they were getting very discouraged, until someone suggested that the hotel might have a Babeuf's Directory of Springfield, Illinois, and Sangamon County for 1874, which might assist in the search.

221

The hotel did, indeed, have the directory, and, although it was divided by Militia districts, it only took a few minutes to find several Thompsons, all of whom were listed in a single district. In fact, in that same district were listed two Josiah Balls – possibly father and son? But there were no Davises or Bensons in that district. Pages of Davises, but not a Benson to be found.

Fortunately, that Militia District was located only a short distance from the hotel. But, by then, Tommy and Laurie were too tired to start anything that evening, and so, after dining, they retired at a fairly early hour.

Tommy and Laurie were so tired from their previous day's journey that they slept late the next morning; they barely had time to get dressed and make it down to the dining room before the end of breakfast (which was served buffet-style; the hotel called it family-style). They were so late, in fact, that no new pans of food or hot biscuits had been put out recently, and everything was cold, including the biscuits which remained. Those cold biscuits had also been picked over thoroughly, too. Fortunately, Tommy preferred the crunchier edge biscuits (of which he had several, being famished), leaving the single more or less soft-center biscuit for Laurie.

After their rapid breakfast of cold leftovers, they managed to get addresses and directions for both of the Josiah Ball residences from the hotel front desk clerk. Tommy went to the stable and harnessed their horses to their new buggy, then drove the buggy around to the front of the hotel. Laurie came out of the hotel carrying a couple of small bundles, which contained a large amount of the breakfast leftovers. (She wanted to make sure that they didn't go hungry while they were hunting for relatives, and had wrapped up the remaining biscuits, a goodly amount of ham, a number of sausages, and several boiled eggs.)

Once Laurie and her parcels were loaded, Tommy began orienting himself, to get familiar with the streets going through the town, and to determine which street to take, following the hotel clerk's directions.

At around noon, the Thompson buggy pulled up in front of a small wooden house in a rather rundown neighborhood. There were no horses, buggies, or wagons evident, and really no place to house them. Tommy climbed down, leaving Laurie holding the reins of their horses, to see if anyone was home. He walked up to the front door, which was closed; the weather was warm enough, it seemed to Tommy, that the door should have been open. But he went ahead and knocked anyway. It surprised him a little bit when his knock on the door was soon answered.

A man, whom Tommy judged to be about ten years older than himself, somewhat stocky, with brown curly hair, opened the door and asked, courteously, "May I help you?" (Tommy was quite relieved, both that someone was actually home, and that the person who was home wasn't unfriendly. He hadn't been sure of either.)

Chapter Thirty-one

Tommy stuck out his hand, and said, "Hello, sir. My name is Tommy Thompson. My grandmother was Louisa Ball Thompson. I have a letter from her, which she sent to my late father, saying that she was going to move in with her brother, Josiah Ball. Does any of that make sense to you?"

The brown-haired fellow looked very serious, and replied, "My name is Josiah Ball, but I'm certainly not old enough to be your great uncle. However, my father, whose name is also Josiah Ball, is old enough. And Dad's sister did live with us, when I was a small boy, but she's been dead for many, many years. I'm not sure I even remember her name. It seems like I remember hearing her name as Emily, though, and not Louisa."

Tommy quickly replied, "Emily was the name of my mother. My mother was born a Davis, and she married Henry Benson, and, after that, my father, Josiah (Jake) Thompson."

The younger Mr. Josiah Ball suddenly noticed Laurie sitting in the buggy watching them, and exclaimed, "Oh, my, I/m being so rude! Please ask your wife to join us. We can go inside, and I'll ask my wife to get us all something to drink."

Tommy thanked Josiah Ball, and walked the few steps to the buggy and helped Laurie climb down. Then he set the buggy's brake, and tied the reins to a branch of a small tree in the front yard, leaving the two horses enough room to nibble on the grass.

Tommy then followed Laurie into the house, in time to hear Josiah finished introducing himself (as 'Joe' Ball) and his wife, Ruthie, to Laurie. Then Joe Ball closed the front door, and directed them to an old, very worn sofa pushed against the wall. Mr. Ball himself went to a straight-back wooden chair and sat down, while Mrs. Ball hurried into the kitchen and lit a gas burner under a coffee pot.

A couple of small gaslights flickered on the wall of the musty-smelling house; the house wasn't dirty, just in need of a little airing out, and the Balls themselves wore clean, neatly patched clothes, and seemed quite nice and sociable. (The reason for the closed front door, and hence the slightly musty smell, became obvious when a large wagon piled high with some boxes went barreling down the street in front, raising a cloud of dust visible through the small front window.)

After sitting down, Tommy came right to the point. "Mr. Ball, is your father still living?"

Josiah quietly replied, "Please call me Joe. Yes, Dad is still with us, praise the Lord, but I'm not sure how much longer. His health is kind of touch-and-go right now."

Tommy continued, but in a more gentle tone. "Joe, we're trying to learn, or at least understand, my family history. My mother, Emily, had died when I was about six. My own father died when I was about twelve years old, and, frankly, I wasn't none too interested in learning about any relatives at that point. I knew we had no relatives anywhere close by; I suppose that was because Dad had gone West, by himself, seeking his fortune – or, at least, to make a living. I sure was hoping you, or your father, could help me."

Joe didn't answer right away, but got a faraway look on his face; then he said, "I've been wracking my brain about those names. Seems like I do remember hearing Dad talking to my aunt, his sister. They talked about an 'Emily' a lot; that's how come I remembered that name, I guess, even if it's not my aunt's name. Seems like it was always the same thing they talked about -- they didn't seem to approve of something or other that she had done, but, if I ever knew what it was that they thought she'd done, I can't remember it now. I'm sorry."

225

Just then, Ruthie Ball reentered the room, carrying four coffee cups and a pot of hot coffee on a wooden tray. Laurie quickly realized she hadn't been gone long enough to make fresh coffee, but she steeled herself to politely "like" some strong, old, bitter coffee.

A few minutes was spent pouring coffee, and apologizing for not having any cream or sugar. Both Tommy and Laurie made a show of not really wanting any cream or sugar, and liking the coffee just as it was (and it really wasn't terrible, although they both would have preferred a little sugar in it).

Laurie, realizing that the Balls, although having very little themselves, were willingly sharing what little they did have, excused herself, got up and went out to the buggy. Tommy was puzzled, but, at a quick look from Laurie, refrained from asking any questions. When Laurie returned, she carried the small bundles, and, telling the Balls that she had gotten some leftover food from the hotel, asked if they would mind if they all shared it with their coffee. The Balls tried to insist that Tommy and Laurie eat it all, but Laurie (now joined by an understanding Tommy) stated firmly that it was much too much for them, that she had gotten carried away when she was picking up the leftovers off of the community table, and that she'd feel just terrible if it went to waste due to her being so piggish.

Needless to report, the Balls both greatly enjoyed the rare and unexpected treat of eating lots of ham and sausage (which Tommy and Laurie professed to have eaten too much of already to be able to eat any more), while Tommy and Laurie each took a hard cold biscuit and pretended to nibble on them with apparent satisfaction. Afterwards, the only remaining food was the boiled eggs, which Laurie asked Mrs. Ball if she wouldn't please put away, if no one wanted to eat them then, since she didn't want to have to go back to the hotel carrying them. Ruthie tried hard not to let her joy at getting the eggs (to eat later, for their supper) show, but she thanked Laurie very sincerely.

Over the impromptu meal, Tommy asked Joe if they could go visit Joe's father, Josiah the elder. Joe replied that they certainly could, but he preferred to be there with them when they visited his father, to make the introductions, so his father would understand the family connection. Unfortunately, he didn't have time right then, however, since he was only home for lunch, and, in fact, he needed to leave the house very soon to go back to work.

Joe explained that his job was some ten blocks away, so Tommy volunteered to drive him in the buggy. (Clearly, Joe walked to and from his job each day.) Since it was only a short distance by buggy, he left Laurie to continue talking with Ruthie Ball, who was clearly grateful for the company. During the buggy ride, Tommy asked if they could go visit Joe's father that evening. Joe agreed, and they made an appointment to meet at the warehouse where Joe worked at around six pm that day. (Joe worked a ten-hour day, six days a week, from seven am until six pm, with an hour off for lunch.)

During the buggy ride, Tommy found out that Joe didn't have a Ball family Bible, but that his father might have one. He dropped Joe off at his place of work, and returned to the Balls' house to pick up Laurie, and to let Ruthie know that Joe would be taking them to see his father that evening, and so Joe would be late to supper.

Then, Tommy and Laurie proceeded toward the address of one of the Thompsons listed in the city directory. (Laurie, in her methodical way, which was so invaluable to Jim at the general store, had carefully written down each Thompson's address.)

When they finally reached the first address for a Thompson, there was no one home. At the second address, the people there denied knowing any of the Thompson names about which Tommy inquired. At the third address, they were slightly successful, but only sort of.

It was the correct family, but they were distant cousins, and were only vaguely familiar with any of Tommy's side of the family. Tommy did learn the name and address of his father's first cousin from them.

But it was too late in the day to find that cousin, so Tommy and Laurie (having given the cold breakfast leftovers to Mr. and Mrs. Joe Ball) found a small store, at which they bought some cheese (which was cut off of a larger wedge) and crackers (pulled out of a bucket) to eat hurriedly, and then headed back to Joe Ball's place of employment.

When Joe finally appeared about a half-hour later than he had told them, they learned he had been involved in packaging up a large shipment which HAD to go out early the next morning.

Joe climbed into the buggy with Tommy and Laurie, and started for the home of the older Josiah Ball.

Josiah's house was larger and had been, at one time, nicer, than Joe's, but the years had taken their toll. Josiah looked the part of a man younger than they had expected, and a good deal of time was spent introducing everyone and explaining the family relationships. Josiah seemed to know even less than Joe had told them. He denied knowing anything which might explain the relationships, or might shed any light on the puzzle which occupied Tommy's mind.

After over an hour of Josiah neither knowing anything nor remembering anything, it suddenly dawned on Tommy that there was a good possibility that the older man simply didn't want to talk about anything which might embarrass Tommy in front of Tommy's lovely young wife.

In desperation, Tommy challenged the older man. "Mr. Ball, surely you must remember conversations you've had with your older sister about my mother and father. We know that my mother was previously married to a Mr. Henry Benson. In fact, there are some

228

people who say my father was Henry Benson. It's vitally important for me to know the truth. Is Jake Thompson my real father, or is Henry Benson? I know that in Ephesians, the Apostle Paul tells us that it is shameful to talk about what unbelievers do in private, but I have to know. I have shared these questions with my wife, too, so please feel free to talk about the matter in front of her."

Mr. Ball was obviously uncomfortable with this line of questioning, and he sat there, embarrassed, as a red color began to creep up from his collar. Finally, he said, "I have never talked about unseemly carrying-on. Of course, I've heard rumors, and I've seen evidence of sinful activity, but it embarrasses me to speak of those things in front of Ladies. I'd also never spread anything which could be a vicious lie, and make folks think someone was sinful, when there was a possibility that they really weren't."

Tommy realized that he was getting close to some important information, and volunteered, "Mr. Ball, if it would help you tell me what I need to know, my wife could leave the room. But, please, won't you tell me? I need to know!"

Josiah Ball looked down at the floor, and didn't make eye contact with anyone, as he talked. "Tommy, my sister, Louisa, was terribly distraught that her son was living in sin, committing adultery. But, for me, I rather think that this sinful activity, if it was, started long enough before your birth that I think you are the son of my nephew rather than the man which Emily left."

Tommy's face lit up, that he finally got the answer to his birth, and he replied, "Mr. Ball, that's exactly what I was hoping I'd find out! But, now, the only problem is that I have no idea how I could ever prove it in a court of law." Mr. Ball simply shrugged his shoulders in resignation, not knowing how to deal with it, either.

Laurie, whose face was also lit up, interrupted then. "Mr. Ball, did your sister leave a family Bible?"

Josiah Ball arose from his chair, and quietly went into what appeared to be a bedroom, and, in a few minutes, emerged carrying a very large, very old Bible, which he handed to Tommy. Laurie got up from her chair, carried the chair over next to where Tommy sat, and, opening the Bible to the family tree pages, they both began to study the writing on there. They only found one entry:

Born: July 17, 1831, Josiah Leonard Thompson

Tommy looked at the entry and said, "That was about 30 years before I was born." He tried not to let his disappointment show, as did Laurie. Although a bit more conversation followed, it became clear that the elder Josiah Ball had no more information to impart (or, if he ever had more, couldn't – or wouldn't -- remember it).

The Thompsons thanked Josiah Ball for helping them, and told both him and Joe that it was very nice to meet such fine relatives, and took Joe home. Then Tommy and Laurie bid the Joe Ball family good night, and started their buggy back toward the hotel.

The day had been emotionally exhausting, as well as physically tiring. Back at the hotel, they were almost as late for supper as they had been that morning for breakfast. Once again, the food wasn't as hot as they would have preferred, but it was plentiful and tasty, so they were quite hungry and ate their fill. After they ate, Tommy looked again through the city directory for Bensons and Davises; there were no Bensons and pages of Davises listed. The Davis name was so common they were scattered all over town except the district where they found the Thompsons.

Tommy and Laurie went to bed fairly early that evening, and they got up the next morning in time to enjoy the hotel's breakfast when it was both hot and fresh. It was really pleasant, except for the dreadful seemingly complete collapse of their mission, which made it almost impossible to fully appreciate the delicious food.

During breakfast, as Tommy looked distractedly at an old copy of the local newspaper, Laurie began telling him about a dream she had the previous night. Tommy wasn't paying much attention to her, until Laurie said the name Joliet, Illinois. He looked up at hearing that, and asked, "What was that you said, Dear?"

Laurie was slightly annoyed, but repeated, "I said that I dreamed last night that I met that Preacher in Joliet, Illinois."

Tommy thought for a minute or so, and then said, "A Preacher in Joliet wrote a letter to my mother, telling her that Henry Benson had said he was sorry before he died, and asked her to forgive him. I wonder what Henry was doing in Joliet. Where is Joliet anyway?"

Just then a hotel waiter came by with fresh hot coffee and cream to refill Tommy's cup. As the waiter poured both coffee and cream into the cup at the same time, to mix them as they filled the cup, Tommy looked up at him and asked, "Do you know where Joliet is?"

The waiter stopped pouring to think, and, after a few moments, replied, "I don't rightly know; I think it's up North somewhere. All I know about Joliet is that's where the prison is located."

Hearing that, Tommy's and Laurie's eyes made contact almost instantaneously, and, simultaneously, they both blurted out, "He was in prison!"

After breakfast, Tommy went to the front desk again. The clerk saw him coming, and had the city directory lying on the desk for him before Tommy got there. Tommy smiled at seeing that,, and said, "Thank you; you've been so helpful, and I really appreciate it. But, this time, I think I just need to know how to get to the Police Station or a Sheriff's Office."

The clerk smiled back, picked the city directory up, and put it away, saying, "Sheriff's Office is at the Court House, but there's a Police Station only about a block away. Just go outside, turn right, and walk about a block. You can't miss it; it'll be on the left."

Tommy and Laurie walked together to the Police Station. The clerk was right; you couldn't miss it, due to the large sign painted on the front. They entered the station and went up to a Police Officer sitting behind a desk, who asked, "May I help you folks?"

Tommy spoke up, "Officer, we're new to your city, and to this state as well. We're looking for records referring to a man who we think was imprisoned in Joliet about twenty-five years ago."

The officer quickly replied, "Sir, we don't have any prison records here. If the inmate was arrested here, we should have arrest records. If he was indicted here, or tried here, the records would be at the Court House. If those actions were taken in a different county, then the records would reside in that county."

Tommy thanked the officer, and then he and Laurie proceeded directly to the Court House, where they spent the rest of the day trying to find any record whatsoever there about a Henry Benson. They looked through arrest records, indictment records, and trial records. But they could find absolutely nothing. Finally, they decided to give up that search as useless.

Since it was nearing time for supper at the hotel, and both Tommy and Laurie were hungry and tired, they returned to their hotel to get supper while it was still fresh and hot. Tommy then went back to the front desk clerk, and, after apologizing for bothering him, borrowed the city directory, and the Thompsons devoted a thoughtful evening to pouring over the directory. They made a list of all the people and addresses with any surnames who might be likely (or even possible) to shed some light, no matter how small, on the growing mystery.

After two more days of talking to various distant relatives, and others who simply had the same last name, and learning zero, Tommy decided they should go to Joliet.

That night, there was a severe thunderstorm, and it rained from right after supper until they checked out from the hotel the next morning after breakfast. Tommy paid their bill, and thanked the front desk clerk profusely for all of his assistance, with the city directory and the wealth of other information the young man had supplied to him (and slipped him some cash in tangible thanks, as well).

The friendly, helpful, hard-working clerk was obviously very grateful for the thanks (as most travelers only gave him complaints, about things totally beyond his control), but overjoyed at the cash (which was most welcome, as he wasn't paid very much at the hotel).

As Tommy and Laurie started out with the loaded buggy, they found their traveling in the city to be very slow. The buggy wheels sank deeply into the mud and muck of the streets, and the horses struggled to find their footing in the mire. Once they made their way out of the Capitol city, however, the going got a bit easier, simply because of the reduced traffic, resulting in not as much stirring up of the wet roads.

Due to the muddy roads, on the first day, they only traveled about twenty miles, and found shelter for the evening with a farm family. The Milstead family, Frank and his wife, Sylvia, were glad to have them stay overnight, and enjoyed the company. (These visitors came all the way from Colorado, and were looking for a dead relative. My, oh, my, would they have a story to tell after church next Sunday!)

The following day was windy and cooler; the drop in temperature was welcome, but the wind shook their buggy uncomfortably. Fortunately, the buggy had a roof of sorts, and sides with curtain windows, but there was very little protection for Tommy, who was driving.

Most of the time, Laurie rode in front with Tommy, but sometimes she went back in the back for some bread and smoked ham for Tommy to munch on. Laurie discovered that she preferred bread and butter with a large dill pickle.

They found a very rocky road for quite a distance, and were able to make it almost to Bloomington by the end of their second day. Everyone had been telling them they should go through Bloomington. Since in about 1870, the city of Bloomington had started paving their streets with bricks; it was quite an innovation, well worth seeing.

After one more night enjoying the hospitality of another farm family, early the next morning the Thompsons were off to see those famous red brick roads. By this time, Bloomington had all of their major streets paved, and the main roads into and out of town were paved to some small degree as well.

Tommy and Laurie practically sailed through Bloomington. Oh, they rattled and shook as they passed over the bricks (even though the bricks were very well laid), but their traveling felt incredibly smooth compared to the dirt roads which they were used to riding on everywhere else (including in Denver). Their horses' hooves made a new rhythmic clop-clop sound as they went over the bricks. Tommy and Laurie agreed that their entire journey of about two hundred and fifty miles would feel so much shorter, and wouldn't be so bad, if all of the roads were like those brick streets.

Chapter Thirty-two

Finally, after a journey of a week, they made it to Joliet. Clearly, the prison was the largest business in town. The guards and other prison personnel lived in Joliet (either as renters or as home owners), the local businesses sold supplies and equipment as needed to the workers personally or to the prison, and the surrounding farmers grew food for the inmates and for the prison workers. The local economy definitely profited from, even depended upon, the prison.

Fortunately, most of the prison administration offices were located in a separate building from the actual prison. Women weren't allowed to go inside the prison. An occasional exception was made for the mother of a condemned man, to speak with her son before he was executed, but, otherwise, the rule was very strictly enforced: No Women Allowed.

Upon inquiry at the front of the administration building, Tommy and Laurie were directed to the Records Office. When the clerk in the Records Office learned the reason for their visit, he was only too happy to search the old records. (He was usually very bored, and so he was glad to have the opportunity to talk to visitors and have a different task to perform than just filing papers.)

After about an hour, and after searching several different places for the desired records, the clerk returned with a smile upon his face, saying, with satisfaction, "You're in luck! And, let me tell you, it was really lucky for you that you came now, instead of later. You see, it was decided several months ago that all records older than twenty years would be moved to a special Archive Building, which was to be built just for housing the old records. Only problem is that they still haven't built the Archive Building! But, fortunately for you, we'd already separated the older records, the ones that need to go into the Archives Building, and put them in a separate area from the newer ones."

Tommy, not at all interested in the future plans for any new buildings, interrupted the records clerk's monologue at that point, asking, "Does that mean you've found what we're looking for?"

The clerk got an embarrassed look on his face and said, "Oh, I'm so sorry. I got all excited, because I'd forgotten about separating out all of those records, and where they were stored."

The clerk then opened up the file, and started reading through it, saying the pertinent facts out loud as he did. (The more recent of the facts were on top, with the older facts below.) "Well, now, Mr. Henry Benson was hanged on April 4th, 1857. He'd been convicted of murder on June 12th, 1854. Apparently, he got into an argument with a fellow from Kansas about Missouri being a slave state, and killed the man. Beat him to death with a bar stool."

Tommy got a big grin on his face, and said, "Well, if he was imprisoned, then he couldn't possibly be my father!"

Laurie threw her arms around Tommy in joy, but then, after a moment's reflection, voiced her conflicting emotions. "Oh, Tommy, I feel awful; we just learned about a gruesome murder and the hanging of a man, and I'm celebrating!"

Tommy pulled her into his arms, and kissed her on the cheek, murmuring, "It's all right, honey; I feel the same way." Then, he apologized to the clerk, saying, "I'm sorry for this unseemly behavior, but, if I can present this evidence in court, it'll save my business!"

The clerk thought a minute, and said, "I suppose we'd need to get a letter from a Judge, or get someone else in a position of authority to write a letter, describing what our official records say…. Hmmmm. Let me look into that."

He left the office, but returned in a few minutes and announced, "The Head of the Prison Registry Department can have these records transcribed, and he'd affix his signature to the authenticity of the transcribed records, then two of the employees of the department would sign as witnesses to his signature, and the official stamp would be put on, by the signatures.

"It'd cost you ten dollars, and it can be ready to pick up the day after tomorrow."

Tommy replied, "That's a whole lot of money, but I agree to paying it as long as there are two copies made for me."

The clerk answered, "Sure; that will be no problem. Pay the fee now, and then come by Thursday afternoon after 3 pm, to this office. The transcripts will be ready for you."

Tommy reached into his pocket, and produced a ten-dollar gold piece; as he handed it to the clerk, he asked, "May I have a receipt for the fee?"

"Yes, Sir, of course you may. Just a minute while I write you out one, Mr. Thompson."

Tommy took the receipt, and, after thanking the clerk for all of his assistance, he and Laurie headed for the door; but Tommy stopped before they went out, turned back around, and asked, "I do need a little more help, if you would be so kind. It's two things – the name of a good hotel nearby, and where the telegraph office is?"

The clerk gave them directions to the old National Hotel on the west side of town, and told them that, if they followed his directions to the hotel, they would go right by the telegraph office.

Tommy thanked the man again, and they left the building, got back in their buggy and started for the telegraph office.

Once they got to the telegraph office, Tommy sent the following telegram to Jim Watson.

DAD CANT BE HOME IN TIME TO ATTEND MEETING DEADLINE STOP HAVE EVIDENCE HG BENSON NOT MY FATHER STOP MAILING ONE COPY TO YOU BRINGING OTHER WITH ME STOP

Then Tommy and Laurie continued on to the hotel, registered, and had dinner. They spent their time, while waiting for the transcripts to be completed, by looking around the town. Mainly, Tommy investigated the local livery stables, while Laurie looked through the general stores to get ideas for the Denver store. They made a few minor purchases, gifts for the folks back in Denver.

On Thursday afternoon, promptly at 3 pm, Tommy and Laurie presented themselves to the Prison Registry clerk. They were a little surprised to find that he had the two copies of the transcribed registry record, all ready and waiting for them, and all duly signed and witnessed. They thanked the clerk over and over again. (The clerk's somewhat flabby chest puffed out noticeably at the praise, and he stood straighter. Ordinarily, he never had any special recognition, and he absorbed it happily, to warm himself with for a long time.)

They stopped by the Post Office and mailed one copy of the transcripts to Jim Watson, c/o the Watson Boarding House, and returned to the hotel for their final night in Joliet, Illinois.

Even though the "golden spike" was driven in 1869, there was no railroad connection from Chicago to Kansas City, Kansas, in the mid-1870s. In fact, Illinois had several railroad projects which were going bankrupt, and those projects had failed to produce a railroad over a long enough distance to be of much value at all.

Tommy and Laurie started on their trip back home by heading for Kansas City, Kansas, where they could board a train headed for Denver, Colorado. This required them to cross Illinois and Missouri in a slightly diagonal way. They traveled back to Springfield through Bloomington (the way they had come to Joliet) in their buggy. Their route then turned almost due West. Their travel plan was an almost exact reversal of the way they had reached Joliet.

The good news was the roads were almost dry on the return trip; but the bad news was that the dried ruts, resulting from wagon traffic immediately after the large rainfall, made the trip rough, noisy, and uncomfortable. The Thompson's money supply was beginning to dry up as well.

By the time they boarded the Union Pacific Railroad in Kansas City (they had their return tickets, but they needed to pay extra for shipping the horses and buggy, too), they were basically broke. There was just a tiny bit of money left with which to buy a little food along the way.

As Tommy and Laurie sat next to each other, watching the country-side slide slowly past, Laurie decided that the time was right to have a discussion. She asked Tommy, solicitously, "Tommy, dear, how are you feeling today?"

Tommy turned to her, and replied, with a puzzled look, "That sure is an odd question to ask me, Laurie."

She just smiled, snuggled up to his side, and, putting her arm around his arm, said, "I was just wondering, considering everything, if you were feeling optimistic now, or if you were still feeling discouraged about the situation; you know, anything like that."

"Oh, I'm most surely optimistic, and very encouraged. I'm not sure I could be any happier, since I'm sitting here next to you, my darlin'! Even if we've hardly any money left to eat on, I feel blessed."

Laurie smiled, more broadly, perhaps a little mysteriously, and asked, "Would this be a good time to share some news?"

Tommy sat bolt upright in his seat, looked intently at Laurie' and said, very slowly, almost dragging each word out, "I can only think of one piece of news which you might have for me."

Laurie grinned very widely, and replied, "Yes, that's it; you are going to be a father."

Tommy leaped from his seat, yanked his hat from his head, swung it around over his head (like you might expect a rodeo rider to do on a bucking bronco), and yelled, "Whoopee!"

Other passengers looked over at them, startled, and wondering whether to expect more celebrating. Tommy, feeling self-conscious because everyone was looking at him, declared to everyone in the train car, "I'm going to be a Daddy!"

All of the other passengers began to smile (even the previously grumpy looking old man sitting a few rows away), and a few men shouted, "Congratulations!"

The disturbance settled down rather quickly, though, and Tommy and Laurie huddled in quiet conversation. Tommy asked, in wonder, "How long have you known?"

Laurie replied, "I've suspected for a couple weeks, but I wasn't sure. Besides, I felt I needed to wait about telling you until your family and business problems had been resolved. But now that your problems look like they're over, and I'm feeling more certain, I thought it was time to tell you. And, as much as I love the folks back in Denver, I sort of wanted some privacy, for us to be by ourselves, when I told you."

The train trip was much faster and easier than the buggy rides, but it still took several days to reach Denver. (It had taken Laurie a considerable amount of talking to convince Tommy that she didn't need to be handled like a rare piece of fragile glass, but he finally settled down, and accepted that she was both healthy and strong.)

After the buggy and the two horses were unloaded from the freight car, Tommy harnessed them to the buggy (noting to himself that the horses had eaten all of the grain he'd left for them). He decided his first order of business at the Livery Stable would be to feed and water these horses a little, and have them walked around for an hour or two, then fed some more. (He was afraid they would overeat if given too much at their first feeding opportunity, and make themselves sick.)

Finally, the Thompsons were driving through the streets of Denver. The horses practically pranced, seeming to know they were nearly at their new home, and to be happy the long trip was almost over. Tommy and Laurie felt pretty much the same way, too.

In less than an hour, they were pulling up in front of the Livery Stable. The first person to spot them was Abby, who was sweeping the front steps. She dropped the broom, ran out to meet them, and hugged Laurie. Laurie, being several inches taller than Abby, bent over a little in order to whisper something in Abby's ear. It was clear to Tommy what she had told Abby, because Abby got very excited, grinning broadly, and jumping up and down (not jumping, really, more like shaking, so she didn't cause Laurie any discomfort).

Davie came out of the barn and greeted them, saying, "I'll take care of the horses and start carrying your things to your room. Y'all go and talk to everyone, and tell them all about the trip. I'll hear about it later."

Tommy said, "Davie, thank you. You know I'm just about busting at the seams to tell Jim and the others all that went on. Oh, the horses have been out of food for a couple of days. Feed them a little grain, and have Timmy walk them for about an hour, then feed them some more."

Davie replied, "Sure thing, Boss."

Tommy and Laurie started into the house, hand in hand, looking for Jim. When they found him, Jim seemed even happier to see them than they were to see him. Jim said, "I've been mighty worried about you two until I got that letter a couple days ago. It came exactly on time, the day before the deadline. The lawyer dropped the case on the spot. It's all over, Tommy!"

"Wow, that's better than I ever imagined!" enthused Tommy. Then he added, "Dad, you're going to be a Grandpa!"

Appendix

Clearly, this is a work of fiction. I hope you have enjoyed it.

All characters are fictitious with the exception of:

1. Crazy Horse: information about him is as factual as I could find.

2. Colonel Custer: including his part ownership in the Whale Peak mining operations is also as accurate as I could find. (Lt.Col. Edwards is a fictitious character.)

3. The Reed Family and other known and unknown victims of the avalanche were buried in Grant, Colorado. (As far as I know, they never had any association with either the Army or the Ute Indians.)

4. The US Army under Colonel Miles did fight the battle of Tongue River as related in the story. (While the Bradshaw family massacre is fictitious, it is more or less typical of some of the violence during the so called Indian wars.)

5. The cemetery at Fort Morgan was moved in the early twentieth century to provide space for a commercial endeavor.

6. The Maysville County Farm (pictured in Chapter Twenty-four) really existed, and served as the Poor House in that county. (The local Historical Society gave me permission to use the picture. The building is no longer in existence.)

7. Biblical references come from the King James Bible.

8. The picture on the book cover came from Shutterstock.com and the artist is ByOksanaMatskovich and the Royalty-free stock

illustration ID: 443526973 and the title is:Sketch of tattoo art, portret of lovely American Indian girl.